Citadel
The Peck Chronicles
Book 2

Paul Murdoch

Published by Strident Publishing
© Paul Murdoch 2016

Printed in the United Kingdom
Cover illustration and design © Ida Henrich

ISBN: 9781-910829-04-2

James Peck, the lead character of the Denthan Series, has asthma.
For help and advice with asthma, please visit www.asthma.org.uk

Typeset in Lucida by Andrew Forteath | Printed by Bell & Bain

The publisher acknowledges support from
Creative Scotland towards the publication
of this title.

About Paul Murdoch

Born in Helensburgh, Scotland, Paul Murdoch grew up beside Loch Lomond, on the very edge of the Scottish Highlands. He studied Zoology at Glasgow University and has always maintained a strong interest in nature and the outdoors. He worked in wildlife reserves for a few years before becoming involved in the sales and marketing side of agriculture.

Always possessing a strong creative streak, Paul played rock guitar on tour in the UK, Holland and America, writing many songs along the way. He then put his talents to use in poetry and short stories, before penning *The Peck Chronicles*.

Paul is also the author of the acclaimed eco-thriller *Windscape* (written under pen-name Sam Wilding) – an adventure novel for young people that impartially explores the controversial topic of wind farms – and a series of picture books for younger children.

Home for Paul is still near Loch Lomond, an easy spot from which to reach the many schools he visits each year.

1 The Keresi

Deep beneath the great, glimmering needle of alabaster that stood proud of Gwendril's skyline, Cimerato's pulse quickened in readiness. The tapping outside his damp, acrid cell was growing louder. The Manimal captain held his breath in anticipation...

A key turned in the lock, and the door creaked open.

As quietly as possible, he moved back against the cold, granite wall and braced.

The door swung inward and the light of a flickering torch filled the room.

He was about to spring forward when he heard a familiar voice call out, "Son?"

Cimerato paused. "Father?" He edged forward. "How did you get down here without being seen by Athelstone's guards?"

"Not every guard is under his control. Not yet." Lord Eldane signalled his men to help escort the still-groggy Cimerato out of the cell. "We need to be quick!"

Following his father and the guards down a set of slippery stairs, Cimerato soon realised that they were heading toward the underground waterways that lay deep beneath the city. "What's your plan, Father?" he panted.

His father's personal guards came to a halt beside a small, rowing boat.

Short of breath, Lord Eldane wheezed, "We must get out of the city!"

"We can't just leave everyone behind!" Cimerato protested. "Where's mother? What about the children?"

Lord Eldane climbed into a small boat and began to untie the ropes. "You must come now. Your mother and the children have already left for the tunnels that lead to Nordengate. As soon as Athelstone used his dark magic on you I knew, in my heart, that he was not the same man we all once loved and trusted. I should have known as much when he banished Mendel." He drew a deep sigh of regret.

Cimerato kept his silence as he boarded the craft. There was nothing he could say that would alleviate his father's shame. They had all eventually agreed to the old wizard's expulsion.

As they took their seats, Lord Eldane made sure he was sitting close to his son. "I've had news from the Yeltans. A small reptilian flyer arrived at my window carrying a scroll bearing the seal of Landris."

Cimerato thought this strange. The Yeltans, a squat race of yellow-skinned root dwellers who were totally driven by protocol and a whole set of complicated 'rules', rarely sent messages by flyer. They preferred the pomp and ceremony of official visits. "What does Landris say?"

"He says that he has found two small boys and a golden-coloured creature called a dog. He writes that these boys are not from our world; that they've travelled to Denthan with Mendel, no less."

"Mendel!" Cimerato punched the air excitedly, causing the boat to rock and pitch perilously. "I knew he'd find a way to get back!" Reaching out, Eldane steadied the boat and the guards began to row. "Apparently, the boys transported Mendel back to Denthan inside a tiny barrel, which they'd suspended round the neck of this dog creature."

"So, even though Athelstone banished him in the form of a goldfish he has still managed to find a way back?"

"With the help of a childling called James Peck," explained Eldane.

"So is the Peck boy a wizard too?"

"That is unclear," said Eldane, with another deep sigh.

"Perhaps Mendel can still do his magic as a fish?"

"Perhaps," mused Eldane. "Landris says that Mendel and the boys have become separated, he says that we should meet them at the Eden Tree on Senegral Island."

Cimerato knew his father was holding something back. Even in the gloom, the old man's Manimal eyes – pure white, with black, vertical pupils – darted about, unable to meet his son's scrutiny. Lord Eldane looked down and busied himself unnecessarily with his robe.

"Father, Landris told you something else in his note, didn't he?" The old man's fingers became tangled in the tie of his purple robe. He leaned over and whispered so the guards wouldn't hear, "Landris has said to take great care around King Athelstone. He is, as Mendel claimed all along, an impostor. The boys have told Landris that Athelstone is actually Dendralon."

Cimerato felt his stomach lurch. He knew, all too well, who Dendralon was. As a child, whenever he had displeased his parents they would say that Dendralon's ghost would come and steal him away. "You mean we've banished Mendel, one of the truest men Gwendral has ever known, on the advice of a Hedra wizard? Worse, this traitor has persuaded us to abandon Gwendral so that all he has to do is open the gates and let his Snakemen walk into the city? How could we have been so stupid?"

"Shhhh," Lord Eldane hushed his son. They would soon be beneath the city walls. "If Athelstone is indeed Dendralon, he must possess very powerful magic to have made such fools of us all for so long."

"He looks exactly like Athelstone," Cimerato admitted, rage rising in his chest.

Lord Eldane sighed. "Son, we have something much more deadly than Dendralon to worry about."

Cimerato didn't understand.

Eldane moved closer to Cimerato in the darkness of the wet

tunnel. "Mendel told these boys that Denthan might only have a few days left before Tealfirth explodes. You can imagine what will happen without our largest sun."

Cimerato shook his head mournfully. "Mendel warned as much before he was banished."

"And we said he was a fool – that such talk was treasonable," said Lord Eldane.

"Athelstone said that, not us," reminded Cimerato, "We'd better get to the Eden Tree fast, and hope that Mendel knows what to do."

Lord Eldane moved even closer. "Landris has said that Dendralon knows of a gateway that can transport thousands at a time from this world to another. These boys say that the Hedra wizard is going to save his own kind at our expense."

Cimerato mulled this over as they passed under the city walls. Sticking to the shadows, the boat edged its way nearer to the River Levan. Slowly, with muffled oars, it glided under the ridge where the Hedra army had set up camp. The small party of Manimals could hear them screaming and banging their war drums above them. Their bloodthirsty yells made Cimerato shiver with dread.

"Get down!" Lord Eldane pulled his son towards the bottom of the boat. His guards followed suit.

Footsteps echoed across the dark waters. Someone was running towards them. A shadowy figure skidded to a halt and then called out in a sharp whisper, "Lord Eldane!"

"It's a Manimal." Cimerato edged himself up.

"I know this soldier. We can trust him," said Lord Eldane.

Beneath a scrap of scarlet sky the Manimal cupped his mouth and in a sharp whisper said, "Someone has unleashed the Keresi!"

"What?" gasped Cimerato. "Why?"

"This is Dendralon's work," whispered Lord Eldane, "he will stop at nothing to destroy Mendel if he thinks he is back in Denthan."

"But how can he know?" said Cimerato.

Lord Eldane helped the messenger into the boat. "If the Yeltans know that Mendel is here, it is fair to assume that the dark creatures of Denthan know too."

"But the Keresi will kill anything they see," said Cimerato. "All creatures are prey to them, even Dendralon and his Hedra." He scanned the ruddy skies above the ridge and wished he was deep inside the great forest of Eldane.

"It will soon be nightfall," said his father, "and we still have another great tunnel to navigate before we reach the forest."

Cimerato knew that their boat would wind its way back under the city and then out beneath the very edge of the ridge where the bulk of the Hedra force was camped.

***

Satisfied that the Keresi would succeed where his assassin, the Wrafnar, had failed, Dendralon was determined to continue with his plan. He had made his way down beneath the city of Gwendral to meet up with the Hedra Leader, King Feldon. As expected, the Royal boat was moored in a small tributary that led to a great underground lake. With the Keresi in full flight, it would be safer to remain below ground for a while.

***

James Peck held The Talisman of Denthan in his trembling hand. It was in fact the detached horn of a creature called Fledha, the most ancient of the Yukplug steeds. The talisman had banished the assassin sent by Dendralon. The Hedra wizard had sent a Wrafnar – a huge insect-like monster that was supposedly impossible to kill. Yet this one had been rendered harmless by James and the talisman. He'd felt Dendralon's pain and frustration. He knew it had somehow upset the Hedra wizard's plans to save his race from the death

5

of Denthan. But could the talisman still save his best friend, Craig? Could it help him again so soon? The Yeltans had tried all sorts of potions and chants to bring Craig back, but to no avail.

Craig Harrison lay on a damp layer of wood-chips that formed the floor of the Yukplug pen. His skin was pale, almost translucent. James could see the veins standing proud on Craig's neck, throbbing with blue, deoxygenated blood. Bero, the faithful golden retriever that had made the journey to Denthan with them, wagged his feathered tail and barked down at his fallen master.

A hornless Yukplug bayed like a donkey and wandered over to sniff at the Talisman in James's hand. It seemed puzzled. It had, after all, shared its whole life with the shed horn. A thick-set animal, covered in orange, Rastafarian-like hair, it began to circle Craig and Bero. A strange mixture of ostrich and highland cow, it looked comical, yet James knew that it was an animal of war. It had a ragged array of yellow teeth and a pair of formidable hooked claws on the back of its scaled legs. The impish Yeltans – small, blue-eyed, yellow-skinned creatures that had, moments before, rejoiced at James's victory over the 'immortal' Wrafnar – were now much more subdued.

"Look!" yelled Landris. The Yeltan leader pointed at the northern horizon.

James glanced between, Craig, the Talisman in his hand, and the darkening sky.

"It can't be," sighed Garlon, a younger Yeltan who had looked after the two boys since the Yeltans had found them. Suddenly more anxious than James had ever seen him, Garlon cupped his mouth and yelled, "Everyone take cover! The Keresi have been set free."

Now babbling and chattering in mass panic, the Yeltans began to disperse. They bolted into their burrows and disappeared, like shadows, between the heavy roots of the tall trees that surrounded the glade.

A sudden breeze ruffled James's tousled hair as he mouthed the words, "What are Keresi?" But there was no answer. Garlon was too busy shouting commands at the fleeing Yeltans and Landris stood dumbstruck staring up at the looming black cloud. James could see now that the Keresi were grouped together in a massive swarm. A strange mixture of ape and insect, the winged creatures issued a low rumbling drone that filled him with complete dread. "Craig!" he moaned, "you have to get up!"

But Craig lay still, his eyes staring blindly.

The Keresi lighted on any creature beneath them like a great flock of locusts. A writhing tree troll had been plucked from the trees ahead and James watched in horror as the horde devoured the wailing giant in seconds. Birds, bats... every kind of creature was easy prey for the terrifying host. Then the massive swarm of flapping, gargoyle-like creatures began to spiral above them. A million leathery wings slapped against each other and a hellish din resonated round the Yeltan clearing. They had long dangling appendages like those of daddy-long-legs, and a head that resembled some kind of deranged ape.

"Use the Talisman!" urged Garlon. Only he and Landris remained. The rest of the Yeltans had taken cover.

"Craig!" repeated James. He held the Talisman over his friend and closed his eyes. A tear rolled down his cheek as he said, "By the power of this Talisman, heal Craig! Heal my friend and let him live!"

"Perhaps it only works against monsters," said Garlon.

Landris gave the young Yeltan a withering glance.

"Just saying," protested Garlon.

Seeing no sign of movement from Craig, James pointed the Talisman at the whirling cloud of flying demons and screamed, "Go back to wherever you came from!"

This time the Talisman vibrated in his hand and began to emit a high-pitched note. A glowing purple mist soon flowed round James's wrist.

"See!" snapped Garlon.

James held the Talisman higher and shouted even louder. "Go back to wherever you came from!"

"It's working!" gasped Garlon, a weird Yeltan smile splitting his mottled, yellow face.

"Go back, I tell you!" James yelled, unable to think of anything better to say. His mind was a mess, his thoughts jumbled. He was sure that Mendel had entered his head the last time he'd used the Talisman. Helped him. Intensified its power. *So where is the wizard now?* He had to be close to perform his magic through James.

The Talisman shone so brightly that it lit up the glade and all the surrounding trees.

The thump of a hundred winged demons landing all around them almost drowned out the single, pure note produced by the Talisman.

A monstrous ape-like apparition lunged down at them with its ragged talons, but James forced himself back onto the damp ground and aimed the Talisman straight at the growling creature.

The Keresi wailed for a split second before its protest was cut short by an airburst of green blood and shattered bones. The creature had literally exploded in front of James, and now more and more beams of deadly lilac light were finding their mark.

High up in the air, the Keresi seemed to be able to dodge the deadly blasts of light from the Talisman, but closer to the ground it tore through the winged demons like a laser.

As before, James felt an incredible power race through him as the Talisman vibrated in his hands.

Landris and Garlon stood back-to-back, slashing up at the

Keresi with their Yeltan spears.

Now the flying demons were forming a kind of tornado above James's head. Round and round they spun, the Talisman at their epicentre, drawing them in.

James felt dizzy and sick at the same time. His chest was tightening.

Bero was trying to drag Craig out of the Yukplug pen, digging his back paws into the ground and shaking his head, his jaws locked onto the heel of Craig's shoe.

Several of the winged demons had lifted Landris off the ground and he was kicking his legs above Craig and Bero.

James swung the Talisman round and a beam of light ripped through at least ten demons before Landris tumbled onto the soft ground. A hardy, thickset creature, the Yeltan leader rolled a few times, found his spear and slashed up at the throng of searching talons once more. Yet the Talisman was fading. Fewer and fewer killer beams leapt from the glowing, striated horn until it juddered to a halt and lay still. Even the single note it sang so loudly waned and then disappeared.

James feared that the screams of the Keresi would be the last thing he would ever hear. A few yards away the baying Yukplug struggled to stand under the weight of the creatures.

Then, as the first winged creature clasped his arm in a vice-like grip, James heard a voice inside his head. A bubbly, grumpy voice that said, 'kill-fire'.

When James opened his mouth to cry out, a trail of gobbledygook that sounded like, "wwwkillwww-wwfiwwreww," spilled from his lips.

The Talisman began to sing again. It actually jumped from of his hand and soared into the swirling mass of Keresi. Then, with a crack of thunder, a million beams of indigo light shot out of the glowing Yukplug horn. The air was thick with the smell of struck matches and fiendish farts.

James heard the sound of a thousand ripping curtains and

then braced as a downpour of hot, green rain drenched him from head to toe.

The whole Yukplug pen was knee-deep in Keresi blood. The surrounding trees were covered, Landris and Garlon were flailing about, trying their best to keep their heads above the gunge, and Bero looked like a walking lump of snot. The Yukplug slipped and skidded until it fell flat on its back with a whimper.

James waded as fast as he could towards the spot where he'd last seen Craig and plunged his hands down into the mess.

He found an arm and heaved his best friend out of the gunge. "Craig!"

2 King Feldon

"Sssire!" hissed Jal, bowing low as Dendralon approached. He recognised the Hedra wizard immediately. Even though Dendralon was still hidden beneath the dead, straining skin of the Manimal king, Athelstone, Hedra could always sense Hedra.

Jal was one of the King's most trusted guards and he had come especially to greet Dendralon.

A wavering flame torch lit the way up the steps that led to King Feldon's camp and Jal was just about to usher the wizard forward when Dendralon turned and slapped him across the face with a small, needle-spiked dragon whip.

"Get more guards down here!" Dendralon hissed in his own Hedra voice. "We don't want any Manimal worms escaping the city through these waterways." Having delivered his order, Dendralon waved Jal aside and continued up the stairwell.

As he watched the wizard climb, Jal's flickering tongue caught the stench of Manimal in the tunnel. Dendralon's magic was struggling to keep Athelstone's skin from rotting, he decided.

Still full of contempt, Jal called after the wizard, "I will call more guards to man the sewers, Sire." But Dendralon was already gone.

Still smarting from Dendralon's blow, Jal looked into the darkness and cursed the dark wizard under his breath. Hunger pangs took hold of his stomach. His last meal, a small reptilian flyer, had merely been a snack. He looked up at the steps on the opposite side of the river and called to the solitary Hedra guard who was slumped in sleep against the wall. "Wake up!"

The Hedra guard almost dropped his spear before standing

to attention.

"Get back up to the ridge and get more sentries down here. Move!"

The guard nodded and scampered up the wet steps to do as he was bid.

***

"What was that?" Cimerato asked. He thought he'd heard some kind of scuffle ahead. "Slow down. Quiet!" He took command of the group. "I'm going to scout round this next bend," he told them. Cimerato turned to his father's guards. "Stay here with my father." He unclipped his yellow armour and slipped into the cold water, swimming as quietly as possible round the bend in the river.

Before long, he saw a small jetty and, beside it, a large Hedra guard who looked agitated and restless.

Cimerato swam closer and noted that there was no one else, just the solitary Hedra giant positioned on the right-hand bank. Behind him, a set of slippery stairs disappeared into the darkness. The opposite bank was deserted. Turning to swim back to the boat, he saw the Hedra guard moving towards the stairs, muttering to himself and belching loudly before disappearing from view.

Dripping with river-water, Cimerato pulled himself into the boat. "Just the one guard, but he's gone now. Row quietly."

The boat edged round the corner of the underground river and soon passed the deserted stairwell. Cimerato drew a long sigh of relief as they drifted out into the night.

"Only ten more minutes and we will be in the estuary of the River Levan," whispered Cimerato.

When they reached the great river, he spoke in a low, steady voice to his father. "I saw one of our Dragons pulled down by the Hedra on that ridge this morning." Cimerato stared up at the dark mass of granite above them.

Lord Eldane scanned the night sky. "There must have been at least six attempts to cross the city walls on the Dragons of Hest. Only one succeeded. One! Some of your richer relations foolishly thought it would be safer than the tunnels."

"That guard back there... I'm sure he had the royal serpents of King Feldon on his breastplate." Cimerato looked up at the glow from a thousand campfires, then back at Gwendral, the 'City of Spires'. A jagged moonlit silhouette, the main citadel was a good hundred feet taller than any other feature. The city looked impregnable from this angle.

"We should have put more faith in our defences," whispered Lord Eldane.

"And in our friends," added Cimerato. "Instead, here we are, fleeing like rats."

Lord Eldane nodded sternly. "Needs must. If we take turns rowing, we should reach the tributary that leads to the Island of Senegral by daybreak." The old man wrapped his cloak round his chest and slumped further down into his seat. He stared hard at the star-spangled sky. "We must make sure that it is our race, the Manimals, that survive whatever is yet to befall us. The Hedra snakes will pay for their treachery."

Slightly unsettled by the sheer hatred that laced his father's words, Cimerato closed his eyes as he pictured his mother making her way through the old tunnels that led to Nordengate. No one had been in those tunnels for centuries. He wondered what dark creatures might still linger in their black pools.

***

Having forgotten his rations pouch, Jal issued a deep growl and doubled back to the bottom of the stairs to fetch it. When he crouched to pick it up, however, he thought he saw the outline of a small boat fade into the inky night. In an instant, an extra set of glistening red eyelids slipped over his cat-like pupils. Jal would see so much more in infrared.

The insects and bats working the dark tunnel were transformed into a mass of flying dots and traces that made it difficult to focus. Before long, though, he saw what he was looking for. In the distance, eight faint red, glowing figures, that could only be warm-blooded Manimals, were rowing into the great forest.

If I confess this to Dendralon now, he'll kill me, Jal realised with a shudder. *He will blame me for letting them escape. So I'll say nothing. Why should I risk my neck any more than I already have?* He started back up the stairs, having convinced himself that he was doing the right thing. When he reached the top, however, he paused and listened carefully.

"What do you mean you never got my message?" Dendralon raged. "I ordered you to find the boys and kill them!"

"But, Sire," exclaimed King Feldon, "we never received any message!" The Hedra King did not like being humiliated, especially in front of his entourage.

Dendralon continued his attack. "I sent it last night, attached to the reptile flyer that you sent to me!"

"But it never returned," said Feldon, shifting nervously.

Hidden in the shadows of the stairwell, Jal gulped as he remembered his snack from the night before.

"We saw the Keresi," said King Feldon, trying to change the subject, "but they disappeared almost as soon as they swept over our heads."

"What do you mean?" hissed Dendralon.

Feldon's wavering tone betrayed his fear. "They circled the hill of Dunnad and then disappeared. They seemed to funnel down behind the hill, as if returning from whence they came."

"Tens of thousands of Keresi cannot simply disappear..." But Dendralon stopped and closed his eyes in thought. "The Talisman is more powerful than anyone realises."

"The Talisman?" enquired Feldon.

14

Dendralon waved Feldon's guards away and continued in a low voice, lest any would hear other than Feldon himself. "Listen to me now. In two days, I will give the command to open the gates of Gwendral. Later that same day Tealfirth will die and our world will be no more!"

"What?" Feldon's slit pupils expanded and blackened in fear. "As soon as that?"

Dendralon gave him a cold smile. "I have already given the order for a mass evacuation of the city. Even now, the Manimals scamper away down their stupid tunnels." He leaned closer still. "Remember, Feldon, only those inside the city of Gwendral will survive the holocaust. Once I have the three crystals in place, the city will transport our race, and no other, to safety. The Hedra will be the only Denthan survivors."

"As it should be." Feldon's nostrils flared with satisfaction at the news.

In the shadows, Jal sensed that the wizard was still troubled.

Dendralon began to explain his thoughts to Feldon. "I now wonder if the combined force of the Denthan crystals will be enough without the Magic Scales."

"The great Scales of Gwendral have disappeared?" gasped Feldon?

"They are destroyed but I will repair them once I get hold of the Talisman," said Dendralon.

Jal did not think that the dark wizard sounded too sure on this point. Carefully, he edged forward until he could see.

"That which tore them asunder may also have the power to restore them," continued Dendralon.

Feldon looked confused.

"However, I must busy myself for now," Dendralon said. "I need to collect all three Denthan crystals. One from the Salt Trolls – the guardians of the sea; one from the Osgrunfs – the rulers of the forests and the tundra; and one from you, Feldon

– king of the Hedra."

Feldon pawed at the thick chain that hung round his neck. "I will bring it to you when you open the gates."

Jal admired the courage of his King. He was not stupid enough to give up the Hedra crystal yet.

Dendralon glanced down at the blue crystal that hung round Feldon's neck and smiled. "Don't shoot their tired Dragons down from the sky anymore, let them flee. Save your weaponry." Dendralon scratched at a peeling patch of pale skin. "In two days, once the Salt Trolls and Osgrunfs have wiped each other out, you can simply walk into an empty city. Have patience, but be ready to move at a moment's notice."

Feldon gave the wizard a nod of satisfaction.

"I have work to do," continued Dendralon, "I must make sure that the Salt Trolls and the Osgrunfs turn on each other. In the meantime, I want you to rid us of those boys. I cannot risk any interventions by that persistent fool Mendel. Is that clear?"

Feldon lowered his voice. "I know that the tree trolls, Ashthat and Ssslathat, were attacked by a pair of small boys and badly wounded. They were the laughing stock of the camp."

"These boys may be more powerful than you think," said Dendralon. They have come here with Mendel."

"But, Mendel is banished, he…"

"Mendel has returned. I'm sure of it. Perhaps in some other form, but he is here and he has helped the Peck boy find the Talisman of Denthan." Dendralon paused, shaking his head in quiet frustration, "They are somewhere close to the hill of Dunnad. Can you find these boys and Mendel? Can I trust you, a Hedra King, to succeed where others have failed?"

Feldon nodded vigorously. "Of course. But you should know that we saw other Manimal-like creatures in the forest. A woman and—"

But Dendralon had disappeared in a swirl of black mist, leaving Feldon open-mouthed.

Unsure of how much the wizard had heard of his King's sentence, Jal continued to watch. He was still trying to make sense of the whole conversation, when Feldon summoned his captain, a savage fighter called Telan, and explained what had to be done. "Make sure that all Hedra have gathered on the ridge. Tell them to stop wasting ammunition on old Dragons." Feldon looked at the spot where Dendralon had stood, his long tongue flicking in and out of his mouth, attempting to sense the wizard's presence.

Seemingly reassured that Dendralon was gone, Feldon gave his next instructions. "Take a troop into the forest and make sure that the archers who fired on that useless Mertol show you where they saw the Manimal woman in the river. Take the Tree Trolls with you and find the two Manimal boys who hide near Dunnad. Kill any creature that accompanies them. Make sure you kill every Manimal you find in the forest, young and old!" Telan made to bow, but Feldon put the point of his sword under Telan's chin, forcing him to lift his head again. "Be sure to kill the Mertol this time too. He failed Dendralon. If he had done his job properly, the strangers would not have entered the forest. Also, once the Tree Trolls have done their work, get rid of them too. Got that?"

Jal suspected that Dendralon would look well on such thoroughness.

Feldon motioned Telan to leave and then called out. "Jal! Jal! Where are you?"

Jal pressed himself against the wet wall as King Feldon shouted down the stairwell that led to the underground river.

"Sire?" To Feldon's annoyance, Telan was still in the room. "Sire, the Mertol killed twenty of our archers today. Its magic is dangerous and unpredictable. And how exactly do we kill a Tree Tro—?" The guard stopped mid-sentence as Feldon whipped round and gripped his throat.

"Sssssssssss. I thought I told you to go. You do not think. You do!" Telan shut his scaly nostrils tight as Feldon's dank breath washed over him. The Hedra King moved even closer to the captain's face and hissed, "Go!"

The Hedra officer tripped backwards, struggling to breathe. He bowed awkwardly, then fell out into the warm night air. Jal could hear Telan's voice outside. "Where are the..." – he coughed – "...the Tree Trolls?"

Not wishing it to appear that he'd listened in on the various conversations, Jal waited a few seconds before slipping from the wet passageway into Feldon's tent. Feldon looked up when his bodyguard entered. "Ah, there you are, Jal. Come here." He sat Jal down, his voice soft when he spoke. "Telan has just left."

Jal smiled. "Yes, my Lord, I thought I heard him."

"He won't be coming back again. Ever." Feldon tilted his head and looked Jal straight in the eye. "Understood?"

Jal blinked his yellow-slit eyes. "I don't quite follow, Sire." Jal had, of course, heard everything, and did follow, but he liked to play dumb. He was less of a threat to the King that way.

Feldon smiled at Jal. "Once Telan has carried out his tasks, I want you to kill him."

"Tasks, my lord?"

"Listen carefully, Jal, and you will understand. I want you to go with Telan—tell him I sent you. Tell him to relay to you every instruction I've just given him. Remind him that he will need more than twenty archers to overpower and kill the Mertol. The useless ape failed to guard the gateway into Denthan and has displeased Dendralon. Only after he has carried out all my instructions are you to kill Telan. Got that so far?"

"Yes, Sire."

18

"And then you may come back and tell me when all is done."

"Another clean-up, Lord?" remarked Jal with a smile.

"That's it, a clean-up. You're good at cleaning up, Jal, but..." – Feldon turned to pour himself a large glass of red liquid – "... make sure you return within two days."

"Do we attack after this, my Lord?"

"Something like that. I'll need you back at my side by then, so just make sure you're here when I need you." Feldon drank deeply from his chalice and waved Jal away with a flick of his taloned hand.

Jal bowed then made his way out into the main Hedra camp. In these last desperate hours, he would have to look after himself. From a young Hedra, Jal had devoted his life to the King, doing his dirty work, protecting him. But that, Jal knew, did not mean Feldon would be doing him any favours in return. When push came to shove, the Hedra King would think only of saving his own skin.

3 Evening Falls

James hauled Craig from the putrid green gunge that filled the Yukplug pen, being careful to avoid an occasional floating wing or disembodied limb as he struggled on. After a final heave, James sat down hard on a moss-covered mound of rock.

Bero swam to the same outcrop as James and immediately began licking Craig clean.

James recoiled in disgust. "Bero...!" Then he looked round his feet and searched his pockets. "The Talisman?" He saw Garlon and Landris on the opposite side of the glade, scrambling up a thick tree trunk, and shouted, "I can't find the Talisman!"

"It's here," said a low voice.

There was a cough at James's feet and he knelt down to cup Craig's head. "Are you okay?"

Craig coughed up another lump of green goo and stared up at his best friend. "Of course I'm not okay, you numpty." He stared at his sodden clothes and picked a piece of something stringy from his teeth. "What is this stuff?"

James barely managed to stop himself being sick. "It's...it's nothing...much...not really." He shook Craig by the shoulders. "I thought you were a goner!"

"Tastes like liquorice," continued Craig. He sat up and wiped his eyes with the back of his right hand.

"Is that the Talisman?" asked James.

Craig nodded and handed it to him. "I told you already."

"Yeah," said James in a bemused tone. "How did you get it?"

"I don't know. It was in my hand when I woke up."

James peeled back Craig's sleeve. "Your wound."

"What wound?" asked Craig, straining to see where James was looking.

"Exactly," said James. "It's gone. You got a nick when we were fighting that immortal thingy."

Bero growled.

"The Wrafnar," said Craig. "It's okay, boy," he patted Bero's head, "we killed it, didn't we?"

"Technically," began James, "we didn't kill it. It was banished to another place, according to the Yeltans, and... Get this. I'm pretty sure that Mendel is here. I heard him in my head. I'm sure it was him."

"Where is he? He told us to meet him at the Eden Tree," said Craig.

James gave his friend a tight-lipped smile. "He did, but..." He took the Talisman from Craig, who handed it over like a hot potato. "I heard him when I was holding this." James examined the striations on the surface of the Yukplug horn. He traced them with his fingers. There were concentric rings on its dull yellowed surface. "It looks just like the horn of a Highland Cow, don't you think?"

Craig looked impatient. More like his old self. Full of energy again. "What happened after I passed out?" Suddenly distracted, he found another piece of green gunge on his leg and peeled it off. "I bet this is like that mossgeld stuff. I tastes pretty good."

He made to put it in his mouth but James lunged forward and caught his hand. "Eh... I wouldn't do that if I were you."

Craig shook the gunge free of his fingers and they both watched it drop on the ground.

Bero took a sniff and growled.

"When you passed out," began James, "the Yeltans told me that you could never recover. I didn't know what to do, so I tried using the Talisman again. But it didn't work. Then, as I was desperately thinking what I could do, this huge cloud of flying demon things appeared in the sky. There were thousands of them. They were looking for me – for the

Talisman or something – because they all veered down towards the Yukplug pen like a tornado. I began using the Talisman against them, and it began to shoot beams of light this way and that. But there were too many so I raised the Talisman and it shot out of my hand. That's when I heard Mendel. His magic filled my head. I felt dizzy and then said some spell or other. There was an explosion and every last one of them split into a million pieces. There was green blood and guts everywhere."

Craig wretched and began spitting on the ground. "And you let me eat this stuff!"

"I stopped you," protested James.

"Not the first time," cried Craig.

"Not the first time," James repeated quietly. "You were too quick for me. I was still confused."

"Yuk!"

"Yeah," said James.

Landris and Garlon approached the two boys.

"Craig is alive!" yelled Garlon.

"How can this be?" muttered Landris.

"Mendel is close by," said James, finding renewed strength. "The quicker we find him, the quicker I will find my dad."

"So, you still think your dad is here?" asked Craig.

"I have to believe it," said James, determined not to get into an argument with Craig. He turned to Landris. "When can we go to the Eden Tree?"

"In the morning," he replied. "The Forest of Eldane is not a place to explore at night."

"But..." began James.

Landris wiped a long stringy piece of something from his shoulder and said, "If Mendel is truly back in Denthan, he will want you to stick to his plan. We will be at the Eden Tree before lunch tomorrow." The old Yeltan then smiled as if he had just put the world to rights. "Bed is this way." He pointed to the buttress of a very old tree that had split in two and had a whole array of newer offshoots. "We must say our chants before bed and tidy up the burrows."

Craig looked at James, a puzzled expression on his face, but James just shrugged and plodded on after the two root-dwellers.

***

Eethan slept soundly on the little raft, his disgusting choking noises only interrupted by lengthy pauses during which the only two awake, Cathy Peck and Father Michael, wondered if he was still alive. Normally, however, a loud snort, followed by a noise like a vacuum trying to suck up a pint of drool, would signal the blue man's continued existence.

"I'm beginning to feel quite queasy," said Michael, as he paddled in the darkness.

"He's disgusting," Cathy agreed. "Maybe I should give him a dig in the ribs before something out there hears him." She pointed into the gloom of the forest.

"No, let me," the Reverend quickly volunteered. "He might scream out if you, um…hit too hard."

She shrugged. "Whatever."

Nodding grimly, the vicar moved over next Eethan. "Eethan!" he whispered into the little man's ear, then instantly drew back.

Cathy felt the chill of the night seeping through her coat. "What's wrong now?"

"His ears smell like rotten cheese." Michael grimaced as he shifted away from the little blue man.

Cathy lifted her oar out of the water and cracked it against Eethan's skull.

"Eeee! What ees eet, nastee woman?" screeched Eethan.

"Wake up. All that racket you're making is going to get us killed," complained Cathy.

"What rackeet?" Eethan rubbed his head and muttered

something in a strange tongue.

"Never mind," snapped Cathy. "Those demon things...?" she continued, "the sky was full of them."

"They ees dead," moaned Eethan.

"So you think my goldfish killed them?"

"Eee thinks so," said Eethan, busy rubbing his left ear.

"So James must be close by?"

Eethan clanked his needle-sharp teeth together, as if testing they were still intact. "Only Mendel can do such big magic. And Mendel ees with James and Craig, ee thinks. But eeeven he would struggle to do thees. Theee only way ee can think of destroying thee Keresi ees by using the Talisman of Denthan."

"So why are we going deeper into the forest?" snapped Cathy.

"Mendel has always said that ee would meet mee at the Eden Tree. Once wee finds Mendel, we finds James and Craig and then maybe you finds your husband and bee much nicer after that."

Ephie, the overweight Drumfintley snoop, who had been drawn into Denthan with them, woke for a second and muttered, "She doesn't know the meaning of the word 'nice'." Then she fell straight back to sleep, snuggled up beside Jean – Craig's mum – and Wee Joe, Craig's younger brother.

Cathy lifted her oar, all set to give Ephie a crack too.

"Mum?" Helen, Craig's younger sister, stirred briefly, but fell back to sleep.

"See," spat Cathy, lowering her oar, "you're going to wake the kids. Just do something to make this raft go faster." She gave Eethan a quick kick to the shin.

"Eee! Nastee woman..." Quite awake now, Eethan mumbled to himself as he slipped into the water. Holding on to the back of the raft, he started to kick and they began to pick up speed.

As the night sky assumed the blood-red hue of dawn, the

raft moved into a much wider section of the river where the current pushed more forcefully against them. They were struggling to make any headway.

"Wees need to turn een there!" Eethan splashed Cathy's face, which annoyed her no end, and pointed to an offshoot that led deeper into the forest.

Cathy's eyes flared with anger and she seemed to be considering giving Eethan another, harder, crack with the oar until she realised that the raft was moving the wrong way. She shook Jean and Ephie awake instead. "Rest time is over, you two. You have to help paddle!"

***

In the flickering light of a Hedra campfire, the Tree Troll, Ashthat, sat sharpening a large tree trunk, a task made more difficult by the huge patch covering his blind eye and his currently unusable hand. As he attempted to work, driven purely by thoughts of revenge, his brother, Ssslathat, poured a great bowl of oil over Ashthat's blooded finger stumps. He nodded with satisfaction as a series of long green shoots pushed through the ends of his brother's severed fingers, bending and flexing as they grew.

"You two!" Telan pointed at the Tree Trolls. "Feldon has agreed to assist you in your hunt for the puny little boys who wounded you."

"They had magic on their side!" protested Ashthat in his deep, woody voice.

"If you say so," Telan mocked.

By this time, Jal had caught up with Telan and his crew. As he had done all his life, he listened carefully, but appeared to hear nothing. He was particularly intrigued by Telan's next instruction. "We'll sniff them out for you, but first you must help us."

"Help?" Ssslathat's massive frame creaked as he

straightened up, the green crest on his head tilting to one side.

Telan flicked his black tongue nervously. "Yes, 'help'. You must help us kill a Mertol that has failed in its duties."

Although he tried to hide it, it was obvious to Jal that the Hedra captain was intimidated by the immense size of the Trolls. He wondered how Telan was going to dispense with these two monsters when the time came.

"You ask the impossible!" growled Ashthat.

"This is not a joke," Telan insisted. "If you want our trackers to help you, then you must kill the Mertol. That is our condition!"

"It is not easy to kill a Mertol," said Ssslathat.

Ashthat let his half-sharpened spear fall to the ground and stood up. He put a heavy hand on his brother's shoulder and said, "I will kill the Mertol. The request for revenge is mine, therefore so too is the condition!"

4 Betrayal

On the River Levan, Cimerato gazed up at the star-filled sky and listened as his father told him more about Mendel's prediction. "Mendel warned the inner Council that Tealfirth would explode and wipe out Denthan. But Athelstone argued that Mendel's calculations were wrong. Then he accused him of scaremongering to retain power. We didn't want to believe Mendel, even those who knew and loved him. We listened to Athelstone instead. Soon after that the attacks on our outer villages began. Centedes, Osgrunfs... And then the Hedra began to move north towards Gwendral.

"Athelstone blamed Mendel for all this too, convincing us that it was the wizard's experiments that unsettled the dark creatures. We stupidly believed the soft words of Athelstone and agreed to banish Mendel. But the sun flares and heat storms continued. In the confusion, the banishment went ahead and we justified it to ourselves, mainly because we did not want to face up to our own fears. I'm sorry, Son..." The old man gripped Cimerato's arm. "Do you remember how that terrible heat storm hit the city just at the point when Athelstone banished Mendel?"

"I remember," Cimerato replied.

"Well, its arrival upset Athelstone considerably and we suspected that all did not go according to plan."

The glow of several far-off campfires lit up the sky as their boat headed further up the river.

"I've been thinking about the last words Mendel said to me," mused Eldane. "He said that if he could return to Denthan, he might be able to save our people by helping them escape through a huge gateway to another world."

"But a gateway can only take a few people at a time,"

Cimerato pointed out.

"That's what I always believed. But after reading the Yeltan letter, sent after the boys told them the truth about our situation, I think now that Athelstone – or should I say Dendralon – has found a giant gateway capable of taking thousands."

"But Dendralon has sent everyone into the tunnels, away from the city," Cimerato argued. "He could just have left us alone to our fate and escaped through his gateway. Why invite the Hedra? Why are the Osgrunfs and Salt Trolls here? I don't understand. He seems to be making things difficult when it could all be so easy for him. Why come back to Gwendral in the first place? Unless..." Cimerato gripped his father's arm. "Gwendral... The gateway must be in Gwendral."

"Exactly."

"But mother and the children and..." gasped Cimerato.

Lord Eldane waved a finger at him. "I've told everyone to wait in the tunnels. They will walk only a mile or so before stopping. They are to wait there for further instructions."

"What instructions?" Cimerato saw nothing in his father's eyes that suggested he had any kind of plan. "You don't know, do you?"

Eldane sighed. "All I know is that Mendel and this Peck boy are our only hope. We must believe that he has managed to return somehow and that he is somewhere in there waiting for us." He pointed ahead into the dark forest.

The muffled oars beat out a steady rhythm as they distanced themselves from the city, passing by the Knoll of Dunnad before slipping into the leafy shelter of the Forest of Eldane.

**

Several Salteths were arguing over the remains of a dead comrade, squashed by one of the Salt Trolls, when they saw

28

something that made them screech and jump back from the campfire. Before them, a ghostly, black-cloaked figure stepped out of the flames and dark smoke. They dropped their weapons and ran blindly, tripping over other sleeping Salteths, which caused an even greater commotion than before.

Dendralon addressed the nearest Salt Troll in his distinctive, deep hissing voice. "Sintor!"

Sintor, who'd been watching the quarrelling Salteths with some amusement, drew back from the strange apparition that had interrupted his entertainment. With a grunt, he raised himself up, soon standing high above Dendralon. "Why does King Athelstone visit my camp?" he boomed.

"I wear the dead King's skin, Sintor, but I am someone else. Surely you can recognise my voice from your dreams?"

Sintor squinted at him. "Dendralon?"

Dendralon opened his robe and pulled a strip of rotting Manimal flesh away from his serpentine scales. "Very soon now, I shall be free of this." He tossed the fragment amongst the Salteths, who screamed and kicked, until one emerged triumphant with the small morsel in his mouth.

Sintor ignored his noisy slaves. "Why are we not in the city yet, Dendralon? Why have you deemed it necessary for my kin to fry in the heat of day for so long? Why?" he bellowed.

Undaunted by Sintor's aggression, Dendralon stepped forward. "As you know, only some will share the treasures of Gwendral. The stars have foretold it." Dendralon peered steadily at Sintor, his dark eyes unreadable. "You are to destroy the Osgrunf hordes. They are not worthy of passing through the ivory gates of Gwendral." Dendralon pointed up to the black ridge in the distance. "King Feldon and his Hedra army will help you."

A displeased murmur grew amongst the Salt Trolls who had overheard Dendralon's words. They raised their massive Gnarwhale spears.

Not intimidated in the least, Dendralon shook his long, black hair from his hood and continued, "I will weave magic that will help you in your fight, but I need something of yours to protect you from my spell." Dendralon lifted his right hand above his head and whispered a small charm.

The trees that had sheltered the sea creatures from the intense heat of the day began to sway and bend in a sudden breeze. The Trolls looked about in fear, then let loose a mighty roar, preparing to attack the wizard at Sintor's command. But the Troll king held up a hand and stayed their charge.

Dendralon pointed a long finger at Sintor. "I need your crystal."

Sintor had worn it since birth. "But why?" he growled, not liking this request at all. The blue crystal was his badge of kinghood. Set in a bronze wristband, the charm shone amber and cerulean blue in the light of the campfire. For an instant, a flash of light from the crystal lit up Dendralon's face, making him squint. Sintor shielded the crystal with his massive, wrinkled hand.

Dendralon held out his hand. "I will, of course, return it after the massacre."

A younger Troll, who'd been watching, hissed his disapproval, "This is trickery, Sintor! Do not trust the words of this necromancer in disguise!"

The dissenter was about to say more, but fell mute as Dendralon fixed his gaze on the young Troll's large silhouette. He moved his hand back and forth in front of the unlucky creature and, slowly, the brute's skin began to tighten. The fire that had brought Dendralon to their camp leaped free from its embers and snaked up the legs of the screaming giant until the flames covered him completely. After several horrifying moments, there was a sickening crack and the fire snuffed out. The Salt Troll stood motionless, little traces of white smoke seeping from his charred form. There was a quiver and a rumble, and then his body simply exploded, black dust showering everyone.

The Salt Trolls stealthily began to back away from the wizard, keeping their eyes lowered. All except Sintor, who remained where he was, dazedly wiping away the black dust that covered his craggy face. "Take it!" he finally hissed. "Just take it!" With a grimace of remorse, he dropped the heavy bracelet into the wizard's outstretched hand.

"Do not worry, Sintor, you will not regret this," said Dendralon. "Now, be ready to attack the Osgrunfs. They were never invited to this place."

Sintor turned, and without looking back at Dendralon, barked to his horde. "Get ready for battle!"

With the Salt Troll crystal tucked safely into his pocket, Dendralon slipped between the ranks of the stunned sea creatures and disappeared into the night.

***

Dendralon knew he had to move fast, especially now that Mendel had returned. Using his magic, he soon entered the part of the Plain of Gwendral occupied by the Osgrunfs. Beside a make-shift tent, he spied their leader sitting on a large throne covered with animal skins.

Dendralon's voice interrupted the din. "Hushna!"

The oversized Osgrunf turned to face the wizard, then called for wine. "Wine for the dream-maker. Wine!" Hushna's blue crystal swung on a heavy black chain round his neck. It sparkled through the matted hair that poked through his armour. "You're not looking your best, Dendralon." Hushna had met the wizard in his disguise before.

With a wave of his flaking hand, Dendralon declined the goblet of wine. "Sorry, Hushna, there is no time to make merry. Not yet. I have come to warn you that the Salt Trolls are planning to move on the city first. They too have had a dream that tells them the city is theirs. And they are greedy for the treasures within."

"What!" Hushna stood up at once and beat his chest armour with a black hooked claw. "So you told them to come to this place too? You have betrayed us!"

"I have not," Dendralon said. He moved in close and whispered into Hushna's ear. "I suspect Mendel summoned the sea creatures here before his banishment." Dendralon spat on the dirt. "I will help you fix this."

Hushna growled at the Osgrunfs that stood beside him as they snarled and jostled to make way for their King and the black wizard.

"What do you have in mind, Dendralon?" Hushna asked, growing agitated when Dendralon beckoned him closer.

Speaking in a low mutter, the dark wizard gave his instructions. "You must attack the Salt Trolls at first light. As your reward I will give you half the treasure of Gwendral. My Hedra army will help you. The stars have foretold our victory. It will signal the dawning of a new age."

Having got what he wanted with a quick sleight of hand, Dendralon quickly stepped back. "I must leave now. Time is short. Remember, attack just after sunrise. I am depending on the legendary fury of your army, Hushna." As Dendralon turned to leave, he checked the blue crystal that hung round the Osgrunf leader's neck. Dendralon stared at it for a moment. Then, satisfied that it looked genuine enough, he backed away with the true gem tucked safely in his pocket.

Dendralon knew Feldon, the Hedra king, had the third and final crystal. It was the oldest and most important of them. With all three, he could operate the greatest of all the Gateways. He may yet need the Talisman to repair the Magic Scales, but he would try his own magic first. Once events were set in motion, no one would be able to stop him, not even Mendel. The appearance of the hideous Salt Trolls and fearsome Osgrunfs at the city gates had been enough to clear the city of the Manimals. Now he would let these armies of Denthan destroy each other. Soon Gwendral would be back in the hands of its original builders, the Hedra.

5 The Trackers

James and Craig stepped out into the remains of the Yukplug pen with Bero, mesmerised by Denthan's spectacular double dawn. The torrent of green goo produced by the demise of the Keresi had solidified and turned into a thick black crust that still covered much of the surrounding area. For the first time since they'd arrived in Denthan, they noticed a few clouds gathering overhead.

"We're ready, Garlon," said James, spotting the young Yeltan. He saw that Garlon and Landris had a sizeable entourage of Yeltans with them. Each carried a couple of bags and two small spears.

"Good morning, boys," greeted Landris. He narrowed his strange light-blue eyes. "Be careful not to touch the spear tips. They are laced with poison."

"Right." James took a step back.

"Are you both happy to travel by Yukplug?" asked Landris.

"*I* am," said Craig, "but what about Bero? He'll never be able to keep up with those things."

"We could leave him here until we get back," James suggested.

"Back from where?" snapped Craig. "Besides, he's come this far." Craig tensed. "I'm not leaving him now."

"Fine!" James looked across to Landris and shrugged. "No Yukplugs, then."

"No problem," said Landris. "We will travel underground."

"How long will it take to get there?" Craig couldn't help thinking of Bero's shaky back legs.

"About three hours, all being well," said Landris. He went on to explain what their route would be. "We will skirt the Centide breeding grounds then travel north to a place known as The Break. It's an off-shoot of the River Levan. For a brief time, we'll need to go to the surface. After that, we'll head deeper into another tunnel system that will lead us to the Eden Tree, which grows on a small hill."

"On Senegral Island?" asked James.

"One and the same," said Landris. "We will travel up under the hill, to the roots of the Eden Tree itself."

"I was there last year!" exclaimed Garlon.

"On your fiftieth birthday," reminded Landris.

"Fiftieth!" the boys blurted out at the same time.

Garlon laughed. "That's nothing! Mendel is said to be more than twelve thousand years old."

Craig's eyes widened and he gave James a friendly punch on the shoulder. "Un-bloomin-believable! You've got a twelve thousand-year-old goldfish, mate!"

James rubbed his shoulder. "It would be a lot bloomin' easier if Mendel were here now. Where has he got to?"

Standing in line, they waited to drop into the chute that would take them to the necessary tunnel.

James checked his belt for the Talisman and then made the leap. "Ooohhh!" he cried out. "This is great!" He loved slides and roller coasters. Moving at high speed, they eventually landed with a bump in the darkness. There was a click off to their left and light filled the tunnel.

Craig turned to James and whispered, "Electricity?"

"I don't think so, somehow. Look!" James pointed to the Yeltans at the front of their group. They held the same glowing branches they'd seen the day before.

Even though the boys ducked low, the ends of long roots clawed at their hair and clothes as they moved through the cramped tunnel system.

In such a dusty, confined space James marvelled at how easy it was for him to breathe. "I still can't believe I've not coughed or wheezed once since we've been in Denthan." He tried not to think of the lost rucksack and the inhaler inside. Just remembering he didn't have the thing was normally enough to send him into spasms.

"Just as well," said Craig, "now that you've lost your inhaler. I mean, you'd probably have keeled over by now. I wouldn't rate your chances here if—"

"Craig!" James exclaimed. "I'm trying *not* to think about it, for Pete's sake!" James forced himself to think about his dad instead as he plodded on. His dad would have loved exploring the Yeltan tunnels and the strange Forest of Eldane. Then he remembered Landris producing his father's jacket and his good mood melted away.

Deep in his heart James knew that his dad was still alive. He just knew it. But did his mum? Did she even want his dad to be alive? Bent double as he navigated the narrow passage, his thoughts drifted to the time when she'd been locked in a toilet on the intercity train between Glasgow and London. His dad had slept through the whole thing. "Six hours and forty-five minutes of hell," his mum had screeched. For his mum, it probably had been hell. She suffered from claustrophobia. When they'd finally arrived at his Auntie Bella's she'd recounted the whole episode at least ten times. "He did it on purpose, Bella. I know he did," she'd moaned, "David likes to get back at me now and again, see me suffer. He knows I can't stand small spaces." He remembered his dad pleading, "No Cathy. I simply fell asleep."

The story in turn reminded him of the shout he'd heard on the hill the morning before. He was sure he'd heard someone yelling the word 'run', and it had sounded just like his mum. But it couldn't have been. She was safe and sound, back in Drumfintley.

James tried to get Craig's attention. "How many teacakes are they on now, back at your place?"

Ahead of Bero, Craig chuckled and shook his head. "I don't

know, hundreds..."

"Ooffff!" James clutched his eye. "Watch where you're pinging those bloomin' roots. That hit me right in the face, dunderheed!"

Craig just laughed as he let another one fly.

"Hey!" yelped James.

***

Telan, Ssslathat, Ashthat, Jal and a whole troop of Hedra light infantry had finally tracked the Manimals' scent and were now following it to its source. The two Trolls waded through the river while the Hedra jogged along in the forest edge. They soon reached the Mertol's cave and slowed their pace.

Telan decided that they should split into two groups – Ashthat, along with one hundred Hedra, would veer east to the Mertol's cave and kill the beast, while Ssslathat, Jal and the rest of the party would push north along the River Levan. They would take care of the Manimals.

The lead Hedra's tongue flicked excitedly back and forth in the morning air. "Sir, we are close!" He pointed to a small, shale beach. "I smell female Manimal and younglings and..." the Hedra tracker closed his slit-eyes in concentration, "I smell some other creature unknown to me."

Swords drawn, Telan and twenty fighters crept up the shale bank and then leapt into a shadowy grove. As they hacked at the hanging moss and jabbed into the thick ferns, they soon realised that their prey had moved on. "Look... There were one, two...four adults, two children and...and that." The tracker pointed to a small, three-toed footprint.

"What's that?" Telan asked.

The Hedra shrugged and flicked his tongue, savouring the scent. "Come, we have to catch up with the others." Telan ran back down the beach but stopped as his eyes caught sight of something. He picked up a smooth, shiny piece of white paper. He held it up to the light and saw some tiny brown grains clinging to the folds and creases. He was completely mystified by the symbols written on its edges, which read: *Galdinie's Hand Made Tablet.* For a moment his long, black tongue probed the creases, then he threw his head back in a hideous laugh. "Ha! As ssssweet as honey! They're going to taste good with this running through their veins!" The rest of the Hedra laughed too as they splashed back into the river to join Ssslathat and the remainder of their column.

***

Near to the Mertol's cave, the other group of Hedra formed a semicircle behind Ashthat. The hulking Troll blinked his remaining eye, then jerked his head back and issued a deep, eerie cry that echoed over the hillside. "Kak! Kak!" He was summoning the Mertol to battle. Crumpled Hedra lay scattered round the cave entrance, victims of the previous day's encounter. The stench of death wafted down through the ferns to the nervous Hedra below. All had slipped feather-light bows from their backs and, with arrows notched, waited for any sign of movement.

Ashthat came to a halt at the opening of the cave and sniffed the air. His heavy limbs creaked as he crouched down low to peer inside.

He saw a few mangled cages hanging from the roof and a shattered table lying in pieces on the damp floor. As his purple eye acclimatised to the darkness, he realised that nothing breathed life in the cave. The Mertol had gone. He backed out of the entrance and looked down the grassy slope at the terrified Hedra. "Nothing there. It's gone! Kak!" He turned, ran, and with an amazing leap bounded over the ducking Hedra. "Back to the river!" he cried. The Hedra sped after him through the forest, not wanting to lose sight of the Troll who could cover such huge distances with every step.

It wasn't long before Ashthat had caught up with his brother and the rest of the Hedra. He explained how he'd found the Mertol's cave empty.

Telan cursed. "King Feldon will not be pleased if we return without the Mertol's scalp." He scratched his scaly head. "There is nothing we can do now but go after the Manimals. They are more important."

The troop headed out, a wave of water pushing ahead of the two Trolls as they marched upstream toward the beginning of the tributary known as The Break. Drops of rain began to fall round them and steam rose up from the forest canopy.

"I hate the rain!" Jal blinked as the raindrops intensified.

Telan shouted up at the Trolls. "What can you see up there?"

Ssslathat creaked as he bent down to speak to the Hedra captain. "The river continues onward, but I can see a smaller offshoot to our left." Ssslathat stood up and asked, "Which way?"

Telan flicked his tongue in the rain. "I don't know. I can't smell anything in this muck! Just stick to the main river and look for any sudden movement. They can't be far now."

6 The Giants

Eethan swam round to the front of the raft, then disappeared beneath the clear water.

Jean quickly woke the children. "Helen, Joe, it's morning!"

"Where's the nose-picker off to now?" Cathy said, remembering Eethan's disgusting habit. She punched Michael's shoulder.

"Ow! I don't know." Michael rubbed his shoulder.

"Why are you always hitting people?" said Ephie.

"Oh, shut up, Ephie! Can you see the nose-picker or not?"

Ephie stretched over the side of the raft just as the rain began to fall and looked into the water. "I'm not sure. I can't really see anything for the rain drops."

"Move out of the way, you useless…" Cathy hissed.

Startled, Ephie pulled herself back from the edge.

Cathy peered over the side herself and muttered, "Go nibble on your tablet. That's about all you're good for."

"Well, I think…" began Ephie.

"That's just the point. You don't think at all, do you, Ephie?" Cathy was now completely at her wit's end. The combination of tiredness and worry had frayed her nerves to breaking point. She was slipping into manic-tyrant mode and now the whole boat seemed to be avoiding her gaze.

"I wish she'd stayed in Drumfintley," sulked Helen.

Jean warned her daughter in a sharp whisper: "Helen!"

Michael confided in Ephie, "I'm beginning to have some very unchristian suspicions about Cathy Peck and her husband's disappearance. She seems capable of anything."

Cathy heard everything and really struggled to quell the frustration building inside her. She was just about to lay into Michael when there was a sudden splash.

Eethan's wet mop of hair appeared through the raindrops on the surface of the river.

"Eethan! What were you doing?" gasped Michael.

"Listeeening. There ees big trouble coming soon. Wee must hide somewhere."

They squinted at the high cliffs that rose above them on their left and then peered into the dark forest to their right. Rain stung their faces, jabbing at their skin like needles. The pretty pink dawn had turned into a dull, drab morning. The trees of Eldane swayed in a sudden breeze.

"Stop!" Cathy cried. She stood up, making one side of the raft dip below the surface. She pointed to the rocky slope beneath the cliff. "Stop paddling now!" Already wet through, Cathy plunged into the river and swam for the bank.

"She has definitely flipped!" exclaimed Jean as she attempted to shelter the kids under her dripping mohair cardigan. "What does she think she's doing?" When Cathy eventually appeared, about ten yards from the shore, she began wading towards a large group of rocks.

"Is she leaving us?" asked Michael.

"I hope so," whispered Ephie.

Cathy lunged forward and caught hold of something.

There was an ear-piercing scream.

Eethan was swimming after her.

A small, cowering yellow-skinned creature with mottled skin and bright blue eyes was babbling, trying desperately to escape Cathy's grip.

"Give it back!" yelled Cathy.

Eethan reached Cathy just as the creature dropped the green rucksack.

"He stole it from the raft!" snapped Cathy.

She threw the creature back into the water and picked up the green rucksack. It was bashed now and heavy with water. She held it above her head like some kind of trophy and shouted at the creature, "What are you, apart from a thief?"

"He is Yeltan," said Eethan.

Now the creature was pointing at Eethan like he was some kind of god. "You have returned to save us. Oh praise be, praise be."

Cathy found the zipper and jerked it open. Water poured out, along with various sweet wrappers, two uneaten apples, and an empty juice bottle. "Never mind him, what have you taken?"

The Yeltan glanced at Cathy and said, "We have your boys."

Jean stood up tall on the raft. "What did he say?"

Eethan tried to stop Cathy but she was too quick for him. She made a dive for the Yeltan, who backed into the water.

"The one called James Peck...he—"

The Yeltan's words were cut short as a red tentacle yanked him under the surface.

The river bubbled white foam and then crimson.

Eethan pulled Cathy back to the shore. "Stay out of theee water!"

Cathy slipped on the rocks and sat down painfully.

The river calmed and Jean gathered the children in close.

The Yeltan was gone.

"Ees a Razorflik," said Eethan. "They neever kill big creatures, only fishes. Neever."

"Well, this one did!" blasted Cathy. "He was going to tell us about James." She opened the front zipper and found James's inhaler and, to her surprise, a rusting can of flea spray. Written on the small label inside the bag was *David Peck*. Gazing skyward, her eyes blazed as the rain splashed her face. "David! Where are you when we need you?" Her voice echoed off the high cliffs that stood proud against the blackening sky.

Scared and cold, she hugged the rucksack close to her chest, relieved that the rain hid her tears. She thought of James being in the clutches of the yellow Yeltan creatures, and of David and the last words she'd ever said to him. *Go on your stupid walk! You're never really here anyway. Your mind's always somewhere else. So why don't you just disappear forever!*

Eethan touched her arm. "Do not bee angry weeth yourself so much, Cathy."

She flicked his hand away.

"Wees have to keeep going. Theere is even beeger danger coming."

"There's no way I'm going back in that water," said Cathy. She stuffed the bits and pieces back into the rucksack.

Eethan waded into the slow-moving water. "I weel protect you from Razorfliks. Beesides ees full up now."

In a daze, and much to the startled amazement of the rest of the villagers on the raft, Cathy sighed and waded through the shallows without acknowledging him. She just stared into the distance until she had to start swimming back to the raft.

Helping her aboard, Michael placed his soggy, black jacket round her shoulders. "Are you okay, Cathy?" He looked at the little green rucksack. "You could have been killed. What were you thinking?"

His question hung in the air, unanswered. Cathy was staring at something behind him, her eyes widening.

The raft jolted as a large wave lifted the bedraggled crew a good two feet above the river and then slapped them back down again. They all screamed, waving their arms in an effort to keep balance.

Jean pulled her soaking cardigan around her neck and teared up. "This has got to be some kind of nightmare, right?" she sobbed.

"What in God's name is that?" bleated Michael.

Helen peeked out from under her mum's mohair cardigan to look. "Giants? They are definitely giants." She turned Wee Joe's head to see, as he was looking in the wrong direction. Behind them, where they'd turned left into the smaller tributary, two gruesome heads bobbed up and down above the treetops.

"Are they made of some kind of wood or...?" Jean stopped when she saw the first thick leg splash into the river.

Cathy screwed up her eyes against the low sun. The giant looked like a tree, but it moved like something living. The first creature she spotted had a gnarled, shiny head and a patch over his right eye. The second giant sported a Mohican-type hairstyle composed of green ferns.

"Mum! Dat one's a punk rocker!" cried Wee Joe. "They're coooool."

His big sister, Helen, wasn't so sure they were 'cool'. Her face was pale, making her freckles stand out even more than usual.

"Paddle quicklee en smoothlee, and don't make anyee more noisees!" whispered Eethan. Still unafraid of more Razorflik attacks, he slipped back into the water and kicked with renewed vigour. The raft moved much faster now, and soon gained an extra twenty yards on the giants behind them.

"Tree Trolls, theys ees. But dee rain is heelping us just now." Eethan glanced behind him and saw the Trolls stop and look up the tributary towards them.

"Kak! Kak!" The bald one jerked his head back, his nostrils pulling in the damp air. With a satisfied nod, he bellowed, "There! I can see them!"

A swarm of serpent-like creatures, dressed in armour, poured round the bend. They milled around the crested Tree Troll's legs like ants.

Everyone on the raft froze, too afraid to move.

Barely a second later, a terrible scream resounded from the reeds at the mouth of the tributary. The bald Tree Troll was lifting a long, sleek boat out of the river. Gleefully, he threw it back down into the water, where it hit the surface hard. Someone was struggling in the water. He picked the unfortunate creature up, and examined him with his one good eye. "It's a Manimal guard!" he roared.

Next to him the other troll crushed the craft beneath his huge gnarled foot.

The serpent creatures cheered.

Grinning, the bald one closed his thick fingers round the guard and tossed his lifeless body into the river. There was a splash, and another cheer.

Jean began to sob as she pulled the kids back into her damp cardigan. Only Eethan continued to kick with all his might as they edged round a bend and slipped out of sight.

7 The Herdigup

When Cimerato heard the thunderous roar of a Tree Troll from the river, he blinked his eyes open.

Lord Eldane sat up. "The boat!"

"Shhh, Father!" he hissed. "Get down and keep still!" Motioning to the others to stay where they were, Cimerato crawled through the nest of ferns that hid them, reaching a point at which he could see what was going on. He sighed in despair. Fragments of their boat floated out in the river while a troop of Hedra and two Tree Trolls searched the trees around him. The rain grew heavier and the ground began to turn to mud as he crawled back into the fern grove where they'd slept.

"Tree Trolls and Hedra...lots of them," he panted. "They'll be here in minutes. We must move now."

"Move where, Son?" said Lord Eldane.

"We must go deeper into the forest and find somewhere to hide," said Cimerato.

Crunch!

A huge foot stamped down, throwing mud all over them.

One of the Manimal guards bolted.

Cimerato watched as Ssslathat immediately scooped him up and threw him back towards his brother, bellowing, "Is this one of the Blinders?"

Ashthat caught the terrified guard and held him up by his leg. He blinked his one purple eye and shook his massive head before opening his needle-toothed jaws.

In a gulp the guard disappeared.

"Not a blinder," said Ashthat, wiping his ragged lips with the back of his hand. "These are Gwendralin morsels. Kuh!" He coughed then picked some of the guard's clothing from his teeth.

As Ssslathat snapped trees and crushed bushes with his club, Cimerato and his men crawled away like snakes, pulling themselves through the mud and rain.

Ssslathat roared and plucked a small tree from the muddy earth, throwing it wildly behind him.

Telan had to duck to avoid the missile but was soon beside the Trolls, hacking at the undergrowth along with twenty Hedra soldiers.

Jal stood motionless on the corner of The Break as a translucent red film of skin slipped over his yellow reptilian eyes. "There's another orange glow at the edge of the trees," he shouted.

Cimerato heard him and froze. His heart pounded hard against the inside of his breastplate.

A third guard had been spotted, but only after he'd dealt with two Hedra scouts, slashing them down with his curved Gwendralin sword. Unfortunately for him, Ashthat's club found its mark. It squashed the guard flat into the mud.

Cimerato winced, fearing the worst for the rest of them. Then he remembered an old trick he'd used when spying on the Hedra in the past. "Scoop up the mud and cover yourselves. Be quick about it!"

The others copied him then remained as still as they could under the debris and foliage. The cool mud would protect them from the Hedra's infrared vision but they could still be stumbled upon or crushed to death by one of the Tree Trolls.

Ssslathat's massive foot crashed into a tree near to where they lay, showering them with leaves, branches and rainwater.

The sharp spike of a broken branch pierced the mud inches from Cimerato's left ear but he remained completely still. The Hedra were everywhere. Any movement would be fatal. The Trolls seemed to be moving back towards the river, muttering to each other in registers too deep to understand. Hedra tongues flicked in the rain, trying to pick up some trace of scent, their eyes scouring the wet foliage for some telltale glow or movement.

Cimerato, Lord Eldane and two guards lay absolutely motionless, plastered in mud and hidden by the debris left behind by Ssslathat and Ashthat. One guard, however, was missing.

The Hedra were still searching, stabbing the ferns with their short swords and prodding the thick bushes with their steel-capped bows only feet from where Cimerato and the others lay.

"Telan!" one of the Hedra called out. "Look what I've found!"

Cimerato saw the Hedra soldier bend down close to where his father lay. His reptilian tongue flicked over his father's face in hungry anticipation, but Eldane remained totally still, his eyes fixed on a spot behind the Hedra.

"You might be a bit tough when I chew on your old hide tonight..." hissed the Hedra soldier, lifting his pointed bow for the killing strike. "But I've had worse."

Shhhunk!

From behind, a curved Gwendralin sword sliced through the Hedra soldier's neck, relieving him of his head...and his hunger. The missing guard had crawled up from the riverbank in time to save his master. Without concern for his own safety, he kicked the severed head away from Lord Eldane's hiding place and began pulling the corpse back toward the river. He was nearly there when a hundred Hedra rose out of the water in front of him.

The exposed guard skidded to a halt, dropping the body. "I will not surrender, so give it your bessst..." Before he could finish his sentence, a flurry of arrows flew fast and furious from the Hedra bows. Courageous to the end, the guard toppled over, his face, even in death, fixed in an expression of defiance.

His back now aching, James reached forward and caught hold of Craig's shorts.

"Hey! Do you mind?" yelped Craig, hauling them back into position.

"Did you hear that?" whispered James. "It sounded like a Tree Troll."

Water was streaming into the tunnel from above and they were now trudging through a thick sludge.

"We must be safe enough under the ground," said Craig in a hopeful voice.

"I wouldn't be so sure," said another voice.

This voice didn't have the same ring to it as the Yeltan's babbling tone. It was high-pitched alright, but precise and clipped, every word pronounced with utter clarity.

"I would say that you are in great danger no matter where you are," said the voice.

Now in a wider part of the tunnel James and Craig squinted up at the roof.

"There," said James, his hand brushing against the Talisman. "It's a millipede or something."

"I am *not* a millipede, young man," snapped the creature, "I am a Herdigup and proud of it."

Craig stared up at the creature above them. It clung to the earthen ceiling, a pair of long, feathered antennae flicking and fluttering over their heads. "Well, you look just like a millipede to me."

The Yeltans had paused ahead of them.

The Herdigup circled above them and said, "Can a millipede do this?" It wiggled its antennae and blew a raspberry.

"Get lost," snapped Craig, wiping his face dry.

"Can it?" the Herdigup persisted.

"No," said James, "probably not."

"And a millipede would probably not be able to tell you

anything about your missing father either, would it?" said the Herdigup.

James froze in shock. "What did you just say?"

"I didn't say anything and I'm not sure I'm going to now either." The Herdigup's voice had adopted a more petulant tone. But then it whispered, "Your parent is very close, young man."

"Tell me more," said James, suddenly feeling drawn to the creature.

Craig pulled him back. "Not too close," he cautioned. He thought about calling on the magic spear Mendel had given him.

"So you have a magical spear called Greenworm, and you…" - it focussed in on James - "have a magical sword given to you by a great wizard." The Herdigup paused in thought. "Your charmed sword is called Firetongue."

"Who are you?" whispered James.

"I will tell you everything if you give me your lucky charm," said the Herdigup. A pair of appendages, previously unseen by the boys, slipped down slowly from the creature's sides.

"This…?" James paused.

"What are you doing?" hissed Craig.

James had unfastened the Talisman from his belt.

The Herdigup began to sing a familiar rhyme: "*The Talisman moves through ancient leaves and yet, at times, stands still. No Denthan eyes can see it, some say they never will.*" The creature wrapped its weird arms round the ancient Yukplug horn and eased it away from James's grasp.

"Eeeeeeekkkkk!"

A Yeltan spear now pinned the Herdigup to the ceiling.

It writhed for a second and then fell limp, dropping the Talisman onto the muddy floor.

"Annoying things, Herdigups," said Garlon. He jerked his spear free of the ceiling then used his foot to hold the dead

Herdigup steady as he yanked the blade free from its lifeless body.

James and Craig watched him, their mouths agog.

"Full of lies and false promises," Garlon chirped.

"But..." began James.

"Wasn't that a bit harsh, Garlon?" said Craig.

Garlon shrugged. "It was trying to steal the Talisman."

"It knew about my dad!" pressed James.

Garlon sighed. "Herdigups rob you of your thoughts and then they rob you of your possessions."

James picked up the Talisman and placed it back in his belt. He felt stupid now, but part of him had liked the Herdigup. He felt sorry for it.

Garlon waved them on. "There's trouble up on top."

8 The Second Wave

"I did not give the order to loose your arrows!" Telan shouted as he scrambled through the undergrowth, but he was too late. "Fools!" The Hedra had seen the Manimal dragging their dead comrade and revenge had raced ahead of reason. Telan slapped the nearest Hedra across the face. "We could have made him talk. Are there any more?"

"Who knows, but we have taken care of four," answered Jal. Staying well away from the fray, Jal had spent his time scanning the area while the others searched. The rain was beginning to ease. To their left, further down the tributary, a glint of sunlight had caught the surface of the river. He was certain that he'd glimpsed some kind of raft before it had edged round a bend. He was also sure he had seen more than four people in the boat they'd just destroyed. He recalled the night before, under the City of Gwendral. This meant that there were probably more Manimals hiding in the undergrowth. For now, however, he would hold his tongue; he would wait and see how things developed.

"Let's go this way," Jal suggested, pointing down the tributary where he'd spotted the raft. Without waiting for a response, he began to move forward.

"Why?" shouted Telan.

Jal could tell that Telan, a captain, resented a common guard telling him what to do, even if he was one of King Feldon's personal minders. "Well, if I was going to skulk off into the forest, I would go down here. That's why."

Ashthat looked worried. "This inlet leads towards the Eden Tree. We don't like that place. It's forbidden!"

Telan glanced up at Ashthat and hissed, "I'll tell you what is, and what is not, forbidden!" He signalled his troops and they fell into line. "This rank," he pointed to the archers who'd killed the last guard, "will stay here. Let nothing pass in or out of the tributary until we return, and search the ferns again! I am sure there are more vermin in there." The disgruntled rank of archers nodded. Without the protection of the full Hedra brigade and the Tree Trolls, those that stayed behind would be vulnerable.

Ashthat looked back at his brother. "I have to find the Blinders." With a deep sigh he turned down the tributary that headed toward the Eden Tree.

Reluctantly, Ssslathat followed.

***

"I'm bored, Mum. I want my toys!" said Wee Joe. Oblivious to any danger, he tugged at his mother's tattered skirt, but Jean was transfixed as she stared blankly into the mishmash of trees behind them.

"We're in real danger here, aren't we?" she whispered anxiously to Cathy.

"What a stupid question," barked Cathy, "of course we are, and so are all our children." She turned away rudely and addressed Eethan. "You there!" Cathy directed her anger at the little blue man. "What were those things doing?"

Eethan winced in a sudden shaft of sunlight and continued to kick his feet in the water. "Wees better keeep going. They weel soon catch up with us."

The raft turned round another bend in the tributary and a strange island came into view. The gorge they travelled through opened out and they gathered speed as the current pushing against them eased.

Eethan climbed out of the water, onto the raft, and said to Michael, "You must keep on going to dee tree." Eethan pointed to a giant, copper-leafed tree in the centre of the island. It stood high on a grassy knoll, twisting upward towards the brightening sky.

"The reever is eeasier now, so you should bees okay. Stop when you reachees dee Island. I will go en deestract dee Tree Trolls." He brushed past Cathy to speak to Wee Joe. "Lookee after your mummy, Wee Fighteer Joe!" Eethan pointed to Jean, winked at the small boy, and then dived into the river.

"Where is he going now?" Cathy's eyes were wide with disbelief. "And he never even answered my question."

"Calm down, Cathy!" said Jean. "You're scaring the kids and…you're making things worse!"

Ephie grunted. "Eethan is crazy. You won't get me splashing into the river like that. Not after that poor yellow creature was killed so horribly."

"It was a thief," reminded Cathy. "It tried to steal the rucksack."

"No one is perfect, Cathy," said Michael.

Ephie found a piece of tablet deep in her pocket and tried to distract the kids. "Joe? Do you want some? What about you, Helen?" Her ploy worked at first but soon the kids were fighting over who was getting the biggest bit.

"I had that bit!" yelped Wee Joe.

"Liar!" Helen ripped the last piece from Wee Joe's fingers and he began to scream like a stuck pig.

"Shhhh! For goodness sake!" hissed Michael, glancing anxiously around.

Ephie fumbled with the wrapper. "Here, give it back, Joe. I'll split it again. Try and share. Please!"

"Everyone shut up!" Jean stamped her foot down so hard on the raft that two of the moss strands that held the whole thing together snapped. The bindings whipped past Cathy's face and she fell back onto her elbows.

The raft slowly began to drift apart.

"Nice one, Jean!" cried Cathy, surprised at the outburst.

They all stared at Jean as two of the main support logs

drifted away. A third log broke free and they all scrambled to hold onto each other as the raft broke apart.

"Grab on to something that floats. Ahh!" Michael fell backwards, cracking his head on a green, slimy log before sinking beneath the surface of the river.

"Michael!" Ephie jumped straight in after him.

Cathy leant over to see as Ephie kicked deeper into the blackness. "What are you...?" She soon realised, however, that Ephie might have been right to go in after Michael. He wasn't anywhere to be seen and the weeds were thick in this part of the river. She turned to Jean and said, "Ephie was a champion swimmer when she was young. When she was thin," she added, wistfully. Cathy peered into the murky water, shielding her eyes.

"There! She's got him," gasped Jean.

Ephie surfaced a few yards away. She had Michael by the collar of his jacket, pulling him away from the weeds with several strong kicks.

"Ahh! Ach! Ach!" Michael coughed and spluttered. As he came to the surface, however, he began to panic. He flailed his arms about and tried to clamber over Ephie.

"Stay still!" shouted Cathy.

But they were sinking again. Now struggling to keep her own head above the water, Ephie gave Michael a brisk, stinging clip across the face and regained control.

Cathy, along with Jean and the kids, clung to what remained of the raft while Ephie and Michael treaded water. In the commotion, they'd drifted close to the green, grassy hill. Cathy looked up at the huge, copper-leafed tree. It towered above them, shading the olive-green waters.

"I can touch the ground now!" spluttered Michael.

Ephie stood up and spread her arms for balance. She swayed for a few seconds, letting the twin suns throw down their warmth on her full face.

Michael tried his best to support himself as he made for the riverbank. The rocks on the riverbed were slippery, causing him to stagger and stumble. When he was on a more even patch, he turned to his rescuer. "Th...thanks, Ephie!"

"No problem. I mean..." Ephie was confused when she saw the genuine gratitude in Michael's eyes.

"Oh, come on," interjected Cathy. She hated unnecessary soppiness. "There could be more of those Razorfliks. Be quick!"

Once they had all reached the riverbank, Michael shielded his eyes against the sun that poked through the clouds and said, "You risked your life..." He wiped the water from his face and stared straight at Ephie. "Your eyes are a lovely colour—"

"Pardon?" Ephie's face turned puce.

"I'm terribly sorry. I didn't mean to... I mean, I'm sorry..."

"Don't be." Ephie gave him a small smile.

Cathy turned and sneered at Michael. "You definitely had a good crack on the head, didn't you?"

Ignoring Cathy, Ephie seemed about to make the most of the compliment when Helen interrupted the tête-à-tête. "You pushed me!" she barked, splashing Wee Joe.

Wee Joe spat at her. "Did not! Pigface!" Like most three-year-olds, Wee Joe had the voice of a town crier and his screech sent three snow-coloured birds flapping skyward.

Cathy scowled at Jean. "Will you keep those kids quiet?"

Jean ignored her. "Michael, are you alright?"

"Yes, thanks to Ephie," replied Michael.

In the shallows, Ephie blushed as she struggled with her sodden, powder blue joggers.

Cathy Peck turned on Michael. "Will you two cool it? Pull some more of that candy floss stuff off that tree and give it to the kids instead of standing around gawping like a pair of love-struck school kids."

Michael staggered up the sandy bank and reached for the

nearest strand of mossgeld. "I am not ashamed to show a little human kindness, Cathy."

Just as Cathy was about to start on him, another wave pushed down the river, tossing fragments of their raft towards them. The debris smashed into the rocks behind them. Jean's eyes widened. "They're coming again!"

"She's right," said Michael. "The same wave hit us before we saw the giants the last time."

Instinctively, Cathy picked up Wee Joe, grabbed Helen's hand and began to move. She growled as they all slipped and skidded on the wet grass that sloped up to the Eden Tree. "I thought Eethan was going to do something about those..." she searched for the right words, "...those Trolls!" She set Wee Joe down and pointed him and his sister in the direction of the tree. "Run to the big tree. Hide amongst the roots."

As the kids ran for the safety of the Eden Tree's giant roots, Cathy rounded on Jean. "Shift yourself, and look after your kids!" Cathy snapped some ferns from the surrounding foliage and thrust them into Jean's hands. "Hide them with these."

9 The Rescue

Next to the River Levan, Cimerato and his entourage lay motionless in the cold mud. Still covered by broken branches and foliage, a sense of hopelessness had washed over them when they'd heard the instructions given to the Hedra archers. If the rain stopped, and if the Hedra archers covered every inch of ground as they'd been instructed, the small group would be discovered and killed. They would have to move. Cimerato slowly turned his head towards his father. He was just about to tell him to make a move when he felt something slippery grab his ankles.

"Arhh...!" Cimerato stifled the cry just in time. He looked down to see a small pair of muddy, yellow hands pulling on his boot. Turning his head to see what was going on, he soon saw that his father and the two remaining guards were also being dragged along under the fallen debris, away from the Hedra. Strangely enough, his father had on his old face a smile that shone through the mud and muck.

They'd been dragged a good fifty yards, and had dipped down into a green, leafy grove, when a low babbling sound came to their attention.

Cimerato caught hold of his father's sodden, purple robe. "Yeltans?"

"And not a moment too soon," his father replied.

Cimerato sat up when he saw the Yeltans' leader, Landris, step forward from the group. They knew each other from past meetings in Gwendral.

Cimerato's father blinked the mud from his eyes and was just about to speak when Landris put a small gnarled finger to his lips. "Not here," he whispered. He pointed in the direction of a moss-covered hatch.

Making haste, Manimals and Yeltan alike slid through the opening and fell down into the darkness until they ended up piled on top of each other at the bottom of the chute. Trying to stand, Lord Eldane struck his head on an overhanging root.

"It is a little cramped," Landris apologised, "but hopefully better than being roasted over a Hedra spit." Landris smiled as he and the other Yeltans bowed respectfully.

Lord Eldane bowed back. "Quite. Thank you, Landris."

Standing to the left of the Yeltans were two boys—one was taller with blond hair and freckles; the other was smaller, with a biggish nose and slight stoop. The strangest things about the boys were their eyes. Coloured and round, they were not like any Denthan eyes he'd ever seen. Other than those oddities, they looked like Manimals, even though they wore strange dirty-white shirts and short leggings that shone like silk.

"Stendelburgh United," said the taller boy, a cheeky smile on his face.

The smaller boy formed a disgruntled expression and said, "He won't know what you're on about. He doesn't care what football strip you're wearing."

Cimerato peered over the small boy's shoulder to eye the hairy animal behind them. "And what is that?"

"A dog," answered the taller boy. "My name is Craig, and this is James." He nodded towards the smaller boy.

"Are you from Gwendral?" asked James.

"Yes, we are from Gwendral. And you are…?" asked Lord Eldane, addressing the yellow-furred creature known as a dog.

"Eh, that's Bero. He can't speak. But he's from Drumfintley, and so are we," said Craig, patting Bero's head.

One of the guards, caked in mud, was the first to reach out and touch Bero's brown ear. "He has the face of a dragon." Cimerato looked at the Yeltans standing round them in the gloom and, to his surprise, saw that they had their elaborate war spears with them. Being a peaceful race, the Yeltans rarely carried weapons of any kind, shunning conflict whenever possible.

"We had a visit from the Keresi," explained Landris.

"Among others," added Garlon.

Landris nodded sternly. "And when we heard the sounds of battle above us, and saw Ssslathat and his brother searching for you, we had to help." He frowned. "I'm so sorry we did not reach you in time to save the others."

Lord Eldane shook his head. "We should have been more careful."

"Did you say 'Ssslathat'?" asked James.

"Did one of them only have one eye?" Craig enquired.

"Yes," Landris answered. "Ashthat, brother of Ssslathat, wore a patch over one eye."

"They said they were looking for the Blinders," Cimerato interrupted, turning to the two boys.

"Well *they* attacked us first..." Craig responded.

"So, you and James are the Blinders?" asked Landris.

"No," said James, his face flushing pink. "Well, not intentionally."

"We *are* the Blinders," admitted Craig. "It's a pretty rubbish name, though. What about the Troll Slayers?"

"We didn't actually 'slay' anyone," whispered James.

"We could have," said Craig, full of unfounded bravado.

"Who are you?" James said quickly, as though trying to steer the conversation away from his friend.

"Your eyes are almost pure white," said Craig, looking closely at Cimerato's eyes. "Are you blind too?"

Cimerato grinned. "I am Cimerato, son of Lord Eldane." He nodded towards his father. "These are our two remaining guards."

The guards nodded at Landris and the boys.

Cimerato turned to face Landris. "We are trying to reach the Eden Tree. As, I assume, are you. My father recounted your letter to me last night. If Mendel is back amongst us, we owe him our help. I only hope that he can save us in the little time we have left."

James gulped and said, "Mendel is here alright. I heard him. He helped me use the Talisman. I'm sure of it."

"You've seen him?" said Cimerato.

James nodded. "We came here from our world with him. But we lost him after we ran away from the giant centipede things."

"Centides," interjected Landris.

Cimerato could see the fear in the boys' faces at the mention of the word. "The sooner we find him again the better it will be for us all."

Landris signalled to his kin and they immediately began to march. The Manimals followed first, leaving the boys and Bero to keep up as best they could.

***

James nudged Craig. "What did you have to tell them about the Trolls for?" He was looking at Craig's muddy shorts again as they struggled along the low tunnel after the Yeltans, not particularly liking the view.

"I was only being friendly," Craig whispered over his shoulder.

"You only went and told them that we're the Blinders, or whatever those Trolls called us. And Landris knew their names and everything. They're probably friends of theirs!"

"Friends?" Garlon had overheard James's whispers. "Friends? Those two Trolls have eaten more Yeltans than... than I care to think about. They are no friends of ours, James."

James felt embarrassed, but less so when Garlon added, "In fact, I was wondering if you could tell me more about your fight with them. If we ever survive this disaster, I could ask the Yeltan embroiderers to do a tapestry. We'd have to have a meeting or two to discuss it, fill in all the correct forms, but it sounds as though you gave a good account of yourselves."

With a grin, Craig assured the little creature that he would tell him everything.

James only groaned. "More procedure. Why do you have to draw things out so much, have so many rules? Even about a tapestry?"

After twenty minutes of crawling through the narrow Yeltan tunnels, they entered a high-roofed cave that smelled of herbs and spices. Landris pointed to a set of ornate ladders. "That is our way up."

Garlon spoke excitedly, "This is where I had my coming-of-age ceremony."

Landris put his finger to his lips to signal silence. "These stairs lead to the island of Senegral, where we will find the Eden Tree," he informed them.

"Please Landris, can I speak to Cimerato?" asked James.

Landris gripped the ladder. "Time is not on our side, James."

James turned to Cimerato and asked quickly, "Have you seen or heard of anyone else like me, here in Denthan? Perhaps with my kind of eyes. I'm looking for my father."

Craig widened his eyes so that Cimerato could be reminded what human eyes looked like.

This annoyed James immensely, but he persevered nonetheless. "I came here mostly to find him, you see. Obviously, I'm sad about your predicament too, and Mendel seemed to need me for his magic, but..."

Cimerato patted James's shoulder. "I'm sorry, boy, but there have been no reports of anyone else like you here in Denthan. But just because I haven't heard anything about your father doesn't mean that he isn't here."

James felt quite inadequate standing beside the big warrior. "Well, I just wondered, that's all."

Landris addressed Lord Eldane, "I've already told the boys that there are more of their kind in the forest. There's a good chance that James's father is amongst them."

Craig touched James's arm. "More of our *kind*? He never said that, did he?"

James shrugged, looking just as confused. "There was the jacket, my dad's compass and his lens cloth, but no real explanation for them."

Lord Eldane placed his hand on James's shoulder. "Well, if Mendel brought you here, anything is possible. However," the old man turned to face Craig, "I don't understand how you two managed to lose track of the most powerful wizard our world has ever known."

All eyes were on the boys.

"As I said, we were running away from..." James managed to remember the name of the creatures this time, "...Centides."

Craig raised a blond eyebrow. "What I can't understand is how you lot were stupid enough to banish him in the first place!"

There was an awkward silence at the bottom of the Yeltan ladder. Eldane, Landris and Cimerato were all struck dumb.

James, well used to Craig's lack of diplomacy, winced as he grabbed hold of the ladder that stretched upwards. For once, though, he actually agreed with his friend. "You tell 'em, Craig," he said in a low voice as he began to climb.

Landris called after him. "James, wait! An official Yeltan patrol needs to check that it's all clear first. It's standard Yeltan—"

"Procedure," moaned James. "How did I guess?"

Garlon shouted after him. "The Trolls could be waiting or..."

But James had reached the top of the ladder and had already slipped the rusty bolt that separated the world above from the world below. Sunlight streamed down into the Yeltan

63

chamber. He pushed against the hatch with his shoulder until the heavy lid fell open, thudding onto the ground above. Dust showered down on the onlookers below making them cough and cover their eyes.

Craig made to follow his best friend, but half a dozen Yeltan hands caught hold of him before he could move.

Excitement building in his chest, James pulled himself through the opening and glanced up to see that he was kneeling between two giant roots. Like the buttresses of a cathedral, they rose above him, supporting the trunk of an enormous tree that must have stood well over two hundred feet tall. It had to be the Eden Tree. He tried to concentrate – to see if he could sense Mendel. He knelt up, closed his eyes and listened for the deep, reassuring voice.

10 Battle Beneath the Tree

Cathy heard a dull thump. It had come from the direction of the Eden Tree. She hesitated, turned to the rest of the bedraggled group and motioned to them to wait.

She could hear the howls and roars of the god-knows-what down in the river behind them, but it was the expression on Jean's face that really threw her. Jean Harrison should have had the terror-struck expression of someone about to be torn apart by a giant Tree Troll. Instead, her face wore the look of someone who'd just won first prize at the village raffle. Staring up the hill past Cathy, Jean's eyes had widened and now a beautiful smile lit up her face. Cathy felt quite sure the woman had lost her mind. "Jean?"

"Mum?" a voice called out. Cathy spun back round to look behind her.

Cathy felt her legs give. "James?"

She saw her dishevelled son peering over one of the giant roots of the Eden Tree. Like he was peering over the garden gate.

"What do you think you've been up to? We've all been worried sick and…" But for once, her lips quivering, Cathy fell silent. Without another word, she ran to James and pulled him close. Holding him tightly, she kissed his dirty face and shook with relief at seeing him again. "James, where have you been?"

Her sobs set James off too. Under the shade of the huge bronze-coloured tree, he hugged her back, tears spilling down his cheeks. He was part of her. She drew back and wiped his tears.

By now, four or five strange yellow faces had appeared

between the huge buttress-like roots behind him.

Seeing them, Cathy gripped James's arm.

"Mum?" James turned to see what she was looking at. "Oh, it's okay, Mum. They're Yeltans."

Not sure which way to run or what to say, Cathy could only continue to stare as a tall man, covered in mud, came into view. He was obviously some kind of soldier; she saw hints of yellow armour shining through the caked-on dirt. A large, curved sword in his hand glinted in the sunlight. "James, don't move," she whispered.

"They're friends too, Mum," he reassured her. "That's Cimerato. He's a Manimal."

She relaxed a little bit, still holding him tightly.

James sniffed back a tear.

***

Everybody—Ephie, Michael, Jean and even the strange onlookers behind the roots—seemed to respect the private moment between Cathy and James, but it was short-lived.

In the river below, James heard a huge splash and quickly pulled free of his mother's arms. A few seconds later, the Tree Troll, Ssslathat, rose up from the waters below, his ridiculous green crest waving in the breeze. An evil smile twisted his splintered mouth. "Blinder! Blinder!" he bellowed in his deep, woody voice. Then he called back for his brother, "Kak! Kak!", jerking his hideous head back in a series of creaks that sounded like a huge timber door being ripped in two.

Scared stiff, Wee Joe and Helen peered from behind another of the Eden Tree's great roots. The Yeltans fell back while Cimerato crouched low, but James, Cathy and the Drumfintley contingent were totally exposed. They stood for a moment on the grassy hillside, like statues, unsure what to do.

Ashthat appeared beside his brother, "Kak! Kak!" Both Trolls jerked their hideous heads back in joy at finding their prey.

Ssslathat was the first to move. He grabbed a small tree, ripped it out of the earth and smashed it against the hillside as he advanced. In two steps, Ssslathat had come twenty feet closer. He ignored the panic-stricken adults. He was after one of the little ones, one of the Blinders.

On seeing James, Ssslathat let out a terrible roar that shook the ground they stood on. He began to close in. "I'm going to tear you apart, Blinder. I'm going to squash you flat!" He thumped his fist down and pulverised a rotting tree stump. Ssslathat twisted round to look down at his brother behind him. "Come, Ashthat, this kill is yours."

James and his mum edged back towards the roots of the Eden Tree. Without once taking her eyes off the Tree Troll, Cathy whispered, "Blinder? Why did he call you that?"

"Eh, now's not a good time to explain, Mum. Trust me." James was looking at something down at the river.

A whole mass of grey-skinned reptilian creatures had gathered round Ashthat. Hissing and flicking their tongues in anticipation, they swarmed round the monster like worker bees round a queen. In the dazzling crimson light of Denthan's twin suns, their black armour flashed menacingly as they moved forward. Most of them had drawn metal-tipped bows, and James heard the sound of a hundred black arrows clicking from their sheaths. Arrows knocked, they waited for the command to fire. Out of the corner of his eye, he saw Landris issuing orders to his own fighters. He was amazed to see the calmness on the little creature's face. When Landris raised his hand, fifty Yeltans immediately rose up from behind the roots of the Eden Tree. When he lowered his hand and said, 'Now!' the Yeltan spears flew into the air.

The Drumfintley group ducked as the shower of spears soared over their heads. In the confusion, Michael, Ephie and Jean found themselves being dragged behind the roots of the Eden Tree by the Yeltans. James and Cathy, still trapped by

Ssslathat, had no choice but to run the opposite way, towards Helen and Wee Joe who were still hiding behind another giant root.

There was a shrieking noise as the Yeltan spears struck home. Six dug into the wooden hide of Ssslathat, three hit Ashthat's face, and twenty Hedra dropped to the ground, killed instantly by the Yeltan poison that laced the spear tips. The rest of the missiles either fell short or simply failed to find a target.

Unharmed by the pinpricks in his tough wooden hide, Ssslathat charged. He reached down to snatch up James, but James wasn't going down without a fight. He had already said his magic word to retrieve his sword, Firetongue, and with a yell, he leapt up onto the Troll's swinging arm. With the power of the magic blade racing through him, he soon reached the Troll's shoulder. He jumped higher again, twisting in mid-air before plunging his sword deep into Ssslathat's right eye. "If you're going to call me Blinder," he shouted, "I might as well live up to the name."

"Arrrrghh!" The Troll crashed backwards and landed on his brother, knocking him on top of the advancing Hedra. James just managed to leap to the ground and roll out of the way so as to avoid being crushed by a flailing arm or leg.

"Watch out, you fools!" Telan snapped at his Hedra brigade. "Fall back!"

"Blinded! Blinded!" Ssslathat covered his wounded eye and screamed in agony. At the same time, Ashthat struggled to regain his feet, his huge legs crushing another group of Hedra coming up on his left.

"Get back, I told you!" roared Telan.

Ashthat was finally able to stand. "You will die now!" he bellowed, full of rage and revenge. "All of you!" Straightening to his full height, he jumped over the squirming body of Ssslathat and forced himself up the hill, his club raised high, ready to crush James.

But James was already racing back to his mum. He had almost reached the cover of the Eden Tree when Ashthat's club smacked hard into the ground in front of him.

The Yeltans snaked round the giant club and the Tree Troll as Landris shouted: "Don't waste your spears on the Trolls. Aim for the Hedra!" He lowered his hand a second time and the last of the Yeltan spears arced towards the retreating Hedra. Another twenty or so screams rose up from the bushes on the riverbank, echoing all around them.

One of the cries had come from Captain Telan, who fell at Jal's feet. "Telan?" Jal caught hold of the Hedra leader's arm but saw that he was quite dead. He released him to drift away on the slow current.

Unaware of anything else going on around him, Ashthat pulled his huge wooden club free of the ground and slammed it down into the dirt a second time. It missed Cathy by inches but landed on three Yeltan spearmen who were trying to scramble back to the open hatch.

James saw Father Michael and Ephie Blake disappear below ground into the Yeltan tunnels, but the Yeltans were finding it hard to restrain Craig's mum.

Jean Harrison was shouting out for Wee Joe and Helen. "They're trapped on the other side of the tree!"

What are they all doing here? thought James.

Ashthat stepped round the trunk and spied him. "Blinder!" he roared.

James looked over his shoulder, into Ashthat's one remaining eye.

"Blinder!" Ashthat bellowed again. He lifted his club, and with a wicked grin, threw it. The large piece of wood whistled through the air as it headed directly for James's head.

"No!" Cathy screamed at the giant Troll. She grabbed James by the shoulders and yanked him backwards.

A few feet away from them, the massive weapon thumped dully into the ferns and mud. The earth heaved upwards throwing James and Cathy away from the Yeltan escape hatch.

As he was falling to the ground, James spotted Craig's mum as she slipped free from the Yeltans. *If Ashthat sees her now she will be an easy target...* "You missed me!" he shouted, hoping to distract Ashthat. The giant roared in frustration and snatched up his club again. Behind him, Jean Harrison dragged Wee Joe and Helen out from a clump of ferns and back to the Yeltan hatch.

James caught hold of his mum's arm. "Keep moving!"

But with a torrent of river water still dripping off the Tree Troll's hide, the slippery mud on the knoll made it difficult to move and they soon fell. Even with his sword, James could not find enough purchase to stand fast.

Ashthat readied himself to make the final blow...

***

"Shut the hatch!" Landris shouted as Jean and the children landed heavily beside him.

"No! Let me past. James is still up there," yelled Craig, his voice full of anger and panic. Then he realised who it was that'd come down the ladder so roughly. "Mum, Helen, Wee Joe! What are you all doing here?"

"We's been wooking for *you*, stupid!" said Wee Joe.

Craig beamed at his little brother, scrunching Wee Joe's hair before dodging another four of five Yeltan hands, all trying to stop him leaping up the ladder. "I'll be back in a minute!"

"Craig! Get down here now!" Jean, still shaking from fetching her two younger children, watched in horror as Craig pushed the hatch open above them and jumped free.

Craig landed right beside Ashthat's left foot.

Incensed, Ashthat screamed down at Craig and tried to

stamp on him.

"Argghh! You're the one who took my eye! You will pay for—"

Ashthat never finished the sentence. Springing to his feet, Craig threw Greenworm into Ashthat's gawping mouth. It sliced off two of the Troll's jagged teeth before flying deep into the back of his woody throat.

Dropping his huge club, Ashthat clutched his neck with his splintered fingers. "Guuurrgg!" He dropped to his knees. "Hhh! Gugg!" The hideous noises that followed sent the Hedra cowering further back into the river. His brother, Ssslathat, looked up the hill in complete terror. Then, clutching his eye in agony, he retreated with the Hedra, further into the river.

"Brother! Ashthat?" Ssslathat shouted up at the Eden Tree. "We were warned not to come here! It was forbidden! Ashthat, fall back..." His voice trailed off into a deep, wooden sob.

11 Ashthat's Revenge

Standing in the river, Jal looked up and pointed to a Gwendralin Captain who'd just appeared from the giant roots. He recognised him as Cimerato, son of Lord Eldane.

The Hedra watched as Cimerato edged past the wavering Ashthat and ran towards the small brown-haired boy who had blinded Ssslathat. The boy was with what he took to be a Manimal woman.

"Fire at the Manimals!" Jal pointed up at the figures on the mound. "We cannot return empty-handed!"

As one, the remains of the Hedra brigade let loose their black arrows at figures beneath the tree.

Jal looked on as the black cloud descended, cutting through leaves and shattering branches. He saw one arrow graze Cimerato's cheek and many more would have found their mark but for the boy. His crimson-tinged sword whizzed with lightning speed, deflecting the arrows an instant before they hit their target.

Jal shouted at his soldiers, "Stand fast! They have Ashthat behind them, Ssslathat is with us and there are only three of them." He held up three scaled fingers. "Three! We are still almost eighty strong!"

The Hedra line wavered. Then, slowly, they all slipped their round shields from their backs and began to walk through the murky, green water again as one. Ssslathat lingered near the far bank as the Hedra regrouped and advanced.

***

James's sword glowed with the fury of the fight. It seemed to feed on danger, gaining more speed and power the worse things got. He was back on his feet, but his arm had just about had it.

James felt his mum staring at him.

"James," she panted, "where in Heaven's name did you learn to do that?" She shook her head in disbelief as she picked fragments of shredded arrow from her long, black hair.

"It's not really me, Mum," said James. "It's the sword." He spotted Craig moving behind Ashthat and jumped up to meet him. "Nice one, Craig."

Craig tapped his lips twice. "Keep it down! He's not dead yet, numpty!"

Ashthat was still coughing and hacking as he struggled to steady himself against the Eden Tree's thick trunk.

Craig glanced at the advancing Hedra before pointing up at the tree. "We have to get back to the hatch!"

"What about Ashthat?" James saw the giant stagger, cough one more time, and then fall.

"What about Mendel?" pressed Craig.

"I've heard nothing," said James.

Craig shook his head. "Just be careful. I lost my spear in his mouth and I'm not sure when it will appear again." As if to prove his point, he repeated the word "Greenworm," several times and stared down at his empty hand.

Craig blushed and winced at the same time when he saw Cathy Peck coming towards him. "Eh. Hello, Mrs Peck," he said.

"Don't you 'Hello' me!" she hissed. "What have you got yourselves into?"

James could tell his mum was going to go off on one. "Mum. Please. Not just now." His face flushed with embarrassment as he glanced at Cimerato

Cimerato grinned and waved them on.

Cathy rounded on the smirking soldier. "And you can take that stupid grin off your face, whoever you are!" Cathy pushed past Cimerato and grabbed James's arm, hauling him up the hill towards the Yeltan hatch. "It's not safe here."

"That's the understatement of the year," James muttered.

She slowed as she approached Ashthat, who was now lying motionless at the foot of the Eden Tree.

A Hedra arrow sank deep into the turf, inches from her heel.

"They're advancing again," warned Cimerato. He looked down at the sluggish green river. "The beautiful lady is right. We should take cover quickly, before one of their archers gets lucky. They're not the best of shots, but they're not the worst either." Cimerato moved ahead of them with his sword at the ready.

"What beautiful lady?" whispered Craig.

James closed the fingers of his left hand and swished them across his throat at his best friend in an effort to silence him.

As Cathy neared the crumpled heap of Ashthat, she gripped James's hand so tightly that it hurt him. "Is it dead?"

The Troll didn't move.

James wasn't sure.

Another arrow smacked into a branch just above Craig's head, causing him to run straight past the Troll without thinking.

"We've got no choice," said James. "Look, Craig's alright. We have to move round him to get to the hatch." He stared at the Troll's open mouth, his huge wooden fist still buried in his throat in an effort to retrieve Greenworm.

As they passed, James couldn't help staring at the Troll's strange, bark-like skin. Gnarled, metallic lumps lined Ashthat's hide and patches of moss and orange algae grew between the folds. When he saw the long, dagger-like fingernails, each at least a foot in length, he shuddered. But the Troll's mouth was even worse. It was full of row upon row of razor-sharp teeth, like those of a shark.

As they inched towards the safety of the open hatch, the stink from the felled Troll's mouth was overpowering. James could see Landris and Craig willing them forward.

Ashthat didn't move, nor did he even appear to breathe, as they walked briskly round the hulking beast.

And all the while, black arrows continued to rain down around them.

Leading by example, Cimerato skirted the felled Troll and made it safely to Landris and Craig. He turned to beckon James and Cathy, but suddenly held up his hand in warning, "Don't move!"

Ashthat rolled with incredible speed and smashed his fist down in front of them, barring their way. James and Cathy stopped dead, shocked by the sudden change in the creature.

"Not so fast, Blinders," he gurgled, the words barely discernible. The Troll pulled himself into a kneeling position.

James lifted his sword, but Ashthat's branch-like arm shot out and caught his mum by the leg.

Still gurgling and very unsteady, the Troll stood up, holding Cathy against his huge belly. James's heart nearly stopped. He couldn't speak.

"Put that cursed sword of yours down, Blinder, or I will squash her dead... Now!"

James dropped the crimson sword and heard it clatter against a gnarled root before it disappeared.

"Magic swords won't hurt us now, will they...Kak, Kak!" muttered Ashthat. Cathy squirmed as Ashthat jerked his head back in an evil laugh. He flicked her over to his other hand before his splintered fingers closed round her writhing body.

Cathy tried to speak. "R...run, James!" She was losing consciousness.

"Mum!" he screamed. He could see Landris and Cimerato through the Troll's legs, hear the hisses and shouts of the Hedra as they climbed up from the riverbank below, their black arrows still thudding into the earth around his feet.

James felt his chest tighten. There was no way out of this.

12 The Inferno

Jal knew they still had a chance to kill the Manimals if he got his soldiers up to the top of the hill right away.

Still in the river, Ssslathat seemed reluctant to follow them. "I have one of the Blinders, Brother!" Ashthat stood up to show his brother below.

As the troll nearest the boy called out, Jal saw that he was dangling a female Manimal in mid-air, swinging her like a rag doll. All seemed to be turning in their favour until a sudden cry echoed up from the river behind them, "Baacckkk!"

Before they could turn to see what it was, an apelike beast leapt up out of the water and onto Ssslathat's back.

"Argghhh!" Ssslathat screamed as the beast sank his long, glistening black teeth into the Troll's woody hide.

Jal looked back to the river. "It's a Mertol!" he exclaimed in disbelief. "It must have followed us here." Jal glanced back and forth between the Eden Tree and the fight in the river.

The Mertol was pounding on Ssslathat's back and biting his neck and shoulders. The wounded Troll, totally unprepared, was fighting to keep his balance, still clutching his eye. Finally finding his feet, the Troll tried to swing round and pull off his attacker, but he couldn't reach. Strips of woody hide flew off as the Mertol tore into him.

Jal gasped as, by chance, Ssslathat grasped a handful of red fur and, in frenzied desperation, spun the Mertol, only half his size, over his head. The Mertol hit the river with a tremendous splash.

As the Mertol struggled in the water, Ssslathat lunged forward and grabbed one of its arms, throwing the beast back behind him this time, toward the trees on the far bank.

Seeing that things were going better for Ssslathat, Jal urged his troops forward again, up the grassy knoll, towards the Eden Tree and Ashthat.

***

"It's a Mertol!" shouted Cimerato.

Mesmerised, James watched from up on the hill as the beast, red fur dripping with green river water, lunged to its feet and raised its ape-like hands high above his head. Ssslathat, hearing the splashing water, roared and turned to finish off the Mertol.

Still panic-stricken over his mum's situation, James saw that Ashthat had become distracted. He remembered the Talisman in his belt and pulled it free.

Just then, however, a small, black ball shot out of the Mertol's right cheek and whizzed right past Ssslathat's head. The Troll looked surprised, swinging round to see who or what the Mertol was aiming at.

James braced himself, but the whirring ball raced straight towards him.

Ashthat screamed as the ball swooped up the grassy knoll, flattened itself to resemble a shining blade, then sliced cleanly through his neck.

Instantly silenced, a look of shock spread over Ashthat's face as his head fell slowly backwards and then rolled off his massive shoulders. His fingers spasmed and loosened. Cathy dropped to the ground as the decapitated Troll's limp body crashed to its knees. Then, like a felled tree, it slammed into the ferns and roots, sending mud and debris up into the branches of the Eden Tree.

Before the earth had stopped trembling, a second ball shot from the ape-like creature's face, this time aimed at Ssslathat. Stunned by his brother's demise, the remaining Troll lost his footing in the river and stumbled. The second speeding ball missed Ssslathat's head by inches, whizzed through his green crest, and then continued up the hill.

James ducked as it flew over his own head and smashed into the Eden Tree. In an instant, green sparks spiralled up the huge trunk and the whole tree burst into flames.

James heard an unearthly cry from the river below.

"No!" Shaking with uncontrollable hatred, the Tree Troll turned to face the Mertol. "You have killed my brother!" With a roar Ssslathat rushed at the creature and landed heavily on its chest. The weight of the Troll forced the Mertol back under the water, its matted body disappearing beneath the foam. The writhing beast attempted to rise up from the waters, but Ssslathat reached out and thumped his jagged fist down on the Mertol's chest, knocking it back into the river again. With a scream of rage, Ssslathat forced the Mertol's face under the water until the ape creature stopped struggling.

With a wail of sorrow that sounded over the roar of the burning Eden Tree, James watched Ssslathat charge up the small, fern-covered hillside towards him and his mum, who was lying motionless on the ground. Determined to reach his fallen brother, Ssslathat trampled several more Hedra as he bounded up the slope.

By this time, Ashthat's body was burning as brightly as the Eden Tree. Strange green flames sparked and popped as the fat beneath the dead Troll's wooden hide caught fire. Above them, the hanging moss burst into flames. Crackling like burning lace, flecks of the glowing fibre floated down the hill and onto the Hedra.

James felt the heat intensify. He hauled desperately at his mum but could barely make her budge.

Craig and Cimerato were waving their hands about, trying to keep the burning moss from landing on her.

Then Cimerato picked up Cathy and began running back to the open hatch. Craig and James stumbled after him, dodging a storm of floating embers.

Ssslathat slid to a halt in the face of the inferno and screamed up at the smoke-filled sky.

"Hurry!" Landris shouted. The Eden Tree was burning with a fury, dying, just like Denthan's tired sun, Tealfirth. Slamming the hatch shut behind them, the three slid down the ladder, landing roughly on the floor of the smoke-filled chamber below.

"Mum... Mum, are you okay?" James coughed as he crouched down to look at her. Cathy's eyes were closed, her face pale. A sizable crowd of Yeltans gathered round him, babbling wildly as tears traced down his sooty cheeks. "Mum!" he shouted.

James rounded on the Yeltans. "I can't hear if she's breathing or not!" The crackling noises and the thump and crash of falling timber on the ground above them wasn't helping either; it was growing louder by the second. The heat was becoming unbearable. He felt his lungs begin to constrict and for a moment wondered if his asthma was returning.

Landris caught hold of James's shoulder. "We have to leave here now! Those bigger branches are going to drop and trap us." He motioned to Cimerato. "Pick her up and come!"

Everyone followed Landris, coughing and babbling as they moved down the passage away from the Eden Tree. James felt an unbearable sense of hopelessness bear down on him as he staggered fearfully after Cimerato and his mum.

Hearing a thundering crash above them, Helen screeched and the Yeltans began their dreadful wailing.

***

Above ground, the whole island of Senegral burned ferociously. Jal steered the inconsolable Ssslathat away from the flames while the Hedra retreated back into the river. Smoke from the fire blew into their faces and stung their reptilian eyes.

Once they reached the water, Jal searched for the Mertol, but there was no sign of the creature. The Mertol had either been swept away by the current or crawled into the trees to die.

Behind Jal, Ssslathat cried out for his dead brother and

smashed his giant fists into the river. "Ashthat! Kak! Kak! Ashthat…"

"There's no time for that just now," hissed Jal, "we need to move." They had to get further away from the furnace – to retreat from the floating cinders that were showered them like flecks of burning snow. Stunned, Jal shook his head in disbelief as he waded away from the blaze. "I have never known such a defeat," he muttered, "Yellow devils; Manimal children with magic swords; and then the Mertol." He fixed his gaze on the grief-stricken Troll and sat down with a thud on the opposite bank. He splashed water into his stinging eyes. "Half the brigade dead and nothing to show for it. I cannot return to Feldon." Jal glanced up through the smoke at their largest sun and spat.

A wounded Hedra soldier called Garazar approached Jal and, after a brief bow, whispered in the ancient Hedra tongue, "You are correct, sir. We cannot return without a hide or a head as some proof." He surreptitiously eyed the wounded Tree Troll.

"Hmmm…" Jal considered the situation. "The brother is probably burned beyond recognition, so we can't use him."

"And the Manimals will have perished with him," added Garazar.

Jal nodded. "Still, as you say, we need proof. We will wait a little longer just in case the Mertol returns. If the Troll kills the beast, we'll use its head as our trophy. If not…" He glanced over at the moaning Ssslathat. "There is always your suggestion."

"As you wish," said Garazar, smiling.

"Whatever we do, though, we must keep moving," said Jal, "for I can assure you that our doom is sealed if we do not return to Gwendral very soon." Jal shielded his eyes against the reddening sun, just visible through the grey smoke, and wondered how all this was going to end.

13 A Cure for Cathy

Ephie Blake knelt over Cathy and immediately began mouth-to-mouth resuscitation. The tunnel where James's mother lay was narrow, but at least they were all well away from the heat and devastation of Senegral Island.

They were, in fact, under the river itself. As James numbly watched Ephie working on his mum, the cold, green water of the River Levan dripped down his neck from the leaking roof.

Father Michael held Cathy's wrist, checking for a pulse and issuing encouragements. "Come on, Cathy. Breathe!"

James was now convinced that his mother was dead. Ashthat had squeezed the life out of her; and what was worse, James hadn't reacted quickly enough to stop him from doing so. He should have tried using the Talisman. He would never forgive himself. He stifled a sob.

At the same time, Ephie paused to wipe a tear from her eye. "It's no good."

"What? No! Keep going!" shouted James.

Ephie looked up at James and sadly shook her head.

"Please, Miss Blake, try again. Please!" James felt Bero's cold, wet nose push against his bare leg.

Ephie sighed, her shoulders drooping. Then, with a determined nod of her head, she pinched Cathy's nose and took another deep breath. Three short blows made Cathy's chest rise again and this time, to everyone's relief, she began to cough and sputter. Her eyes blinked open. "Cugh! Cugh! Agghhh…!" She seemed to recognise the sizable outline of Ephie Blake leaning over her.

James braced himself for her inevitable reaction.

"Yuck! Get off me you tub of lard!" Cathy coughed and pushed Ephie away.

"Mum! No. She...she saved your life!" James was crying with relief but red with shame.

In the bright light of the Yeltan torches, Ephie steadied herself. "What did you just call me?"

Michael stepped forward to comfort Ephie. He was shaking with anger. "I think you owe Ephie an apology, Cathy!"

Jean appeared out of the gloom, holding Wee Joe over her shoulder. Amazingly, the little boy had fallen fast asleep. "Everybody just calm down. Getting angry isn't going to help," she said, "We're not exactly in a normal situation here and we must do our best to stay focused." Jean edged nearer to Michael and whispered, "What will these people think of us?"

Helen nuzzled in beside her mother and in a loud voice said, "Mum, why is James's mum always so angry? She's such a pig to everyone."

Everyone looked at Helen.

Right there and then James knew that she'd said aloud exactly what they were all thinking. He cringed with the shame of it.

Even Landris, who'd known the conscious version of Cathy for less than ten seconds, nodded his head in agreement. "Truth often spills from the lips of the young," he sighed. "However we have to get going right now."

Garlon edged his way forward. "The tunnels beneath the river are not safe."

Landris waved them on. "I would prefer to get back to our home. We've lost too many in this struggle; I don't want to lose any more."

James's voice cut through the gloom. "But what about Mendel? We've got to go back and look for him. He said he would meet us at the tree!"

Craig edged forward. "There's no Eden Tree anymore, mate."

"It's not safe!" Landris exclaimed. "There are Hedra everywhere and—"

"Never mind safe," interrupted James. He felt totally drained, both physically and emotionally, but he wasn't going to give up now. He looked into his mum's eyes. "Mum, I think dad might be here somewhere. He could be up there right now." James pointed to the low, dripping ceiling above his head.

Cathy Peck's hazel eyes narrowed. "Son, your dad isn't up there. Your dad is in deep..."

"Deepest France?" finished Craig, a toothy white grin creasing his dirty face. "You see, Mrs Peck, I've told James not to worry too much. Mr Peck's probably just taking a break."

"Taking a break from what?" Cathy Peck drew Craig a deadly stare.

Craig moved off and muttered, "Eh... I don't know."

James jabbed Craig in the ribs. "Not helping." He pointed to the tunnel ahead. "Landris, where does that tunnel lead to?" The dark passage veered off to the right and James could see the rungs of another ladder.

Landris put his yellow hand on James's shoulder. "It leads up to the forest opposite the island. It would take you right into the middle of the Hedra. Please take my advice..."

But James had already made up his mind. He looked back at his mum. She seemed confused and disoriented. "Are you okay, Mum? You see, I have to go..."

"You aren't going anywhere!" Cathy was still weak and not quite sure where she was, but her voice was as strong as ever.

"But Mum..." James pleaded. Half hero, half kid, James felt torn in two. He knew that Mendel was the key to his dad's safety, the key to *all* their safety. The goldfish was the only chance they had of surviving this mess. "I know that if we don't find Mendel, we'll all die," he said simply.

Cathy raised herself up on her elbows. "Don't you dare move an inch, James Hamish Peck!"

"Hamish?" Craig snorted.

"I'll be back soon," he told her. Then, ignoring Craig and

avoiding any eye contact with his mum, he dashed off down the tunnel towards the ladder.

"James!" Cathy's furious voice filled the tunnel, but James pushed on regardless, never once looking back, knowing full well that he was in serious trouble when he got back. If he got back...

Cathy pulled herself up into a sitting position, but instantly winced in agony and clutched at her ribs. "I've not come all this way to lose you now." Again, she cringed in pain. "You little..."

Craig turned to *his* mother. "Mum, I have to go with James."

Jean grimaced, then looked at Cimerato. "Could you go with them?"

Cimerato smiled at Jean and the children. "You two," he summoned the remaining Manimal guards. "Come!"

"Son!" Lord Eldane protested. "I should be the one to go."

"Father, it is better that you go back with the Yeltans. We will return soon. The boy's right. Mendel is our only hope."

Craig squeezed his mum's arm and ruffled Helen's hair before setting off after James. He shouted over his shoulder, "We've got magic weapons and a Talisman that can kill just about anything. So, don't worry!"

The Manimal fighters followed Craig down the passage and were soon climbing up the ladder behind the boys.

***

Cathy Peck rounded on Jean. "Are you just going to let him go like that? It's taken us days to find them and you're just going to let them go? Get a backbone, Jean!"

Jean made an effort to stay calm. "Cathy, you can't control everything. All your shouting and hitting and threats won't make any difference in the long run. I know I'm a bit soft on them sometimes but..."

"A bit soft! You deserve all that's coming to you when that boy grows up - if he grows up. You'll pay the price. They need to know the rules, the boundaries. And by letting your son go, you've just undermined me in front of mine. You deserve..." Cathy began to cough.

Jean knelt down and looked Cathy right in the eye. "James didn't see me letting Craig go after him. He was already gone. When anything goes wrong or something happens that you don't like, you always turn on some poor sod and heap the blame on them. Craig's gone because he wants to help his best friend, because he wants to try and save us. This is like some really bad nightmare, and I don't want them to go either, but they know more about what's going on here than we do, so stop... Just stop it..." Jean stood up. She saw Helen looking at her with wide eyes and apologised, "I'm sorry you had to see that, dear."

Helen smiled and gave her a little clap. "No. It was good. Well done, Mum!"

The atmosphere in the cave was tense as Cathy tried to pull herself to her feet. She spied Michael, still trying his best to console Ephie. "If you were a real gentleman, you would help me up."

Father Michael flushed. "Oh, I beg your pardon, Cathy. Here, take my arm."

"Don't bother!" she snapped.

Cathy's rebuff caused Michael's mouth to drop open. "But I thought...?"

"You thought you would cuddle into Podgy, and let me struggle with my cracked ribs, here in this..." Cathy faltered. Anxiously, she grabbed the Yeltan leader's arm. "Where are we?"

"We're about four feet below the River Levan, in a Yeltan tunnel that's rarely used and has seen better days." Landris traced the low ceiling with his stubby fingers. "We'd best get moving, madam."

"Tunnel?" Cathy began to shake. "I can't be in any kind of

tunnel…" Her voice shook with fear. She pulled Landris close to her. "Get me out of here. I can't…I can't…"

"Garlon!" Landris called the young Yeltan across. Garlon pushed his way through a cluster of Yeltans, fumbling for something in his jacket pocket as he hurried along.

Cathy had gone from being practically dead, to blazing tyrant and then to quivering wreck, all in a matter of minutes.

Helen looked up at her mum. "She's bonkers, isn't she, Mum?"

"Not bonkers, Helen, just not very well," corrected Jean.

"Whatever." Helen shrugged her shoulders.

Garlon produced a small, wooden bottle from his belt.

"You have the Lugpus?" Landris asked.

"Indeed, I do," Garlon answered.

"Excellent. I think it should do the trick." Landris took the bottle and knelt down beside Cathy. "Madam? James's mother?"

Half delirious, Cathy squinted up at Landris.

Landris offered Cathy an encouraging smile. "Take this drink. It will make you feel better. At least until we get above ground."

In between sobs, Cathy at first only sipped the yellow liquid. Then, liking the taste, she downed it, soon emptying the bottle of every drop. "Humph!" Cathy sniffed, then began to smile as a look of contentment brightened her face.

When they at last began moving through the tunnel she did not make one complaint or rude remark. She even giggled a little and began to hum a catchy tune.

"Mrs Peck should drink that stuff all the time, shouldn't she, Mum?" said Helen, her big blue eyes sparkling in the light of the Yeltan torches.

Jean smiled reassuringly. "Just keep moving, Helen. We'll soon be home. I hope…"

14 The Battle of the Grove

Craig caught up with James, finding him just outside the hatch. James didn't say anything when he saw his friend, but he looked very relieved, which was good enough for Craig.

Both boys called for their magic weapons as Cimerato and the two remaining guards climbed out of the hatch. Together the small group crept to the edge of the tall ferns. Acrid smoke still blew through the trees and little grey flecks of ash floated through the grove like fairies dancing in the breeze.

"It's like a dream," said Craig, blinking in the amber light. Suddenly frowning, he looked up through a break in the canopy at the large orange orb that was Tealfirth. "It's getting bigger," he remarked, twirling his green spear.

James followed his gaze. "Much bigger," he agreed. And then he whispered quietly, so the others wouldn't hear: "I think that's what stars do before they explode. Or implode. Or however it is that they end."

"Get down!" said Cimerato. "I can hear voices."

James and Craig quickly crouched low. They could hear the voices too.

***

Hissing and spitting, several Hedra soldiers moved to within a few feet of their position. They were so close that James could actually smell them—a mixture of damp dog and rotten fish.

A strange voice hissed through the bushes and trees. "Jal, I can still taste them. The Manimals."

The one called Jal's slit nostrils opened wide. "The breeze is pushing the smoke and their scent towards us. We need to move onward to Gwendral."

"But I can still taste them," mused the voice.

"They burned on the island," hissed Jal.

"It doesn't smell like cooked Manimal," hissed the voice.

Ssslathat moaned in pain, uttering deep resonate wails as he marched along. "Ashthat…oh no…oh no…"

Jal looked up at the wounded Troll, the expression on his flattened, scaly face scornful. "Keep it down, or that Mertol will find us again."

Ssslathat shuddered and creaked as he traced his wounded neck with his long fingers. "I finished it off," he replied. "I made sure it was dead." He eyed the smoked-filled forest suspiciously, as if he didn't quite believe his own words.

Suddenly Ssslathat's deep voice boomed, "Stop!" He pointed a long sharp finger at the fern grove to his right and jerked his head back to test the air. "Kak, kak…"

***

James looked across to Craig who was lying beside Cimerato in the undergrowth. To his left, a Gwendralin guard slowly pushed himself up onto his knees. The guard put his fingers to his lips to signal silence and then, sword in hand, edged forward to where the Troll stood with his back to them. They could see the deep marks left on the creature's shoulders and neck by the Mertol. The bushes around them began to rustle as more and more Hedra came back to support the Troll.

"We've walked right into this one," whispered Cimerato. He held his sword at the ready and slowly joined the first guard. "It's always better to strike first," he whispered. He signalled James to go to his left and Craig to his right.

James was terrified, but knew he could trust in his magic sword, Firetongue.

Craig's spear, Greenworm, as always, had returned to him. It shone like new in his hand and looked no worse for having been stuck in the back of Ashthat's throat and then having been burned to a crisp under the Eden Tree. Both of the magical weapons glowed and jerked in the boys' hands, ready for the fight.

James wondered about trying to use the Talisman but decided to trust his sword instead.

In front of them, Jal drew his sword. The remaining Hedra slithered and hissed, their grey scales flashing through gaps in the undergrowth as they prowled about. Suddenly, there was a heavy crash, just in front of James. Craning his neck upward, he saw Ssslathat's thirty-foot hulk towering over him. His massive foot had sunk into the leaf litter about three feet from Craig's head. *Just one more step and he'd have been strawberry jam,* thought James.

Thud!

Cimerato's curved sword slammed into the left heel of the Tree Troll.

Thud!

The smaller guard's sword bit deep into the right heel. They'd cut out two huge notches of woody flesh. Shocked by the attack, Ssslathat began to topple backwards.

James and Craig rolled out of the way as Ssslathat smacked down amongst the ferns. He missed the boys, but several of the approaching Hedra were not so lucky.

The bigger Gwendralin guard charged out of cover only to stop dead, skewered to the hilt on the Hedra leader's sword. The snake-like eyes flashed bright yellow as he pulled his sword free.

"Jal has killed a Manimal!" shouted one of the Hedra.

All hell broke loose.

James's sword brought five surprised Hedra down at once, slicing through scales and bone as though they were butter.

Close by, Craig jumped up onto the toppled Ssslathat. Using the Troll's chest as a vantage point, he tried to pick out the Hedra who looked to be in command. When he saw Jal, he let the spear fly. Jal dodged to his left, escaping with a cut that oozed black blood. Instantly, the spear reappeared in Craig's hand. At the same time, Ssslathat moaned and turned, sending Craig flying as the giant hauled himself up onto his elbows.

"Blinders!" Seeing the spear in Craig's hand, the Troll automatically covered his good eye.

Craig stumbled to his feet and loosed the spear once more at four charging Hedra. It passed right through the attackers, leaving them slumped and twitching in the ferns.

Cimerato spun and ducked as he moved forward, slashing at the advancing Hedra while making sure to keep space between himself and the recovering Tree Troll.

The remaining Gwendralin guard was less fortunate. He parried several Hedra swords well enough, but in the mêlée the guard failed to see Ssslathat's heavy fist before it was too late. With a sudden rush of air, it flattened him, along with the two Hedra he'd been fighting.

Jal and Cimerato ran at each other, locking swords before pushing away. The Hedra guard was an excellent swordsman and he soon gained the advantage. Once, twice, three times he parried Cimerato's thrusts and cuts. Then he went on the offensive. With a hiss he thrust forward, twisting his sword at the last minute so it cut down into Cimerato's shoulder.

"Argh!" Cimerato bit his lip in pain as the black Hedra steel buckled his golden armour and took a chip out of his collarbone. Cimerato kicked himself free, but he was badly hurt.

Jal's tongue flicked with excitement when he saw the Gwendralin captain stagger backwards. As he fell, however, Cimerato lunged at Jal's legs, catching Jal's shin guard. Jal wavered but quickly regained his stance and raised his sword for the kill.

With a yell of exertion, Cimerato rolled onto his knees and got to his feet. He managed to switch his sword hand and block the blow but blood was pouring down his chest from the cut on his right shoulder. His yellow armour glistened crimson.

Jal ducked and threw his sword at Cimerato's legs. A blur of steel, it spun forward and smacked against Cimerato's weapon, forcing it back between his legs. Cimerato winced.

Moving in for the kill once more, Jal lizard-crawled along the ground. James was too busy fending off his own attackers to help the struggling captain; he could only hope Cimerato could hold on. Just as Jal was about to pounce, the Gwendralin captain yelled and jumped over his opponent.

Jal twisted his head as Cimerato flew over him, his reptilian teeth biting upward.

Cimerato met the bite with a powerful jab of his heel, which caught Jal's nose hole and smashed his mouth shut. Jal hissed in pain as Cimerato sprung off his back and landed, cat-like, behind him. As his Hedra attacker stood up, black blood trickling from his scaly mouth, Cimerato readied himself for the Hedra's next move.

With a roar, Cimerato raised his sword and charged. A nearby Hedra fighter flung his blade to Jal and the leader caught it. Once more, he and Cimerato locked swords. They stood, steel against steel, pitting their weight against each other. As they pushed and skidded in the mud, however, Cimerato's strength began to give. His left shoulder was growing numb; his right arm was useless. In one last furious effort, he smacked his head into Jal's face. Jal merely blinked once then smiled.

"No!" screamed James, seeing that Cimerato was beaten.

Jal's black tongue traced Cimerato's face, and the Gwendralin captain turned his head away.

James was also weakening as he cut and parried his way through the Hedra fighters. Almost reaching Cimerato, he heard a roar behind him. Instinctively, he ducked and the air rushed past his neck as Ssslathat's wooden fingernails took a swipe at him. Fortunately for James, the Troll skewered two more Hedra who'd been about to attack him from behind. As he turned to fight, he saw Ssslathat stagger back on his weakened heels and sit down heavily on the forest floor.

Craig, taken by surprise, barely managed to throw himself clear, but his magic spear now lay trapped under the enormous weight of the Troll. "James, help!" he shouted. But James could do nothing for his friend. He was too busy spinning and cutting his way through the encroaching mass of Hedra. There were just too many of them.

"James!" Craig cried again.

Worried for his friend, James turned back to see Craig edging away from his trapped spear and the Tree Troll. It was only a quick glance, but the distraction was enough for the nearest Hedra soldier to take his chance and move in. As James turned back round, the Hedra brought down a fierce two-handed killing stroke.

With amazing speed, James's right arm shot up and blocked the blow. The swords locked in a spray of sparks and James found himself staring into the hypnotic eyes of his opponent. Unable to blink or break free, his mind grew fuzzy and he felt himself drift away from the fight. Sensing his advantage, the Hedra soldier brought his scaled knee upwards and caught James in the stomach.

"Unghh!" James fell hard. Winded, he lay helpless as another four Hedra notched their bows and took aim. Despair made his gut churn when he realised he had no choice but to surrender.

Cimerato, seeing what had happened to James, shouted, "Hold your fire! We surrender!"

"Halt!" Jal stood over Cimerato and waved his hand, hissing the command once more to his agitated troops. "Lower your weapons!"

Jal glanced down at James's magic sword. "Drop it now, or your friends die!"

Reluctantly, James dropped his sword. The Hedra nearest to James all jumped back in amazement when they saw it dissolve into the forest floor.

"Stay there, all of you!" Jal ordered. "Do not move." One of them kicked Cimerato in the ribs before binding him and retrieving his curved sword.

The deep voice of the Tree Troll, Ssslathat, filled the forest. "Now you will pay, Blinders." Grabbing hold of Craig, Ssslathat lifted the boy high above him. He examined his captured enemy curiously. "Such a little morsel. Hardly worth eating."

Craig, desperate for his magic spear, called out, "Greenworm! Greenworm!" But nothing happened.

"No good calling me names, boy. I won't kill you any quicker." Ssslathat laughed at his own joke, then threw Craig up into the air. He flew a good twenty feet above the forest canopy, spun round in mid-air then tumbled back down, screaming all the way. Ssslathat crouched, catching him with his other hand just before he hit the ground. "Lucky for you I can still manage well enough with the one eye you left me."

James knew it wouldn't be long before their time was up. His mum had been right. They should have stayed below ground with the Yeltans.

"Thirty-two, thirty-three..." Jal finished counting the dead bodies. "Another thirty-three killed by..." Jal looked down at the spot where James's sword had disappeared. "Magic, I presume. However, before I kill you, I should like you to tell me where the other Manimals are hiding. I need to finish this job. King Feldon will be disappointed if I only bring three heads back to our camp."

The rest of the Hedra hissed and gurgled with laughter.

"Then you may as well kill us now, because we will tell you

nothing!" Cimerato spat at a Hedra guard standing over him.

James wished Cimerato hadn't been quite so unwilling to negotiate. Not that he would talk, but maybe they could at least pretend they would, buy themselves a bit of thinking time. James was, after all, the one who had dragged them into this mess in the first place. Since he'd let them all down, it was up to him to fix things.

James's heart pounded as he racked his brain for a plan.

***

Jal pointed at James "You first!" he shouted. Then, turning to a Hedra guard, he issued an order. "Take him behind that tree."

Craig couldn't believe that after all their trials – after all the dangers he and James had faced together – their demise would be so cold-blooded.

He was stuck, powerless to intervene, and could only look on as the Hedra leader who had given the instructions stepped behind the tree, to where James had been dragged by the guard.

And then the most sickening words Craig had ever heard carried to him from behind the tree's trunk. "Time to die, boy!" the Hedra leader hissed.

There was a sickening thud, the meaning of which was only too clear to all who heard it.

15 The Magic Hand

"Who will be next?" Jal's voice echoed through the forest as he reappeared. He was toying with the Talisman, seemingly unaware of its significance.

It had all happened so fast. Craig couldn't believe it. "No!" Stunned, he cried out again, then dropped down to his knees in despair. Ssslathat whipped Craig over into one hand and thumped his other hand against a nearby tree trunk. Leaves showered over Craig as Ssslathat's purple eye burned with rage. He addressed Jal. "Why did you kill the other boy? He was mine. He killed my brother!"

"He did not. The Mertol killed your brother with his magic. And besides, I am in charge here, not you!" Jal signalled to his troops and they fixed their aim on Ssslathat.

Ssslathat drew back. "Do not threaten me. I'm killing this one!" He lifted Craig high and opened his hand. Craig looked up to see the Troll's fist above him, ready to drop down in a deadly crushing blow. Just as the Troll's arm tensed for the kill, Craig heard something strange coming from the thickset tree where they'd taken James.

"Woowwwdwwright!"

Ssslathat jerked back, a startled expression on his face. Roots began to sprout from the Troll's toes. They twisted out from his feet and burrowed themselves deeply into the soil. Ssslathat screamed as his shins wrinkled and cracked. His skin, Craig realised, was morphing into brown, knotted bark. With every second that passed, a hundred new roots sprung out from the lower half of the Troll's body. Ssslathat tried to twist free, but he was stuck fast.

A loud crack exploded in the quiet woods. "No...!" Ssslathat screamed as his torso became solid wood. "Not tha...!" His voice was cut short as he jerked his head back for the last time. "Ka! Ka! K-" Gnarled woody branches covered his face, cutting off any further protest. He'd become a tree, a proper one, indistinguishable from the others that surrounded them in the grove.

***

James felt the knock, knock, knocking sensation fade and now dared to look out from behind the broad tree. He saw Ssslathat – or what was left of him - holding a bemused Craig in what had been the Troll's outstretched palm.

Tentatively, James whispered the wizard's name, unsure if he'd really said the strange word. "Mendel?"

There was no reply. Just the hisses of the Hedra soldiers. Spooked by what had happened to the Troll, Jal and the others, backed away.

"Hello again, my young friend." James heard the familiar voice and began to laugh with relief and joy.

"Where are you, Mendel?" James shouted as he stepped out from behind the tree.

Hearing James's voice, Craig screeched with delight and began clambering down the Troll. "Thank God you're alive! I could never have faced your mum if…"

The Hedra rounded on Jal.

The warrior Garazar, standing near him, gave Jal a puzzled reptilian stare, his tongue flicking erratically. "Why did you spare the boy?" He snatched the Talisman from Jal.

"I was keeping him for the Troll, Garazar, nothing more." Jal shrugged his shoulders.

Garazar tightened his grip on the Talisman and took a step back, his eyes flicking between the petrified Troll and Jal. "But you said we were going to kill the Troll if we could not find the Mertol, so why try to appease him?"

"He has tricked you all!" accused Cimerato.

The Hedra all began snapping their jaws together loudly.

James's eyes were still fixed on the Talisman.

"Get back in line!" Jal shouted.

But the Hedra, unnerved by the death of Ssslathat, now eyed their leader warily.

"Get back in line, now!" Jal repeated.

But the Hedra were already slipping back into the forest. Garazar shouted, "Flesh and steel are one thing, but magic cannot always feel the bite of the sword."

Another Hedra voice sounded from the trees – "We don't want to be turned into trees or bushes!"

James still didn't understand why Jal had spared him, but that wasn't what was foremost in his thoughts now. He ran to Jal. "The Talisman!"

Jal gave him a puzzled glance.

James watched in horror as the Hedra soldier with the Talisman faded into the forest.

"The Yukplug horn," James pressed, "it's something very special. We need to get it back."

Jal stood hissing at the retreating Hedra. "Garazar is a fool. They will never make it back alive without me. And even if they do, they will be put to death for failing."

"Could you please get that Yukplug horn?"

Jal looked straight at James, roared in frustration, and then ran after the retreating Hedra.

"James?" said Craig. "Let's untie Cimerato while we still can."

"Where are you, Mendel? I can hear you but I..." James felt a wave of hopelessness wash over him. He turned to Craig. "Things are worse than ever. The Eden Tree has burned down, the Talisman is gone and we still haven't found Mendel."

Craig caught James's arm. "We're alive." He stopped and peered up into the canopy. "Look!"

A little blue man, with a shock of white hair, was spinning

down from the treetops on a long strand of moss like a spider.

James gasped. "Mendel?"

The blue creature bumped onto the forest floor, took a bow and began to giggle.

"Sorry about the delay, boys," Mendel apologised, his voice filling their heads.

"Why are you still talking in our heads? Are you frightened that the Hedra will hear you?" asked Craig.

"Ha!" said Mendel. "I can choose who hears me, boys. I thought I'd explained that before?"

Craig shook his head. "No. Not that. You're not—"

"It's called 'inter-atomic selectivity'. I can direct sound waves using the sub-ether airwaves that—"

"Mendel!" snapped Craig. "You've only been here a few seconds and I want to..." Craig made a fist. "We don't need the science. It's just that you're not moving your lips."

James knew Mendel could choose who heard his voice. His magic, on the other hand, could only be done through someone who had actually made a physical connection like he had. "And I thought you were a Manimal before you were a fish," pressed Craig.

Confused, James stared hard at the frail creature before him. "What happened to you?" he demanded. "Why did you leave us?" He was still shaking with the shock of battle.

Craig approached the little blue man. "I think I preferred you as a fish," he remarked after looking the odd creature up and down.

The little blue man smiled, and in a very different voice said, "Eee...I ees not Mendel. This ees." The creature produced a small bottle from behind his back.

Craig and James, slightly relieved to hear this, peered down into a little jug, which appeared to be made from amber-coloured leaves.

"MENDEL!" Tears began to roll down James's cheeks.

"Calm down, my boy," said Mendel.

"But you're back," blurted James, quickly smearing his wet face with the back of his hand.

"And you're still a fish." Craig stated the obvious.

James drew his friend a warning glance. "You could at least tell him you're glad to see him after all we've been through!"

"No, no, no..." said Mendel, "Craig makes a very good point. I am still a fish, which means I must continue to do my magic through you, James."

"See!" said Craig, smugly.

James narrowed his eyes.

"Now that the Eden Tree has been destroyed," continued Mendel, "I can't see any easy way of getting back into my own body again." Mendel splashed his tail, spraying the little blue creature. "This is Eethan...Eethan Magichand."

James nodded, remembering the Eethan from the Yeltan tapestry.

Cimerato interrupted the boys' conversation. "Who are you talking to? This is not Mendel." He pointed at Eethan but his strange eyes were mainly set on Jal.

Water splashed out of the makeshift jug as Mendel circled round.

"James, tell Cimerato to behave or I will make him recite the periodic table." James realised that Cimerato could not hear Mendel's voice.

With a sigh, he screwed up his face then turned to Cimerato. "Mendel says to behave or he'll make you recite the periodic table." Cimerato's expression changed in a flash. He moved closer and peered into the bottle.

Eethan held it up for him to see.

During all this Jal remained motionless, apart from his tongue, which darted in and out of his scaled lips.

"Tell the Hedra fighter, Jal, that he can either run and catch up with his comrades or else join us." Mendel's voice once again filled James's head as he issued the command.

"Ask him to join us?" James peered into the flask in disbelief. Then, on receiving no reply, he turned to the Hedra and said, "Em, well, Jal. That's your name, isn't it?" Jal nodded, his tongue still flickering.

"Mendel says that you can either run now and catch up with your lizard men, or else join us."

"Join you?" The Hedra's eye-slits narrowed and his nostrils flared as he stared back at James.

"There is no way that any Hedra scum are coming with us." Cimerato's white eyes widened.

Eethan tried to reassure Cimerato. "Ees good scum, ee thinks."

"Don't be stupid, little man. The only good Hedra is a dead one."

James shook his head. "Wait a second! If Mendel has asked him to join us, that's good enough for me. Besides, he spared my life back there when the others would have killed me. I'm not exactly sure *why* he did that, but he did."

Jal looked as if he was smiling when he pointed to Cimerato and said, "I have spared *you* twice, great captain."

"What do you mean, twice?" Cimerato lifted the point of his sword until it twitched menacingly under Jal's chin.

"I saw you and your guards slip out of the sewers in your boat. I said nothing." Jal stepped back from the tip of Cimerato's sword.

"But you followed us, with two Tree Trolls! I was there when those Trolls and your Snakemen killed my guards!"

"The Trolls were looking for those two." Jal pointed to Craig and James. "And anyway, I was not in command at that point, Telan was."

"Telan?" Cimerato questioned.

"I'm afraid your little yellow friends took care of him," said Jal. "Saved me the job."

"Who *are* you?" Cimerato pressed.

"I am Jal, Royal guard of King Feldon. I was asked to take care of Telan after..."

"After your Snakemen and the Trolls had disposed of us and any other loose ends. Isn't that right?"

"Exactly!" Jal gave Cimerato another snaky grin.

Cimerato moved closer to Jal. "So why should I trust you for one second?"

Undaunted, the serpent guard continued, "Your King Athelstone is an impostor."

"So it seems," replied Cimerato.

"The dark lord, Dendralon, killed your King and now wears his skin."

James could see that Cimerato was unimpressed.

Jal hissed and said, "Feldon, our King, is ready to take Gwendral..."

Cimerato pointed up through the canopy at the reddening sky. "If there is time."

Jal moved forward. "I despise Dendralon, and have been treated no better than a slave by Feldon all my life." The Hedra giant looked up at the menacing sky. "Dendralon has said that we only have a matter of days before our world is destroyed."

"Twenty-three hours, according to Mendel." James's voice seemed small in the forest, though his words struck fear in them all.

Jal knelt down on one knee and bowed his head. "I will gladly join you, if you will have me."

"Ha! You must be joking!" Cimerato looked round at the boys and Eethan in complete disbelief. "You're joking, right? He's a Hedra."

"He spared James's life," said Craig.

"He's just a plant!" moaned Cimerato.

At this, everyone glanced up at the woody remains of Ssslathat.

Craig laughed. "Bad choice of words, mate."

Mendel's voice filled the boys' heads. "Jal is telling the truth. Let this be the end of it. We must go and find the others now. Oh…James?"

"Yes?" James answered.

"Show me the Talisman."

James felt the blood drain from his face. He pointed into the forest. "One of the Hedra took it with him." He began to stutter. "Jal took it from me and then the Hedra guard took it from him. I was confused. There was so much going on, and…"

Mendel let out a deep sigh. "We need to get the Talisman back. When you destroyed the Keresi, you also, I suspect, destroyed the Magic Scales of Gwendral."

"And?" said James, in a small voice.

"And unless the Talisman is used to repair the Scales, we are all doomed."

James glanced up at the smoke-filled canopy.

"What do we do with the Hedra?" pressed Cimerato.

Eethan waved a glowing hand over Cimerato's wounded shoulder and said, "He comes with us."

"I don't understand, Mendel," snorted Cimerato, rubbing his shoulder and making circles with his arm. He made his way past Jal and, without looking at the Hedra directly, warned, "I'll be watching you, Snakeman."

By this time, the wind had picked up and the forest rustled and creaked menacingly. James looked back one more time at the twisted tree that had once been Ssslathat. He felt a pang of sorrow. He also felt a little guilty. He and Craig were the Blinders after all. And now the Troll would remain frozen like that forever. James shuddered.

"I suppose you could say he's gone back to his roots," joked Craig, snickering.

James punched Craig's arm. "That's not even funny."

Finding the Yeltan hatch again, they slipped down the ladder and dropped into the small chamber they'd emerged from only half an hour earlier.

Above them, Eethan took one last look round the forest, then fastened round his skinny waist the little leafy pouch that held Mendel. A few steps down the ladder, he pulled the hatch shut behind him.

James wondered what kind of creature this Eethan Magichand really was.

Mendel seemed to read his thoughts. "Don't be concerned, James. He is an old friend."

"Eee, very old friendeee. Yes, James, yes," Eethan tittered as they crawled onwards. A faint blue light shone out from Eethan's left hand as they scrambled through the tunnel.

"I'm sorry about the Talisman, Mendel," James whispered.

Mendel made a splashing sound with his golden tail. "It will most likely be halfway to Gwendral by now. We are in no fit state to race after a troupe of Hedra. In a way we'll have to hope that Dendralon gets hold of the Talisman. He will know that he has to fix the great Scales before he has any chance of saving his skin." Mendel chuckled to himself and added, "Not that it's his skin anyway."

James frowned. "But he might use the Talisman against us."

"He might indeed," mused Mendel.

16 Whindril

Dendralon had two of the crystals he needed to open the giant gateway – one from the Salt Troll, Sintor, who had offered it freely, and the second from the Osgrunf leader, Hushna, who was still unaware that he had a forgery. The third was with Feldon, the Hedra King.

Dendralon would soon be ready to test the power of all three if he could repair the Magic Scales. He looked down at the shattered Scales and wondered if the pieces had moved. It seemed that the various shards had gathered together, clustered around the original centre-point of the Scales. Perhaps he was imagining it, or perhaps the Talisman was moving closer. It was even conceivable that the crystals themselves had the power to regenerate the device they were destined for.

Although there were many smaller crystals that opened doors to other worlds, it had been thousands of years since anyone had opened the giant gateway of Gwendral. Once the city was safely back in the hands of its rightful owners, Dendralon would take it, along with all its powers, to another world – a world where the Hedra could rule and realise their full potential.

So far, his mock invasion of Gwendral was serving its purpose. The ruse had drawn the crystal-bearers to the city and had emptied Gwendral of its Manimal parasites. It was now time to follow through on the rest of his plan.

He scratched his left arm and looked down at the pink skin. It was beginning to flake and peel. He pulled his sleeve further down to cover the small patch of grey scales that now glistened in the candlelight.

Dendralon stepped out onto the great balcony of the citadel

just as dawn was beginning to spread its fingers over the Denthan landscape for the last time. He was pleased to see that at last there was some movement.

The giant Salt Trolls had grouped together, surrounded by their Salteth slaves. Their long whale-tooth spears flashed white as the first rays of Tealfirth caught the polished blades. The Salt Trolls always let the vicious Salteths engage first before they committed themselves fully.

The Osgrunfs only had one tactic when it came to warfare— one huge berserker charge, en-masse and at maximum speed. A solid brigade of steel and muscle, they could trample and defeat most of the foes before the poor fools even knew what had hit them.

"This will be an interesting fight," he murmured to himself, his long black tongue forking through the dead Manimal king's dry lips.

Looking beyond the campfires to the Forest of Eldane, he sniffed at the air. Smoke still seeped up from the forest near Senegral Island. Feldon's search party must have found the intruders, he decided. The Hedra king would be back soon, bearing the news Dendralon wanted to hear.

"King Athelstone, my Lord." A nervous-looking Council Secretary stood behind his king. "The Salt Trolls have begun to group."

Dendralon retracted his flicking black tongue then turned, pulling his sleeve down a little further. "Yes, I know. How many Manima—I mean, how many of our people still remain in the city?"

The Council Secretary blinked. "Only your elite guards at the gates and a few soldiers on the walls, my lord. All the people have now left by the tunnels or have flown north on the Dragons of Hest."

The wizard looked down at the cowering Secretary – a Manimal by the name of Elgry, who had served him well.

"Take my dragon, she will see you and your family to safety."

"Your dragon? Whindril?"

"Yes. But before you go, tell the soldiers on the walls to leave by the tunnels. I shall remain here with my elite guards until the end. There is one last spell I may try—a dangerous one. It is our last hope."

Elgry bowed his head respectfully.

Dendralon's hair flicked round his face in the early-morning breeze as he listened, impatiently, to the Secretary's mutterings. "Thank you, my King. I will make sure your bravery will be forever told. I will do all that you ask."

***

Sometime later, the Secretary emerged from the bottom of the citadel. Whindril, Dendralon's royal, white dragon, was chained to the courtyard wall below. The beast was magnificent. The youngest of the Dragons of Hest, her wings were still intact and her eyes sparkled like diamonds. Gleaming white scales covered her majestic form. Soft downy hair hung from her neck like ermine and poked up in little tufts between her powerful talons.

Whindril had once been famous for being the dragon that had borne his enemy, Mendel, in his victory over the Hedra all those years before. The creature had never truly bowed to Dendralon's will. Her tail flicked as the scampering Secretary approached and undid her heavy chain. Dendralon would have no use for Mendel's dragon where he was going.

***

"Come, Whindril," Elgry said, far down below. "You are to take my family to safety. You must fly high over the spires, then even higher over the spears and arrows of the Hedra."

"Oh, Father!" Elgry's little boy, Davado, squealed with delight as he and his mother approached the dragon.

As Elgry's son marvelled at the animal his wife moved closer and caught his sleeve. "The Hedra have shot down too many of these beasts already," she whispered, not wanting to frighten the boy. "They showed no mercy. It might be safer to go the way we planned, through the tunnels that lead to Nordengate."

"This is Athelstone's own," replied Elgry. "She is the youngest of the Dragons of Hest, and the best. Please..." He looked into his wife's eyes and placed his finger on her reticent smile. "We must stay calm for the sake of Davado."

The little boy tugged on his sleeve. "I want to hold the reins. Can I?"

Elgry's wife sighed when she saw the look of exhilaration on her child's face. Begrudgingly, she nodded her head. "When we are far above the Forest of Eldane, your father will let you hold the reins."

Making haste, they packed what they could and scrambled up onto the large, decorated saddle that sat between Whindril's elegant, silky wings. Then, with two huge flaps, Whindril rose up from the cobbled streets.

The dragon gained height quickly and they all hung on tightly as she veered round and round the main citadel. As they passed the highest balcony, they saw King Athelstone, transfixed and oblivious to all except the armies massing below. Far above the citadel, they were too high now for the arrows and spears of the Hedra on the ridge.

Below them, the Salteths shrieked and charged the Osgrunfs. This did not suit the Osgrunfs, as they relied on charging first, but they soon rallied and turned back on the Salteths with their cutlasses and claws. The ever-present cloud of black flies lifted as the armies engaged and the stench of death was soon heavy in the air.

"Don't look, son!" Elgry shielded Davado's eyes and cuddled him in close to protect him from the freezing cold and the carnage below. He peered down at the battle beneath them and shouted across to his wife, "Why are they fighting amongst themselves?"

His wife, holding on tightly to Whindril's seat, pulled her crimson robe around her shoulders. "Take us away from here, Elgry. We might not be high enough."

Elgry strained to hear her voice. It was lost in the flapping of Whindril's giant wings.

"Athelstone said that there was one last spell he could perform. Perhaps this is his magic. Our old King may save us yet."

Elgry's wife closed her white eyes and shielded her face against the whistling winds. "Just fly high over Eldane, Elgry. Take us to the safety of Hest."

17 Salt Trolls & Osgrunfs

Dendralon was engrossed in the battle. He watched as Hushna, the leader of the Osgrunfs, pushed to the fore and smashed into the first line of Salteths. Each swing of his huge cutlass sent five or six Salteths flying back on top of their own kin. It wasn't long before bodies were heaped high all round him. Hushna's ferocity was legendary and he nodded approvingly as the giant cut a bloody swathe with the fury of his berserker charge.

Eventually the Osgrunfs and Salteth alike made way until it was only the completely stupid, or those off balance, that staggered into Hushna's deadly path. The Osgrunf troops had gained ground and soon the Salteths were struggling against the warriors' greater stature and incredible strength. When the Salteths began to falter, Dendralon heard the trumpet call that signalled they should split into two groups.

Peeling apart from the rear, a channel opened up to form a passageway leading all the way to the front line. Sintor, the King of the Salt Trolls, brandished his white whale-tooth spear as he took in the scene before him. More than three times the height of any Osgrunf, Sintor raised his royal hand high in a mailed fist. "Charge!" he bellowed.

Dendralon sensed the Troll King's anticipation. He tapped the base of his gnarled staff on the floor of the balcony in excitement as almost two hundred giant Trolls thundered toward the Osgrunfs. Hushna was at the front of his troops, standing alone in the circle made for him by his own and the enemy. He was still slashing, carelessly, back and forth, when Sintor's spear skewered him.

Hushna wriggled like a worm on a hook, a mixture of surprise and anger on his twisted face as Sintor lifted him high into the air. Hushna's body jerked several times and then, with a final scream of defiance, he flopped limply like a rag doll.

Sintor whipped the corpse of Hushna high into the air and let out a terrible roar. Hushna's body fell amongst his own soldiers and a huge cry of fear rose from the Osgrunf ranks. But they did not run. Instead, their fear seemed to meld into a burning rage that forced them onwards, like one giant beast, toward the killer of their King.

Dendralon smiled. Everything was going beautifully. Even the Centides of Eldane had joined the fight. Several of the bug-like creatures wriggled through the ranks of the raging Osgrunfs and began to climb the thick legs of the Salt Trolls, nipping and piercing as they went.

Gaining momentum, the main bulk of the Osgrunfs roared as they smashed into the Salt Trolls; cutlasses, pikes and heavy maces, all slashing a gory path. When they were close enough, they dug their claws deep into the Trolls' salty hides and climbed up their bodies, tearing at flesh and hacking at bone. They didn't discriminate in their fury, cutting down any Centides or Salteths in their path. No creature was spared.

Through the sheer weight of their numbers, the Osgrunfs soon toppled the giants, who were then finished off by a hundred slashes. Unsatisfied, the Osgrunf mass pushed further into the midst of the Salt Trolls. Always ravenous, the Salteths became crazed by the smell of blood, pouncing on any wounded creature they could, feasting there and then, completely unhindered by the battle around them.

As the dead piled high around him, Sintor, king of the Salt Trolls, scanned the ridge. Seeing the Hedra army poised but uncommitted, he screamed, "Now, Feldon! Charge now!"

The Hedra, however, made no attempt to help. They remained deaf to the pleas of the Troll king.

Just then, an enormous Tree Troll slammed into Sintor,

knocking him backwards. Rolling over and over, the two giant creatures crushed countless Salteths until Malkor, the brother of Sintor, forced himself forward and jammed his whale-tooth spear through the Tree Troll's hide. Pinning him to the ground, Malkor stamped down hard until the attacker's backbone cracked and dark green blood spilt thick across the mud. The Salteths swarmed over the felled Tree Troll and finished him off, tearing chunks of bark from the twitching beast.

***

High on the ridge, King Feldon looked on, as Dendralon did, with unreserved delight. He'd cheered when he'd seen Hushna's corpse fly high through the air. He'd bellowed jubilantly when Sintor had stumbled. But when his Hedra troops stepped out of their lines, he checked his own fervour and stood up high on his chariot. "Stay at the ready! Don't you dare move until I say so!"

When they'd settled back into formation, he squinted up at the citadel where the dark figure of Dendralon stood on his balcony, still dressed as the Manimal King. "The old Hedra wizard's plan is working well," he hissed proudly. "We will soon walk into the city, unopposed."

Dendralon, the last of the true ancient ones, continued to stare down over the battlefield as sunlight spread over the growing piles of dead.

King Feldon, without once taking his eyes from the battle below, addressed his charioteer. "We Hedra are the only true species. The first to evolve, we will be the last to survive. You are fortunate to be at my side to witness our return to power."

The charioteer hissed excitedly, bowing his head to Feldon before reining in his reptilian steeds. "Hold fasssst," he snapped. "Not much longer!"

***

The sounds of war filled the skies as Whindril banked to her left, soaring high over the Hedra. "Look, Father!" Elgry's little boy exclaimed, "The grey Snakemen are making big lines on the ground."

Elgry hugged Davado tightly as he stared down at the sheer size of the Hedra army. Long supply lines, like wriggling grey tentacles, stretched back all the way to the Southern Marshes.

"There must be more than a hundred thousand of them and..." – Elgry pulled Whindril round to get a better view of the horde below – "...they don't have any siege weapons. As far as I can see, they only have piles of furniture and belongings. King Athelstone told me they had siege weapons."

"They don't look like an army intent on destroying Gwendral," his wife shouted in his ear. "They look as though they are about to move in."

Davado stared up at his father. "But Father, how will King Athelstone stop all those Snakemen?"

Elgry gripped his son tightly as a bank of warm air wafted up from the forest below, filling Whindril's massive wings. "Don't worry, Son. We must trust our King." Gripping a tuft of dragon mane, he looked north to the cliffs of Nordengate and beyond to Hest. "We've dallied long enough. It's time to go." For a brief moment, he glanced across at his beautiful wife, then flicked Whindril's golden reins.

***

Dendralon stood transfixed as he whispered a very ancient spell. This Hedra magic allowed him to focus in on the battle detail. He watched the Osgrunfs continue to drive the Salt Trolls back towards the Gorton Sea, their sheer animal determination proving more than a match for their larger foe. Sintor struggled to stay upright as time after time Osgrunfs leapt up onto his heavy armour. He kicked at his green-haired assailants and struck out at them with his ivory spear, but he was growing weary. Finally, a particularly determined Osgrunf, leaner than the rest and sporting an especially long set of hooked nails, managed to find a piece of exposed hide. He plunged his sloth-like claws deep into the Troll King's flesh.

Dendralon watched excitedly as Sintor tried to flick the wretched beast off. But before he could, more Osgrunfs jumped up onto his arms and legs. Within moments, their combined weight caused him to stagger and sway. At the same time, one of the Osgrunfs had reached Sintor's shoulders and was now biting and clawing at his neck. The Troll began to bellow in agony. "Get them off of me!" he shrieked.

Hearing his cries of distress, two large Salt Trolls kicked their way through and were soon pulling the vicious Osgrunf attackers from their King's neck. They stamped the writhing assailants into the dirt before guiding Sintor away from the front line. Edging back towards the sea, they supported their King with one arm while with the other they swung their Gnarwhale spears in huge arcs in an effort to keep the oncoming Osgrunfs at bay.

Sensing a change in their fortunes, the Salteths suddenly ceased fighting and feasting. With a high-pitched wailing, they began to run back towards the sea. They darted between the Salt Trolls' legs, screaming curses as they ran. Many were trampled in the rush.

Still possessed by the need for revenge, the Osgrunfs ran ahead of the routed Salteths and Salt Trolls, stopping as many of them as they could from reaching the beaches in the distance.

It was not a pretty sight, but Dendralon loved every minute of it. He hissed with glee when a Salt Troll stumbled or toppled over in the mad dash to the sea. These fallen giants were easy prey for the Osgrunfs. Once down, they couldn't right themselves in time to use their deadly spears against the onslaught of swords and pikes.

In the midst of the battle, a small group of Osgrunfs carried the body of their King high like some gruesome puppet mascot. Over and over again, they chanted his name, proclaiming the battle as "Hushna's victory".

Fools, thought Dendralon. *Entertaining, but fools, nonetheless.*

By retreating, Sintor had surrendered himself to defeat. The King of the Trolls must have known that his only hope of survival was to get back under the waves of the Gorton Sea. Finally at the shore, Sintor turned and looked directly at the great citadel of Gwendral.

Dendralon met the Troll-King's gaze and heard his voice enter his mind – "You promised to help us, Dendralon, yet your army holds fast? You have betrayed us!"

Dendralon issued an indifferent sigh. He saw Sintor glance up at the reddening sky one last time before slipping beneath the crimson waves of the Gorton Sea.

Around him, the waters bubbled with Salteths trying to escape. Following their King, several Salt Trolls dived into the red waters, sending huge waves crashing against the shore. Many more fell before they could reach the sea, and still more sank below the waves and scarlet foam, no doubt to die. Across the Plain of Gwendral, millions of flies filled the noxious air, their continuous drone intensifying as they pestered the wounded and hindered the dying.

Feeling triumphant, Dendralon raised his gnarled staff high into the air. "This is the beginning of the end for Denthan. The Hedra will soon have a clear path to the city gates." Dendralon toyed with the heavy gold chain around his neck, revelling in the power of the two blue crystals. Turning toward the Hedra King, Feldon, he gave his signal.

Feldon nodded and relayed the instructions to his captains. Neatly and swiftly, three long lines of Hedra Archers moved forward and knelt in position.

They were ready.

18 The Yeltan Grove

After an uncomfortable night spent in the tunnels, James could tell by the babbling sound of the Yeltans and the occasional high-pitched voice of a whining child that they'd almost caught up with the others. James, Craig, Eethan, Cimerato, Jal and, of course, Mendel could at last see daylight as the passage opened out before them. Up ahead, James saw the Yukplug pen, miraculously free of Keresi gunk. And there, just at the mouth of their tunnel, the unmistakable figure of Wee Joe. He was giving his mum a hard time.

"I don't like dat puke! It's not wogurt, it's not!" Wee Joe spat another blob onto the sandy ground.

Jean dipped her finger into the white goo and tasted it. "Look Joe, it's lovely."

"Yuk!" Wee Joe moaned. "Now it's got your germs nin it too. It's agusting! What nelse food is der?"

When James and his group emerged from the tunnel, the babbling stopped instantly as all eyes alighted on the Hedra giant. Hundreds of little swords slid noisily from their scabbards.

Lord Eldane stepped forward, his curved Gwendralin sword at the ready.

"Wait!" James held up his hand and stepped out in front of Jal. "He's here to help us."

Jean held a spoon in one hand and Wee Joe in the other, but the three-year-old slid off her knee, splattering white Yukplug yoghurt all over her mohair cardigan. "Joe!" she bleated. "Be careful!"

Landris moved alongside Lord Eldane.

Tall, even for a Hedra, Jal towered above them all. Flicking his black tongue, he smiled and stooped down to offer a handshake. He quickly pulled his scaled hand away when Landris raised his spear.

The Yeltan leader had seen the dried bloodstains on Cimerato's shoulder and, thinking this was a trap, had made himself ready. He expected to see a Hedra patrol emerge from the gloom at any moment.

The Yeltans' babbling intensified.

When Eethan finally stepped out from the shadow of the tunnel, the noise instantly ceased. He held up the jug made of copper-coloured leaves. To James's surprise, an audible gasp rose from the watching crowd. All eyes were on the little blue man.

"Here, en thees flask, ees Mendel, thee only one who can save ees. Ee has said thees Hedra," Eethan touched Jal's arm, "ees one who can help us too." Eethan spoke slowly and waved the bottle in front of him for effect. He turned to Landris and Lord Eldane, smiled, and then gave them an exaggerated bow. This move seemed to appeal to the Yeltans. To James's amazement, they began to clap.

Craig whispered in his ear. "What's going on now?"

James shrugged. "I don't know, but Eethan seems to have struck a chord."

The Yeltans were looking at Eethan in awe and wonder. Some of them even knelt down before the little blue creature.

Lord Eldane steadied his son, staring at his shattered armour and wounded shoulder. "Who did this to you, Cimerato?" His son had never been beaten in a fight.

Cimerato sat down heavily. The Yeltans, seemingly always prepared, surged toward him with packs of cold moss and river mud to put on his wound. He pointed to Jal. "Our guest over there. He's pretty good."

Landris, still wary of the Hedra giant, gave him a wide berth as he walked over to Eethan and took his hand. "He has returned!" he cried exultantly. He lifted Eethan's hand up high.

"You'd think he'd won the bloomin' Olympics," sniggered Craig, nudging James.

"Yeah," said James. "And how do you think they got this place tidied up so quickly?"

Craig shrugged.

Landris continued, "This is Eethan Magichand, friend of Mendel. He is the one depicted on our tapestries."

"He's the nose-picking twit," Cathy cried out, suddenly roused. "The one who got us into this mess in the first place. And you..." Cathy pointed to James, who tried to look away, "... you are grounded!"

James cringed and turned to face her. But to his surprise, by the time he caught her eye, her expression had shifted from rage to indifference. She tittered, smiled, and then collapsed back onto a pile of animal skins. His mum had fallen fast asleep.

"Mum?" Concerned and embarrassed at the same time, James didn't know how to react, though he thought he had better see if she was alright. As he approached, he felt a renewed twinge of embarrassment when he saw who was sitting beside her.

"Hello, James."

"Eeh!" James yelped. "I mean, em...eh...hello, Father. I mean, Reverend, I mean..." What the heck were Father Michael and the churchwarden's sister, Ephie Blake, doing here? Could this get any weirder, or more embarrassing? He groaned as he thought back to his swift kick that had felled the Rector outside their house days earlier. "I hope that your, um, well... I mean, I'm sorry about the way I acted back in Drumfintley and everything. The gargoyle..." James became tongue-tied.

Michael looked puzzled. "You know who stole the gargoyle from the church tower?"

"Well..." James didn't know what to say. "Not exactly stole..." He stopped again.

Father Michael simply sighed and covered Cathy with a soft, yellow blanket. "She's tired, James. They gave her something called Lugpus. I asked that one over there." Michael was pointing to Garlon. "She began to panic in the tunnel, you see, and..."

"And that must have calmed her down a bit, I suppose," said James.

"Yes, it did." Michael stood up. "You've got a cross to bear there, my son," he mumbled, before moving over to sit down beside Ephie Blake, the village snoop.

Ephie was chewing on some sticky bread. "Mmm, not bad." She offered some to James, who was taken aback. Only weeks before, Craig and he had been involved in an 'apple-stealing incident' and the last thing she'd said to him was, "Reform School, that's where you two will end up. As sure as fudge!"

James took the sticky bread from her. "Eh, thanks," he said, as politely as he could. He munched on it as he scanned the crowd for Craig, who he spied sitting with his mum and siblings beside the Yukplug pen. James joined them. As he walked along, he spotted the Yeltans slapping some kind of goo on Cimerato's wounded shoulder, Lord Eldane watching on.

A pang of jealousy gripped James. Father tending son; Mrs Harrison hugging Craig; Helen and Wee Joe laughing. No one seemed to give a damn about his dad, and his mum was 'out of her tree'. Even if she were awake, she'd probably be more of a hindrance than a help. No one here seemed to like her much. He could only imagine what kind of commotion she must have made in the tunnels after he'd run off to find Mendel. He really wished she wouldn't get so angry all the time. His life would be so much easier. "Flippin' heck" he muttered to himself.

Okay, so maybe he wasn't the only one who was feeling out of it, James decided as his eyes fell on Jal, standing a few yards to his left and holding a plate of raw meat. James guessed that sticky bread probably wasn't a Hedra's cup of tea.

James sighed and continued walking. As he drew nearer to the Yukplug pen, however, Garlon appeared with Bero. The Golden Retriever was wagging his tail excitedly. James noticed something hanging round his neck. "Craig, look!" said James.

Craig turned from the kids and waved, but then he saw it too. The plastic brandy barrel was back in its rightful place, swinging below Bero's neck, as good as new.

Garlon winked at the boys. "I'm good at fixing things."

"And tidying up," said Craig.

"Most of the mess had disappeared by the time we got back," said Garlon. He stared down at James's belt. "What happened to the Talisman?"

James sighed. "It fell into the wrong hands."

"Hedra hands," added Craig.

"But the gateway...?" gasped Garlon.

James spoke quietly. "Mendel thinks that the Talisman will find its own way to the Magic Scales."

"The Magic Scales?" enquired Garlon.

"Mendel says that they operate the giant gateway. Says that the Talisman probably destroyed them, but that it can fix them again." James widened his eyes, bit his lips together and shrugged at the same time.

Eethan joined them, having escaped from his adoring fans.

"Garlon's fixed Mendel's barrel," James told him.

"Weeell, it looks a leetle beetter than mine. Eeee..." Eethan examined the flask he'd made from leaves, then glanced over at the sleeping Cathy. "Ees your Motheeer?"

"Yes," said James, feeling slightly ashamed.

"Ees a tough ladeee, but shee has a kind heart inside— deeep inside."

"Yes, she can be kind." James racked his brains for an example, but was unable to come up with one. He decided to ask Eethan about his dad instead. "I was wondering if you might have seen my dad? He's about this high…" He waved his hand a good foot above his own head.

Eethan unexpectedly reached out and touched James's temple with his middle finger. It made James jump. "Hees lifeblood and yours are as one. Ee feel here ees still a connection here." James wasn't sure what that meant.

"I think he's trying to tell you that your dad's okay," Craig explained.

"Ah-hem!" Mendel interrupted. "I think I should like to go back into my barrel, please."

Eethan immediately unscrewed the lid and poured Mendel back into the barrel.

"I suppose I'd better get used to being in here for a while longer," said Mendel, as he splashed about.

Before Eethan screwed the lid back on Craig popped some crumbs into the barrel.

"Snug ees a bug," said Eethan, patting Bero's head.

Craig knelt down beside the barrel. "Mendel, I have to admit that I've missed seeing those googly eyes of yours pressed against this window. Just knowing you're there makes me feel so much better." He grinned and Bero panted and whined with excitement.

"How touching," Mendel replied dryly.

Craig's smile broadened. "It was, wasn't it?"

The wizard flipped his tail. "I'm glad that I make you feel so much better, Craig, because we must get into Gwendral today."

"But, Mendel…" said James. He thought back to the hordes of Osgrunfs and Hedra he'd seen from the top of Dunnad.

"Don't worry, James. Jal will get us into the city through the sewers."

James looked over at Jal, who appeared to have several irate Yeltans shouting at him. The Hedra giant was pleading his innocence and pointing to his stomach.

Cimerato, now looking much better, walked over to the

boys. "Your friendly Snakeman has just eaten one of the Yeltans' pet parrots."

"Not one of the little blue parrot things!" Craig yelped. "How did he manage to catch one in the first place?"

"One flick of that black tongue of his and it was gone," said Cimerato.

"Call him over," Mendel instructed.

Eethan scampered over and took Jal's arm. "Come, eets time to prove your loyaltee."

19 Eethan's Reunion

Jal had to stoop under several low branches as he made his way through the disgruntled Yeltans. He gave a large belch as he stopped in front of Bero. His nostrils flared. "What is this creature?"

The hackles rose along Bero's back.

"He's a dog," said Craig. "My dog. And what's more, he's not for eating. Not for breakfast, not for lunch, not for dinner. Not even as a snack. Okay?" Craig scratched the green serpent on his palm, prepared to call his spear if he needed to.

"Whatever you say, little one." Jal eyed Bero curiously before turning to Eethan. "So, blue man, how can I prove my loyalteee?" He mimicked Eethan's pronunciation, his serpentine mouth grinning widely.

As the others gathered round the Hedra giant, James felt a tingling sensation, which meant Mendel was about to speak to everyone around him.

"We don't have much time. Tealfirth has grown in size and reddened."

Everyone squinted up at the large, red ball in the morning sky.

"In less than twenty hours, it will explode and most probably wipe out all life on Denthan. We have to get inside Gwendral if we are to have any chance of survival.

Eethan, you should use your magic power to see if the Talisman in nearby."

Eethan nodded and scrunched his face into a mass of wrinkles. "Ee weeel try."

Michael crossed himself.

Landris spoke up. "I think we should go down to our deepest tunnels. Surely it will be safer there than in Gwendral?"

"No," said James. "Mendel is saying that Denthan will disappear. The tunnels won't do you any good." Mendel splashed in the barrel, his golden tail flashing past the plastic window.

"Can't we just go back the way we came, through that square door? Back to Scotland?" asked Michael.

"There's no guarantee that will work, and no time to experiment," relayed James. "Mendel says that Gwendral is a giant gateway, capable of transporting itself, and all within its walls, to other parts of the universe."

"I heard Dendralon speak of such a thing," said Jal.

All eyes turned on the Hedra giant.

Ephie and Garlon belatedly joined the group as James continued to relay the information as clearly as he could, but he was having a hard time making himself heard over all the muttering. "Mendel says..." James made his voice louder. "Mendel says...!"

The racket stopped.

James swallowed. "Mendel says that Dendralon intends to take his Hedra army back to Drumfintley, to Earth. And that he probably has the three crystals needed to operate the giant gateway. However, Mendel thinks that the Talisman destroyed the Magic Scales. Without those the gateway won't work."

Everyone, especially the humans, gasped loudly.

James was struggling to believe the words coming out of his own mouth. *Dendralon wants to go to Earth?* Stunned, he could only whisper the last part of Mendel's message. "Our only hope is to get inside Gwendral and somehow fix the Magic Scales." His shoulders slumped. It seemed an impossible task.

"And what happens if the Talisman doesn't turn up?" Helen asked in a small voice.

"At least we can say we tried," said Craig, cheerfully.

Everyone drew him the same unimpressed glower.

Landris spoke up. "Our scouts report that a battle has begun outside the walls of Gwendral. We should make for Dunnad. It is on our way, and it will give us a vantage point."

"Landris, tell your people to gather only the most essential of possessions," instructed Mendel.

James remained where he was. He couldn't stop thinking about the Hedra army spilling out over Bruce Moor. Worse, Mendel had said nothing about his dad. It was as though his dad didn't even exist. Everyone had forgotten about him.

When they were ready to go, the disheartened group, including a very sluggish Cathy, followed Landris and the Yeltans to Dunnad Hill.

As they approached the rocky knoll, James nudged Craig and whispered, "Look, the snakes are still here."

As before, a huge gathering of serpents guarded the slopes of Dunnad Hill, hissing and slithering this way and that. James thought about calling on his magic sword, but Mendel stopped him. "No, James, I will take care of this," he said.

"Wwwswerpwent Swwleewwwp!" James's voice echoed up the rock face.

As soon as the sound reached the snakes, their tongues stopped flickering and their heads lowered. Every last one of the serpents fell asleep.

Thud!

Startled, they all looked behind them.

There, in an unsightly pile, lay Jal, snoring his head off. He had slumped down beside Cathy, who was snorting and twitched as though she was having a nightmare.

"Oops!" said Craig. "Nice one, Mendel."

Cimerato laughed. "Perfect. Let's just leave him."

Many of the Yeltans eagerly nodded their agreement, but James was already moving toward Jal. On instruction from Mendel, he touched the Hedra's scaly temple with his forefinger and watched as Jal began to stir.

"Argh!" Jal opened his yellow slit eyes, then snapped

ferociously at James, causing him to jump back in alarm.

"Wow! I was only trying to wake you," exclaimed James, making a mental note never to get as close as that to a Hedra again.

Muttering what sounded like curses, Jal climbed to his feet, holding his head.

Cathy continued to sleep as the party made their way up through the unconscious serpents to the top of Dunnad Hill, only a short distance away.

James pushed ahead and soon saw the battlefield in the distance. "What's going on?"

"The Osgrunfs have routed the Salt Trolls and their Salteth slaves," Mendel informed them.

"Look at that!" cried Craig. "It's just like a huge, black tidal wave washing over the others."

After glancing back to check that his mother was alright, James joined the others at the top of the hill. As his eyes adjusted, he spotted a group of Tree Trolls lumbering toward the sea and shivered. He saw the disgusting Centides too. Both groups were joining the fight against the retreating Salt Trolls.

"Don't look, Helen." Jean covered her daughter's eyes. She couldn't keep Wee Joe back, though. He kept pushing to the front of the group, mesmerised by the sights and sounds, as if one of his computer games had actually come to life.

Lord Eldane looked over to his son. "What's going on, Cimerato? I don't understand."

Before anyone could respond, James noticed something flying high above them. "Wwwhinwwdril!" he shouted, startling the others. As soon as the words slipped out of his mouth, the white dot banked away from the mountains in the distance and sailed back towards them.

"Mum, look!" Helen pointed. "It's...it's a real live dragon!" Wee Joe and his sister both looked up at the reddening sky. The dragon was dropping fast, spinning down through the morning air.

In his head, James heard Mendel say, "Whindril is a Dragon of Hest. Let's see if we can put her to use."

The dragon was close to them now and when she flapped her enormous wings, a huge blast of air slammed into their faces. The ensuing dust-cloud blotted out the rout on the plain below.

Finally, the white dragon landed, her razor-sharp talons scraping on the rock. Once settled, she folded her silken wings and swished her long tail. Impressive and imperious, Whindril was probably the most beautiful creature James had ever seen.

"Mum, I'm scared." Helen snuggled into Jean, but she couldn't take her eyes off the wonderful animal.

In a fit of excitement, Craig rushed over to the dragon but Jal stopped him before he got too close. "Be careful, boy! They bite," he hissed.

Cimerato yanked Craig free from Jal's scaly hands. "They only bite Snakemen like you, Jal," he growled, as he guided Craig forward.

Recognising the man on the back of the dragon, Cimerato called up to him. "Elgry!"

Elgry's face lit up. "Cimerato! Lord Eldane! It is good to see you alive and well. We were making our way to Hest when Whindril suddenly turned back to land here. It is just as well. I can update you on what is happening. Right at this very moment, Athelstone is trying to save the city. Look!"

James tried to see, but there was too much dust still swirling about the knoll.

"I think his magic has caused our enemies to turn on each other," said Elgry.

"He didn't need magic to do that, my friend!" Mendel's thoughts echoed round in James's head. James wondered what the wizard meant.

Elgry continued, "The King said we could take Whindril as

he is going to remain behind. He is going to try to use his magic to save the city." Elgry glanced down at Whindril. "I haven't stolen her," he added nervously. He seemed a little scared of Cimerato.

Cimerato called the man and his family down. "The thought never occurred to me, Elgry. Come now. You'd all better dismount until Mendel decides what we should do next."

"Mendel?" said Elgry. He looked confused enough, but when he saw Jal, standing unbound behind Cimerato, he tightened his grip on his wife's shoulder. "Why is there a Hedra amongst you?" Elgry pointed to Jal.

"Yes, well, I'm not too happy about him, either," said Cimerato. "But you'd still better come down. Whindril was always Mendel's dragon."

"And why do you speak of Mendel?" Elgry protested. "He is gone."

"Actually, he is here, with us, Elgry. And Athelstone..." Cimerato moved closer to Whindril's heaving breast, her scales shifting as she breathed. "Athelstone perished a long time ago. We have been led astray by Hedra trickery and witchcraft." He sniffed scornfully at Jal then helped a confused Elgry down from the dragon.

"Madam," Cimerato addressed Elgry's wife, holding her hand as she dismounted. "If you will please take your boy back there to the crèche..." Cimerato pointed towards Jean and the kids, a disgruntled look on his face.

Whindril snorted and yawned, exposing her long, translucent fangs. After shaking out her snowy mane, she began to sniff the air.

"Ssith ta he ttesh, Whindril!" Although James didn't recognise the words coming out of his mouth, he noticed that Mendel had said them in a kind way, as if talking to an old friend.

When Whindril began to waddle towards him, however, he

thought of calling for his sword again.

"No, James," said Mendel. "It is alright."

At that moment Bero barked.

The dragon turned her huge head to the side and peered down at the old dog. Her eyes blinked slowly as she studied the strange animal.

Bero barked again.

"Ttesh na ta Ssith, Mendel?" The dragon's voice was soft and deep as she addressed Bero.

"Yes, I am before you, Whindril," Mendel laughed. "But I am not the dog. I am the small goldfish trapped inside the barrel that hangs round the dog's neck. Your new master did this to me."

"Arggg Ssssss…Ttishnta nar Athelstone." Whindril exposed her teeth again and flicked her scaly tail twice.

"Quite!" agreed Mendel. "I need you to do something for me, Whindril. You must take the two boys, this dog, and myself back into Gwendral, without being seen."

James could see that Craig, like himself, was almost bursting with excitement at the prospect. He'd been wondering for a while now, if his dad was actually in the city. He wondered, though, how a forty-foot dragon was going to sneak into Gwendral without being seen by the guards or, for that matter, the mass of screaming creatures covering the plain below.

By now, Eethan had scampered over to Whindril and was stroking the fine scales nearest her flattened ears. Flecked with golden ridges, the scales glistened in the strange Denthan light.

"Ttesh na ta Ssith, Eethan," said Whindril, lovingly brushing her head against the little blue man.

"Eee bet you thought you'd seen dee last of mee girlee, eh?" Eethan trailed his fingers through the dragon's fine mane and tittered.

While Eethan and Whindril became reacquainted, Mendel

asked James to get Jal's attention. James was still wary of the hulking Hedra who'd snapped at him earlier, so he kept his distance when he said, "Jal, Mendel would like you to take everyone you can into Gwendral by way of the sewers." James paused to listen to the wizard's next directive. "He says you should hide them under blankets and mats and go in a convoy of boats. Tell your Hedra comrades that you are in charge of supplies for the city."

"It's broad daylight," Jal replied, squinting up at the waxing orb of Tealfirth. "But it might work," he added. "Though, if any of my troop of archers have managed to make it back to the city, Dendralon will be ready for us."

Landris spoke again. "We don't think that any of your brigade survived. Last night our scouts informed us that they ran into a part of the forest thick with Centides. They're most likely dead or, worse still, wrapped up for later."

James felt his chest tighten as he thought about the Talisman. "Mendel?"

"We shall make a small detour," said Mendel. "The Centide nest is close-by."

James thought back to the swinging black Centide pods and shivered.

"Besides," Craig spoke up, "your Hedra brigade all ran away before you declared your loyalties, Jal. They're going to assume you were either captured or killed."

James looked at his friend in awe, surprised by the way he'd made his point. "Nice one, Craig." Amazingly, he hadn't managed to insult anyone.

"They wouldn't know," Craig went on, "that you simply got scared and bottled out when Mendel killed the Tree Troll." A toothy smile creased his freckles.

"Sssss..." Jal hissed at Craig contemptuously. "I did not show any fear when the Troll perished."

James sighed deeply.

20 A Short Flight

"I want to go with you this time," said a familiar voice. Cathy, finally awake, had appeared beside them, her green cardigan wrapped tightly round her. She stepped forward and placed her hand on the dragon's mane. "I would like to go with my son, please." She seemed unusually calm and collected. James was immediately concerned.

"Mum?" He knew he had to say sorry for disobeying her or he'd be paying for it for weeks, if not months. "I'm sorry for leaving you in the tunnels like that, but..."

"I've told you a thousand times, James. Never say the words 'sorry' and 'but' in the same sentence. They cancel each other out. Anyway, we can discuss that later." Her words were spoken, not shouted or yelled in her customary way. James braced himself, waiting for a change in tone, but it never came. She turned towards Eethan, who was busying himself picking his nose again, and asked, "Now, how do we get home?"

Eethan, examining something disgusting on the tip of his thumb said, "Eee es not me who will decide. Ees Mendel." He pointed to the barrel round Bero's neck without looking at her directly.

His mum glanced down and James's stomach did a somersault.

"My barrel!" She reached down to retrieve it but suddenly stopped herself. "You've filled it with water and there's a bloomin' goldfish swimming about inside."

James was about to explain but his mum carried on.

"Your father gave that to me as a gift. How dare you put that stinky fish in there!"

James couldn't help thinking back to the 'flying rings' incident that had followed this particular gift from his dad.

She'd had some kind of argument with his dad over him staying an extra night away in Switzerland, and had thrown her wedding rings out of the window in a rage. It had taken his dad two days to find them.

He knelt down beside his mum and toyed nervously with Bero's crooked brown ear. Bero began to pant. "Mum, this fish is the reason why we're all here."

"Oh dear," sighed Craig.

James scowled at Craig. It wasn't the time or the place for one of his stupid remarks. "He's a wizard called Mendel," continued James.

"Ees my friend," Eethan added, rather unhelpfully.

James gave Eethan a quelling look and the blue man shrugged before returning to his nose-picking. James continued, "As I was saying, he is a wizard and I can hear him in my head." James looked into his mum's deep brown eyes as he said this, hoping she would see that he wasn't crazy.

"So can I!" Craig interjected. "He kind of decides who can hear him and who can't. Bit rude, if you ask me."

"Ees can heers him en mee head too," Eethan added, rolling something rubbery between two fingers.

Bero gave a small woof and wagged his tail, as if to let Cathy know he could hear Mendel too.

Cathy looked at them all and nodded. "Fine, I'm standing beside a forty-foot white dragon, looking down on a city surrounded by an army of goblins, or whatever they are, and I'm talking to a three-foot-high, blue man. Not to mention *him*." Cathy pointed towards Jal, who was standing beside Landris. "Or them." She flicked her fingers at the Yeltans. "So, I'm quite prepared to believe that this goldfish, who's swimming in my barrel, is actually a wizard. Okay! Whoever it is I'm talking to, just get me and my boy home because my life is complicated enough as it is. I don't need this." She bent down and peered into the barrel. "Got that, fish? And by the way, from now on wherever James goes, I go. Okay?"

"I think we better take your mother with us too," Mendel sighed.

"Then you better make sure she can hear you," James warned. "I don't want to be the translator all the time."

Mendel sighed again.

While Craig and James strapped themselves onto Whindril, Cimerato and Jal lifted Bero up onto the wide saddle.

"It's a bit like being in a horse-drawn carriage," remarked Craig, grinning widely. He was ecstatic at the prospect of riding on a real live dragon. However, when Whindril arched her snake-like neck and turned to look down at her new passengers, Craig shrieked and drew back.

Last aboard was Cathy, who still looked drowsy after her Lugpus. "Remember to hold on tight," she lectured as she wrapped the golden tether round her wrist and leaned back against the ornate leather back-rest.

"Remember to hold on tight," Craig mimicked into James's ear. Then he added, "Or mummy will smack your bottom!"

"Hardee-har-har, Numpty!" James was about to turn away when Craig jabbed him in the ribs. "Look, I've still got some."

James saw the top of the small, black bottle that Garlon had given him the day before. "Garlon actually gave you some Lugpus?"

"Yeah," whispered Craig. "A drop in her tea every morning and your life is sorted, mate."

"You do talk the biggest heap of dross!" James growled, though a treacherous part of him was considering the suggestion seriously.

"What was that?" Cathy demanded.

"I said, I wish Dad could have done this with us," James lied.

"Hmm," said Cathy, nonplussed.

James's eyes widened. "Mum, where did you get that?" He'd

132

just spotted his green rucksack.

"I found it on some rocks beside the river." Cathy looked at her son's dirty face and wiped away a tear from her cheek.

"You okay, Mum?" asked James, suddenly concerned. He felt a tinge of sadness and wondered if maybe she really cared about his dad after all. They'd never really discussed his disappearance properly. Maybe it was less painful for her that way, he decided.

James reached for the rucksack, but Cathy increased her grip and unzipped it. "I suppose you'll be needing this." She produced James's blue inhaler.

"No, Mum. I've been fine here, so far." James grabbed on tightly as Whindril shifted her position. "Mendel says that there's more oxygen here, or something." His mum, however, remained silent. She had always thought that his asthma was a put-on, to get out of chores or bunk off school. "About Dad," James broached. "Do you think he's here?"

Cathy looked at him but couldn't speak. She just gave a half-hearted smile and shook her head. "No."

"Why not?" James blurted. "I mean…he was up on Bruce Moor too. We came through the Jesus Rocks and—"

"So did we," interjected Cathy, "but he's not here. I just know."

"But…"

"James," warned Craig.

When everyone was on board, Whindril unfolded her wings and extended them to their full sixty feet. She tested the air, causing the Yeltans to shield their strange blue eyes from the dust and debris. The dragon placed a knowing eye on Eethan as he jumped up beside the boys. Then she stretched her worm-like neck and shook her white mane before leaping up into the heavy Denthan air. An updraft caught her immense wings, making them tense and fill. After an initial jolt, she soared higher and began to sail effortlessly over the forest.

Cathy was now wide-awake, her lips set in a childlike grin.

Craig held onto Bero's fur and Cathy's green cardigan. "Wow! Yeah!" he shouted.

Far below, James could see Michael and Ephie waving up at them. They looked strangely out of place amongst the little Yeltans. Jean was trying to placate Helen and Wee Joe, who were crying because they didn't get to ride on the dragon. However, they were soon distracted by offers of more Yeltan sticky bread.

Holding on as tightly as he could, James listened to Mendel as the wizard's words formed in his head, "Fly higher, Whindril. Fly high, and away from Gwendral." The dragon obeyed. "Get ready!" Mendel cried as he prepared his spell. The knock, knock, knocking sensation of impending magic began to build in James's head. "Wwwinviswwabllwwittwwor!" The words burst awkwardly from his lips and were soon lost in a rush of wind that made them all hold on so tightly that their knuckles turned white.

The weird words were still echoing in his head when all of a sudden, Whindril's snout started to shimmer. Just like heat haze over a hot road, the dragon's head flickered, distorted, and then disappeared. The dragon's neck was next, only wavering momentarily before fading away. James could still hear the sound of her huge wings beating somewhere nearby, but he certainly couldn't see the dragon, or anybody else for that matter.

"We've disappeared!" Cathy screeched.

James looked down. It was totally disorientating being invisible while suspended in mid-air.

Mendel gave a second command. "Quickly, Whindril! Take us down to the forest. There, next the rapids. The Centide nest is at the top of the ridge."

Whindril banked down to their left and James felt as if his stomach was in his mouth.

"Whoooo!" shouted Craig.

Down and down Whindril spiralled until her great claws brushed against the treetops.

Birds flew up in fright, scattering in every direction, while enormous bats howled like phantoms, taking to the air in complete disarray. Their leathery wings reminded James of the gargoyle he'd seen on his front lawn, back home.

Then, with a loud hiss, Whindril, still invisible, snatched up a great chunk of foliage.

Grasped tight in Whindril's invisible talons, James could see a mixture of branches and swinging pods. These were not black and shiny like the Centide cocoons they'd encountered before. They were fibrous and oddly shaped.

"Every one of these pods has a Hedra inside," explained Mendel.

James caught a glimpse of a grasping reptilian hand protruding from one of the dull pods. Another had a Hedra bow sticking out of the bottom. "What am I supposed to do now?" yelled James.

"If the Talisman is amongst this sample, you will feel its presence," said Mendel. "Call on it!"

The strange clump of vegetation and gruesome cocoons continued to sway below them. Holding their position, Whindril flapped hard to keep them steady.

Feeling completely stupid, James shouted out, "Talisman! Where are you? Come to me!"

"What are you doing?" said Cathy, still spooked by the whole experience.

James ignored her for a moment as he tried to sense something.

"Anything?" pressed Mendel.

"Nothing," moaned James. "This is pointless. What the heck am I—"

"Drop them and try again!" commanded Mendel.

James watched in horror as the mixture of branches and Hedra-filled pods tumbled down and smashed through the forest canopy.

"Again!" urged Mendel.

Whindril swooped down and scooped up another chunk of the forest canopy.

This time, even before James got a chance to say anything, he felt a sudden tingling sensation in his fingers. When he forced his hand down towards the swaying pods the feeling intensified.

"You need to climb down and get the Talisman before Whindril drops it back into the forest," Mendel instructed.

"Who said that?" yelled Cathy.

"I have allowed you to hear me, Mrs Peck," said Mendel.

"Oh, honoured indeed, I'm sure. But there is no way that my son is going down there."

"But mum, if I don't get the Talisman we could all die," said James, his head still spinning at the thought of climbing down an invisible dragon's legs.

"James!" shouted Cathy. "Where are you?"

But James had taken his chance. He had slipped over the side of the hard saddle and was desperately trying to find something to grip.

Above him, his mum's voice was full of despair. "James!"

For a second he caught hold of something that felt like fur, then he lost his grip.

The warm Denthan air rushed past him as he fell.

21 The Battle in the Sky

James landed with a crash, face-down onto the floating platform of leaves and branches. Winded and still suspended beneath the invisible dragon, he fought for breath. His fingers groped until he found a something to hold onto.

"James!"

He looked up but there was nothing above him.

"It's me! Craig! We can see you!"

James looked down and saw his bruised knees and torn shorts. He was visible. He screwed up his eyes and began searching the cluster of branches for the nearest Centide pod, the wind still wafting into his face.

"Quickly!" urged Mendel.

James could still feel the power of the Talisman, or at least a trace of it.

"Boy!"

James jumped back and waved his hands in an effort to keep his balance. A Hedra face, covered in sticky strands was staring straight up at him.

"Boy, release me. I am Garazar."

The Hedra soldier was barely conscious. The rest of his body was covered in long, sticky strands of hessian-like material that bound him tight.

James called on Firetongue and the crimson sword appeared in his hand.

"Yes... That's it. Please... Cut me free and you shall have your Talisman," gasped Garazar.

James got to work on the strands but felt the whole platform shift as Whindril banked to her left. He looked up. "What are you doing?"

His mum shouted down at him. "Be careful, there's

something coming up from the forest."

"Centides!" yelled Craig.

In the same moment, the blue man, Eethan bumped down beside him.

"Yous geeet thee Talisman. Eee weell fight thee Centides!"

Shaking with panic and fear, James hacked away at the tough strands as the first of the flying Centides appeared on the floating platform. Two whirring gossamer wings buzzed loudly and then stopped as the creature landed with a thump. It twisted its head round and snapped its mandibles at him.

Eethan threw a blue ball of light that stuck like glue in the creature's mouth and it was soon writhing, trying to prise its mouthparts open.

James tried to ignore the unfolding scene as he stuck his hand into the Centide pod and caught hold of Garazar's scaled hand. "Give me the Talisman first."

Garazar hissed and then snapped down with his needle-sharp jaws on another of the strands that bound him.

A second Centide caught Eethan by surprise and knocked him onto his back.

"Eeeee!"

The weight of the Centide rocked the floating platform and half of it broke away, spinning down towards the trees.

James could feel Whindril's wings beating harder above him as the dragon tried to hold its position.

Eethan dodged a piercing, crimson antenna and managed to hold on to the remains of the platform.

Firetongue flicked back in James's hand as a third Centide clambered over the side of the platform. With a whoosh, it lopped off its bulbous head.

Garazar was almost free.

James brought Firetongue round and shouted, "Give me the Talisman!" The feeling that the Talisman was near, somewhere on the platform, was still there.

Garazar eased away from the point of James's sword. "I cannot. A Herdigup stole it from me down there." He pointed to the canopy below. "It promised to set me free.

Still more Centides buzzed the fragile platform.

"I had it in here." Garazar held up a tattered leather pouch before letting it fall.

The sensation that the Talisman was close by began to fade away.

"No!" yelled James. They would all die on the doomed world, and it was his fault.

"Climb back up, James." shouted Mendel.

Almost at the same moment his mother's arms poked down above his head from nowhere. "Catch hold!" she shouted.

"Wait," hissed Garazar, "take me with you."

A large Centide bounced onto the remains of the platform and folded its long wings, as if performing a masterful piece of origami, tucking them neatly beneath a pair of hard chitinous flaps.

"Please!" pleaded Garazar.

"We have no time," Mendel interjected.

As Firetongue parried a deadly jab from the circling insect, James felt sorry for the Hedra soldier. "We can't leave him here for the Centides."

"Grab hold of your mother's hands and return to the saddle," urged Mendel.

"No!" yelled James.

"I have more information," snapped the Hedra. He was lashing out at another Centide. "About your father," he added.

Cathy suddenly appeared beside James and caught hold of the Hedra by the throat. "What do you know? Where's my David?"

Garazar's yellow slit eyes widened in shock. "The... Herdigup told me that Dendralon had sent him to another world to steal from a human boy. It told me that it took a jacket and a shiny pin, and..."

Just then a vicious barb shot out from the circling Centide and thudded into Garazar's chest-plate.

Cathy and James jumped back, both of them teetering on the edge of the abyss.

The Hedra soldier buckled and sank to his knees. "It told me..."

"It told you what?" snapped Cathy.

But life was ebbing away from the stricken Hedra. He closed his strange eyes and bowed his head.

Eethan and Craig both caught hold of Cathy and James just as Whindril dropped the jumbled platform.

Silent, Garazar remained kneeling all the way down until the clump of fibrous pods and Centides crashed through the canopy below.

"We should have helped him!" wailed James.

"We did," said his mum. "Those things were going to eat him alive."

James flayed about for the giant saddle. Invisible again, he struggled with the waves of nausea that washed over him. "Mum?"

"I'm here, son."

James found his mum's soft, warm hand and squeezed it tight. "I'm sorry mum. I'm sorry for bringing you here. I don't understand why Dendralon would want to hurt our family so much."

"You didn't bring me here, James. And neither did your father. I..." Cathy wavered, "I love—"

"Fly fast and fly high!" interrupted Mendel. "We will fight Dendralon in the great citadel."

At that moment James couldn't care less about Denthan, Dendralon or the weird array of battling creatures on the far off plane. He was convinced that his mum had almost said that she loved him. Mendel had spoiled the whole thing,

140

snuffed out the moment though. His mum had just released a beautiful, delicate butterfly and the stupid goldfish has squashed it dead before its silken wings had even caught the breeze.

"So what if Dendralon has the Talisman," said Craig, still panting with exertion. "He can fix the Magic Scales himself."

James heard Mendel splash around in the invisible barrel beneath the muzzle of the invisible Golden Retriever. "I am worried that Dendralon will unlock the full power of the Talisman."

"Hees won't have time," Eethan reassured, "Hee will have to geeet thee Scales working or hee weel die."

"Will you please tell this dragon to fly more quickly," said Cathy, her voice lower than usual. "I'm going to throw…"

There was a terrible retching sound followed by a wet splash.

"Ewww!" gasped Craig. "You've just spewed over my leg, Mrs Peck."

There was a loud cough followed by a drawn out moan and the single word, "Good."

Bero woofed over the battlefield below.

"Wees still have a chance," blurted Eethan. "Wees can still survive the broken sun."

James squinted up at Tealfirth, the tortured star. A big, drippy tear was rolling down his cheek and he was suddenly relieved that Craig couldn't see it.

22 The Hedra Attack

A scuttling sound distracted Dendralon from the battle on the plain. The citadel was over two hundred feet high and its walls were made of smooth alabaster. There were few creatures able to scale its heights.

"I have done all you have asked, Dendralon," said the voice.

A pair of white, feathered antennae wiggled over the balcony before the long, segmented body of the Herdigup came into view.

His skin burning from wearing Athelstone's hide for too long, Dendralon scowled down at the creature. He knew it had come for its reward. "I told you that I would give you the gold after the battle."

"I want more than you promised, and I want it now," said the Herdigup.

Dendralon made to swat the creeping creature off of the high balcony.

"Wait! Look what I have brought you."

Dendralon paused. His long serpentine tongue flashed out of Athelstone's dead lips. "You have found it?"

"*The Talisman moves through ancient leaves and yet, at times, stands still. No Denthan eyes can see it, some say they never will.*" A pair of red appendages unfolded from one of the creature's segments. It held a simple horn about six inches long.

"This is a Yukplug horn," he snapped.

"No Denthan eyes can see it for what it is," whispered the Herdigup, brimming with supercilious pride. "It had moved through the leaves of Eldane until it stood still. I freed it from a leather pouch that dangled from a Hedra belt. A Hedra who, along with his troop, was about to be eaten alive by a swarm of Centides."

Dendralon stared hard at the Yukplug horn before reaching out to take it.

The Herdigup drew it back. "This is the Talisman of Denthan. The very charm you instructed my kind to find. The Hedra soldier confirmed it. He took it from the boy called James Peck. The very same boy who rescued Mendel."

Dendralon snatched the Talisman from the Herdigup and drew his black sword. "Come with me, my loyal lady. You have earned your gold this time." Dendralon was beginning to feel the power of the Talisman. It filled him with renewed determination and energy. Athelstone's skin tightened and flushed pink, invigorated by its power.

The Herdigup scuttled about excitedly, picking up the gold coins that Dendralon threw her.

There was a sliding sound, a tinkling, and then a whoosh, as if a giant chandelier had crashed to the ground.

Dendralon turned and hissed a sigh of amazement as he watched the shattered Scales of Gwendral reform. A million tiny shards rushed into one central spot and then reassembled in exactly the correct order.

The Talisman glowed purple in his outstretched hand.

He closed his grip around the hilt of his sword but saw that the Herdigup had gone. A mind-reader and a thief, the creature must have guessed his intentions and fled. No matter. It could enjoy its short-lived success. All he needed now was the third crystal. The one that hung round King Feldon's neck. The giant gateway would open and the Hedra would escape the death of Denthan. Now, with the extra power of the Talisman, no one – not even Mendel – would be able to stop him.

***

"Whindril, take us back towards the city before the invisibility spell wears off!" urged Mendel.

James hung on as the dragon banked round and flew towards Gwendral.

"Look, James!" cried Craig. "Look at the city spires. What do they remind you of?"

James looked hard, then said it at the same time as Craig, "The Jesus Rocks!" The positioning of the spires and citadels exactly matched the pattern of stones on Bruce Moor. No wonder the city had looked familiar to them up on the knoll.

"Well spotted," said Mendel, chuckling as he explained. "The stones and spires are both set to a certain pattern. The alignment is critical. Hold on!"

As Whindril circled the main citadel, the boys saw a black-cloaked figure move out on to a high balcony. Transfixed by the battle beyond the walls, the figure stood motionless, dark and threatening, as he watched the destruction below.

After the slaughter on the seashore, the Osgrunfs were now racing back to their positions, though only five or six thousand remained intact, a third of their original number. Their encounters with the Salt Trolls and Salteths had taken their toll, but the Osgrunfs were still a sizeable force. The Centides did not follow the Osgrunfs, preferring to stay behind and feed off the dead. The Osgrunfs were on their own.

The Hedra archers were arranged in three long thin lines and stood ready for the returning Osgrunfs. James realised that the Hedra had stayed well out of the battle between the Trolls and the Osgrunfs.

"I can see Feldon, the Hedra king," Mendel said. "We are in luck! I think I can see the third crystal. It still hangs round his neck. And the figure on the high balcony is Dendralon, wearing his Manimal disguise. The Hedra are about to take advantage of the Osgrunfs. They will loose their arrows on them. Get ready to head in closer everyone!"

"A talking fish..." Cathy mused, "Bizarre."

"You're not wrong there, Mrs Peck," sighed Craig.

For once, Cathy didn't rebuff Craig.

James didn't think his mum would like the intrusion of a talking fish inside her head.

When everyone was holding on tight, Mendel began to speak to the dragon in her own tongue, which James found he could actually understand. "Fly over the battlefield, Whindril. Get as close as you can. We need to slow things down a bit— keep that last crystal away from Dendralon for as long as possible."

The dragon snorted and then dived down the side of the citadel before flapping up and over the city gate at the last minute. When the unexpected displacement of air caught Dendralon's elite guards on the gate towers they looked terrified.

The dark figure on the balcony noticed the confusion at the gate and scanned the horizon to see what was causing the trouble.

James stared hard at Dendralon and shivered.

Unaware of what was coming his way, King Feldon lowered his mailed fist and five thousand arrows ripped through the air. When they reached their zenith, they came together to form a black cloud that looked like a swarm of deadly locusts.

Whindril had flown right into the path of the arrows on purpose.

"Wwwrongwwflyw!" The power surge from Mendel's magic made James's head feel as though it was splitting and this, combined with the disorientation of being invisible, made him lose his grip on the tether. "Ah!" he yelped, struggling to hang on.

Hearing James cry out, Dendralon turned toward their position, narrowing his eyes as though he could see them. Whether he could or not, the Wrongfly spell was already doing its work. The needle-sharp arrows flew left and right, bouncing off of Mendel's force field in an explosion of sparks and vapour trails.

The Osgrunfs took advantage of the confusion, gathering into one huge herd and charging the Hedra archers, snorting and spitting with anger.

Witnessing the powerful magic that had come to the rescue of the Osgrunfs, the Hedra hissed in fear. They struggled to nock their arrows as the Osgrunfs pounded toward them.

James tried to grab onto a tuft of dragon hair as Whindril lost height. "No!" he cried out as a sudden turn caused his fingers to slip free.

Sensing that her son was falling again, Cathy snatched out blindly and somehow caught hold of his arm. Panic-stricken, James kicked in mid-air, only a few yards above the Hedra below him.

King Feldon shouted across the battlefield at Dendralon, high up in his citadel. "What magic is thi—?" But his words were cut short as a gust of displaced air slammed into his face. The Hedra king ducked and scanned the skies, confused by the sudden blast.

James felt his mum tug hard on his shirt, yanking him back onto the dragon seat. Dripping with sweat, he gripped his mum so tightly that he heard her gasp.

"You're soaked through!" she scolded, holding him close to her.

Through everything, Dendralon seemed to pick out his mum's piercing voice, and James flinched when the wizard raised something very familiar in his right hand.

"I have you now!" The voice sounded in James's head and he recognised it as that of the stranger he'd met in Drumfintley. A second later, a ball of lilac fire raced out from the Talisman, skimming the city wall. It was heading straight for them.

"Turn, Whindril! Turn!" Mendel shouted.

The invisible dragon dipped one wing and dropped to within a few feet of the Hedra army.

Fear shook the reptilian archers as they felt another unexplained rush of air knock into them. They hissed and growled at their unseen tormentor, some of them loosing their arrows in panic.

James felt nauseous as the arrows flew past them. "Wwshieldwwbarww!" Mendel's voice roared in his head.

Dendralon's speeding blue ball of fire smashed against this second invisible shield, spreading over them in a huge ball of lightning. Flashes and bolts of blue showered onto the Hedra below and they screamed in agony, the noise terrifying.

"Dendralon will try again, and my power is waning," said Mendel. "Climb high, Whindril!"

On hearing Mendel's command, the faithful beast beat her wings furiously and climbed up into the morning sky.

Dendralon, however, had been distracted by the renewed screams below. The Osgrunfs had hit the first line of his Hedra archers like a battering ram, trampling them into the hillside before smashing into the second line just as ferociously.

King Feldon, however, had prepared for the unthinkable.

The third row of archers had another defence against the Osgrunf's berserker charge. Twenty feet behind the third line, a thousand light infantry leapt forward and caught hold of their ropes. With a nod, the third line of archers nocked their bows and unleashed a point-blank onslaught. Unfortunately for the first and second lines of Hedra archers, the new wave of arrows did not discriminate, and slayed Hedra and Osgrunf alike, piercing armour and bone.

Frantic screams filled the morning air and the "Harka!" cry of the Osgrunfs grew louder and more manic. Dendralon was pleased that their thick, matted hair proved useless against the arrows at such close range, but despite this weakness, the charge did not falter.

It was now that the light infantry acted out their well-rehearsed plan. Just at the point when the Osgrunfs were within feet of hitting the third line, they pulled on their ropes, each of which was attached to a long, jagged pike. The black-bladed weapons swung up and caught the Osgrunfs as they slammed into the breach.

In an instant, thousands were skewered, yet still more Osgrunfs scrambled over their own dead to reach the Hedra lines.

The King summoned his personal guards. "To the ships. Now!" he roared.

23 The Citadel

They were still circling above the fight when Craig called out. "Look! Some of those Hedra things are running away!" Hearing this, Mendel, quite uncharacteristically, bubbled with excitement and splashed about in his barrel.

The Osgrunfs, now only hundreds in number, continued to cause havoc in the Hedra camp, tearing through tents and routing the Hedra followers.

"This is horrible!" cried Cathy. "Do we have to stay here and watch?" She groped about until she found the barrel round Bero's neck. She rapped the plastic with her knuckles and screamed, "I don't want my son to see this!" But her words were lost in the warm wind that rushed by their faces. Whindril flapped her gigantic wings and took them even higher into the Denthan sky.

"Mrs Peck!" Mendel pleaded. "Please refrain from knocking on my barrel again!" His voice sounded shaky. "Whindril, bank left towards the river. We'll head off Feldon there."

James hung on for dear life as they glided for several hundred yards, losing height the whole way. In seconds they were hovering over a long, sleek river galleon, decorated with gold and protected by polished black armour plate. The deck teamed with grey-scaled Hedra scrambling to untie the mooring ropes.

"They know the battle has turned against them," said Mendel. "They're making ready to sail."

"Wees have to deelay them," said Eethan.

Whindril flapped down to the ship and settled on the stern, her polished talons scratching deep into the wooden deck. The movement almost tipped the boat, lifting the bow clear of the water.

The Hedra deck-hands slid backwards as the vessel splashed back down again. They fell in a heap, kicking and struggling to right themselves.

The helmsman turned round to see what was going on and Whindril snapped forward. She caught him in her mouth and gulped him down with two flicks of her head, crunching and hissing as she snacked.

"Yuck!" James thought he was going to throw up.

"No way!" protested Cathy.

Bero whined.

On deck, the Hedra were in a total panic. After seeing one of their own disappear into an invisible mouth in two huge gulps, many of them screamed and jumped overboard.

A Hedra sailor dressed in green armour, who looked to be the captain of the boat, froze when he heard the sound of Whindril's thunderous footsteps on the foredeck. The planking warped beneath the dragon's weight as she moved forward.

James prepared to turn away rather than see another Hedra eaten alive.

"That's King Feldon," announced Mendel. James saw a Hedra on a chariot, dressed in fine black and green armour.

The Hedra king called out to the ship from the river-bank, "Get ready to sail!"

But the terror-struck captain was still staring at the bending floorboards.

Surrounded by a hundred Hedra archers, Feldon screamed, "I said, get ready to sail!" The Hedra king looked terrifying in his battle dress. His large green plume flickered in the breeze as Whindril's invisible wings began to flap.

James saw Feldon shield his eyes.

"Tetsh Hee!" Mendel's dragon-tongue command sprung from James's own lips.

Soon after the words were spoken, they began to rise high into the air again. They were flying back towards the city.

James heard Craig retch. "I'm feeling sick. I need to get off."

Mendel ignored Craig's pleas. "Whindril, we must go round the citadel and land in the Royal courtyard."

As Whindril climbed higher, James noticed that Dendralon had left his vantage point.

"Where'd he go?" James asked.

"He will have gone to get the gateway ready," replied Mendel. "We've done enough, for now."

"Why deed you not kill Feldon at de reever?" Eethan wanted to know. "Why deed you not take de third creestal?"

Mendel sighed. "That would've been ideal, but Whindril has been hit."

They felt the great dragon pitch forward.

"Whindril," urged Mendel, "try to get us over the city walls."

As they swooshed over the parapets, they all flickered into view for a second. James wondered if the invisibility was a power that came from Whindril rather than Mendel.

"But we need to get up to the top of the citadel," said James.

"All is not lost, James. There are other ways to get inside the citadel."

"And what about King Feldon's crystal?"

"I'm quite sure that King Feldon will bring the crystal to the main hall himself. In the meantime, we can get ourselves in place to intercept him."

Whindril gave a loud groan as her tail clipped a cluster of chimney pots.

There was a loud swish, like the drawing of a huge curtain, and they were all visible again. Immediately, James felt like a huge weight had been lifted from his shoulders. The whole time he had been invisible he had been tense and nervous, like he wasn't completely in control.

Whindril landed on the cobbled courtyard with a jolt and James slipped off the ornate saddle. He noticed the sheer relief on the faces of his mum and Craig.

Eethan immediately found a black arrow protruding from the dragon's neck. "Eee lucky shot. Ee can feex eet."

"There is likely to be poison on the arrow tip," said Mendel. "Let Whindril rest. She has done enough for now."

The courtyard was deserted and the adjoining streets totally empty. Although the sounds of battle echoed down into the city they could still hear the squeaks and chirps of flying reptiles as they foraged for abandoned scraps. Many of the market stalls had been left behind, their contents already rotting away..

Feeling exposed, James quickly decided that he might want his sword close by. He whispered the word, "Firetongue," and soon felt the reassuring weight of the crimson sword in his hand.

"Put that away. Now!" his mum yelled, grabbing his wrist and looking him straight in the eye. James's fingers unravelled to reveal part of his crimson tattoo. She saw him glance down and followed his gaze. "What on earth is that?" she screamed.

"But Mum..." he protested, "I had no choice."

"Mrs Peck," said Mendel, "that is the magical mark that connects James to his sword. We will need all the protection we can get."

"Yeah," added Craig. "So... So don't..." His bravado was faltering.

"Don't what?" snapped Cathy.

Mendel interjected. "Dendralon will not be in the best of moods. He knows we are here and is bound to have a few surprises in store for us."

Uncharacteristically, Mendel's words seemed to calm Cathy. She relaxed her grip on James's arm.

"Now," continued Mendel, "we need to get to the top of the citadel."

They all craned their necks in an effort to see the top of the main citadel. It stood two hundred feet high and looked impossible to climb or enter, being fashioned from the smoothest stone that James had ever seen.

"Bloomin' heck! How are we going to get in there?" Craig asked. He snapped his fingers and Bero shuffled up behind him.

"We'll use the door, of course," replied Mendel.

"I don't see any door! Nothing but this stuff." Craig ran his hand over the smooth surface.

"There are two ways into the citadel," Mendel explained. "Via the main stairs to the Council Chamber, which will no doubt be heavily defended, or through this door right here."

They all stared at the flawless alabaster surface of the citadel.

"I don't see any door, Mendel," said James.

"Put your hand on the stone," Mendel commanded.

James moved closer and touched the cold, marble-like surface. "Like this?" He looked down at the barrel.

"Yes. Quiet now. I must concentrate," said Mendel.

James grimaced as the knocking sensation began to build in his head.

"James, what's wrong?" asked Cathy. She stepped forward.

In the grip of magic, James was unable to answer as he braced himself against the smooth wall of the citadel.

It was at that precise moment that they heard the shout.

24 The Black Lake

Underground, a long line of Yeltans and Yukplugs made their way down a steep set of slippery steps. The tunnel walls glistened with damp, green algae and the roof dripped continuously. Stalactites stabbed down through the dank air and the taller members of the party – Jal in particular – had to duck.

Father Michael caught up with Landris and asked the obvious question. "There are so many of us. How many boats do you have?"

"We do not have any boats," said Landris.

"What!" Michael cried. "Then how do you expect to cross...?"

Lord Eldane cut in. "The Yeltans are very literal. They really do not have any boats. We Manimals, on the other hand, have plenty of boats at the harbour. There were over three hundred the last time I saw the inventory."

"Three hundred and twenty-one, to be precise," remarked Elgry. He'd entrusted his family to Jean and Ephie, who were further back with the Yeltans.

"But how..." persisted Michael, "...how do you propose to get three hundred boats, full of all these people and their animals, into the city unseen and under the noses of the Hedra?"

Landris tried to stifle a smile. "The Hedra do not have any noses."

Michael glanced at Jal before nodding.

Landris placed a yellow finger to his lips, then pointed at the flickering torchlight in the distance. "Please keep your voice down. We are in enemy territory right now."

"Michael?" Ephie's call echoed up the tunnel walls.

Cimerato and Jal both stopped and turned to look at her.

"Can you keep it down, Madam?" asked Cimerato. "No need to alert the whole world to our presence."

Ephie's face flushed scarlet as she reached Michael. He patted her arm sympathetically.

She gave him a grateful look.

Without warning, Jal pushed forward and raced ahead until he reached the bend in the tunnel.

"What's he doing?" Cimerato hissed. "I told you he would betray us!" He began to run after the Hedra but swiftly stopped and flattened himself against the tunnel wall.

***

In front of Cimerato, only yards away, Jal was addressing a Hedra guard. "Anything to report?" he snapped.

The frightened Hedra guard recognized Jal and instantly drew back.

Jal's heart quickened. Maybe someone had made it back from the battle at the Eden Tree after all.

"Sir... I mean, no Sir." The guard had only been startled and promptly slapped his upper arm in a Hedra salute.

"Get back to the surface. Be quick now!" Jal pointed to another set of steps. "We have to get all of our supplies, some of which are King Feldon's personal items, into the city by way of the waterways. I am putting you in charge of keeping all unnecessary Hedra at bay."

"Yes, Sir," hissed the guard.

"First take your comrades, the ones down there..." Jal pointed to the flickering torches beside the underground harbour. "Take them up to the surface with you. Things are not going well for us. We are going to need all the troops we can get. I will load the boats with my own soldiers," explained Jal. "They have been specially chosen by King Feldon."

The Hedra sentry gave another salute and began to shout his commands at the guards below.

Soon, the stairs to the river and the harbour were empty and Jal turned back to where the Yeltans were waiting. As he turned round the bend he came face to face with Cimerato.

"Mmm...not bad, Snakeman," whispered Cimerato. "So why are you helping us?"

"Why not?" replied Jal. You think we're all a bunch of deranged killers, don't you?"

Cimerato raised his eyebrows, as if this was a particularly stupid question.

"Feldon wiped out my family when I was just a child," continued Jal. "My father wanted to make peace with the Manimals and paid for the suggestion with his life. Don't forget, Manimal, we built Gwendral when you were still leaping from tree to tree, scratching your backsides."

Cimerato gave Jal a wry smile. Only Mendel had ever dared to remind the Manimals of their true past. "If you don't mind, Snakeman, I think it's time we got to work."

***

Cimerato eventually managed to persuade the Yeltans to leave as many of their belongings behind as they could, and soon the long lines of Yeltan families were filing down to the harbour and onto the waiting boats. There were only a few dozen Yukplugs. At the front of their column, a very old specimen led the way. White with age and missing a horn, the Yeltans fussed over the creature, as if it were royalty.

Finally, the Drumfintley contingent lined up on the pier, trying their best to keep the children from falling into the black water. Cimerato helped the young ones onto a boat and untied its ropes. Elgry and his family jumped into the last boat along with Jal, Lord Eldane and Cimerato.

Before long, all three hundred and twenty-one boats were under way. In the darkness, they could hear the battle cries in the distance, echoing down through various fissures in the walls. The boats pushed on regardless, eventually passing under a low-ceilinged section of tunnel that Cimerato knew marked the foundations of the city walls.

Several minutes later the flotilla arrived at the Black Lake. It lay directly beneath the centre of the city. Cimerato recognised the set of stairs that led down from the cells; the same stinking cells where his father had found him only two days earlier. Amazingly, there were no signs of any guards or sentries here and Cimerato wondered if his kin still held this part of the city. There could only be a few left now who hadn't already fled by dragon or secret passage.

The Yeltans' incessant, high-pitched babbling began to drift over the still surface of the lake, annoying and worrying Cimerato. He wanted to shut them up, but knew that any reproach of his would have to be louder still.

Through the din, Jal's deep hissing voice reached his ears. "Over there!" Jal stood up in the boat, beside Elgry, making it wobble in the darkness. "About fifty yards ahead of us... There's a heat trace... It's definitely Manimal," he added. "Give me one of your spears, little root-dweller." He held out his hand in anticipation, but Cimerato reached across the boat with his sword and flicked the Yeltan spear away. "No chance, my friend. Not until we know what we're dealing with."

"Hmmm... Well, there are too many now anyway!" Jal retorted. A hundred torches flared into life along the underground shore to reveal at least three times as many Manimal archers, their arrows nocked.

Cimerato stood up beside Jal and shouted across the expanse of cold water towards the bank. "Hold your fire!" Several archers had spotted Jal, however, and let loose their arrows.

"Get down!" Cimerato pulled Jal to the ground as the first arrow ripped past his scaly neck. Cimerato stood up again and waved his hands. "Stop firing!" But more arrows flew from the shore. "Father," he called. "They think we are Hedra!"

"Stop!" Lord Eldane's rich voice ricocheted off the cavern wall and the arrows finally stopped flying.

A voice called out in the darkness, "Lord Eldane, Elgry, Cimerato!"

Cimerato began to row his boat toward the edge of a long, underground jetty.

As more Manimals appeared on the quay, Cimerato called out to them. "Help us to unload these people and their belongings."

His fellow Manimals began to gossip and chatter when they saw the Yeltans. "Why do you bring these creatures into our city?" he was asked by a young archer called Fetrand, whom he knew. "Don't you know the Salt Trolls have been crushed by the Osgrunfs? They all began fighting amongst themselves," Fetrand continued. "Even now, the Osgrunfs are fighting the Hedra archers. Our enemies are falling, but the sentries on the walls say there are still more Hedra on the way. That's why we loosed our arrows. We thought you were..." His voice trailed off as Jal stepped from his boat and gave him a small bow. The Hedra giant then proceeded to lift the three children out of the boat, followed by the adults.

When it came to her turn, Ephie shuddered and protested. "It's alright. I can manage!" And she did, though not before almost falling into the water. Michael caught her just in time.

When they were all off the boat, Lord Eldane addressed the young archer. "Why are you not in the tunnels that lead to Nordengate? Where are the others?"

Fetrand replied, "Once we were sure that our old and young were safe, some of us returned to help. We thought we might buy you some time if we held the Hedra a while longer. You should know, though, that some of the people in the tunnels grew impatient and have begun their journey on towards

Nordengate."

"I told them to travel for two hours only. They were told to wait!" Lord Eldane's eyes blazed with anger and fear. He beckoned to the Council Secretary, Elgry. "This is your chance to be a hero, Elgry. Take this man with you." He pointed to the young archer, Fetrand. "Run to our people in the tunnels. Go as fast as you can! They must come back into Gwendral now, or there will be no hope for them. As a Council member you have the authority to order them back. Now, go!"

"What of my family?" Elgry hesitated. "What about Athelstone, I mean Dendralon?"

"Mendel is the only one who can challenge Dendralon now," Lord Eldane replied. "We must climb up to the citadel and await his instructions."

Jean looked across at Elgry and smiled reassuringly. "I will stay close to your wife and son." She moved to stand beside Elgry's beautiful wife and took his young son's hand in her own. Wee Joe, who held her other hand, stuck his tongue out at the boy. Davado returned the favour.

Elgry stooped and kissed his wife, and then his son. "I will see you both soon." He turned away and began running – the young archer at his side – down the jetty and along the ledge that led deeper under the city and to the tunnels of Nordengate.

In the meantime, the Yeltans continued to stream from the boats, carrying all they could possibly manage. Before long, the dark, rocky shore was littered with clusters of the babbling creatures. Only a few remaining boats waited for space to dock and unload.

"Don't wike dat!" Wee Joe's voice cut through the din.

Wee Joe seemed to be pointing his little finger straight at Cimerato who wondered what he'd done to upset the little one.

"Not you. Dat!" Joe pointed past Cimerato toward the direction of the lake. Everyone followed his gaze.

A large, black boat had slipped round the bend of the river and was drifting into the underground lake, its oars muffled.

***

High up in the citadel, in the Council Chamber, Dendralon was setting up the gateway using precise specifications. In the alcove that housed the newly repaired Scales of Gwendral, he'd placed the Osgrunf and Salt Troll crystals into the cup on the left. It seemed to hold them perfectly.

In the half-light of the hall, Dendralon now prepared to place the third and final crystal into the right-hand cup. The Hedra crystal, the largest of the three, would balance the other two perfectly. He'd already written the pre-Hedran dragon script in the correct places within the alcove and on the walls, and in the correct colours: black and green. He wondered if he'd missed anything...

His patience was wearing thin, however, as he waited with growing anger for Feldon and the last crystal. He paced the hall, and eventually ducked behind the curtain that led to the upper balcony to see if he could find out what was going on.

Feldon's ship was no longer at the river. It would be under the city by now, he decided.

The battle between the surviving Osgrunfs and a new battalion of Hedra infantry was almost over. The Hedra were simply picking off the hundred or so Osgrunfs with their spears. They had even sent two of their large Raptor pets into the fray to speed up the job. The Hedra often used these ancient beasts, descendants of the Saurs. He wondered why King Feldon had not used them sooner. In fact, Dendralon wondered how much he should have relied on Feldon to protect the last crystal. What should have been the easiest crystal to procure was rapidly becoming the most elusive.

There was no longer any sign of Mendel, nor of any invisible beast. What if the creature had seized Feldon and the crystal while Dendralon had been preparing the scales inside the Chamber? Paranoia washed over him as he looked once more at the huge, blood-red sun, Tealfirth. In the last two hours it had grown rapidly, blistering black and red like an angry wound. Its dying light was giving Denthan a red tinge. It had turned the Gorton Sea a deep crimson. "A sea of blood," he whispered.

25 Sintor's Revenge

Down in the underground lake the Hedra ships came into view."

Hedra!" shouted Cimerato.

A tall Manimal archer pulled the children behind a large rock and nocked his longbow. The few Yeltans still floating on the lake began to wail. Amongst the mêlée of arrows, they splashed and scrambled for the safety of the jetty and the rocks behind it. Four of their boats were rammed, smashed to pieces by the full force of the Hedra attack.

Cimerato hauled Jal down beside the women and children. "Be careful, your kin might get lucky."

Next to him, Jean was shaking and Ephie was whimpering. Before Michael could duck, an arrow caught his left ear. "Arrgghh!" he cried. Blood streamed down his neck.

Behind the first three Hedra boats, Feldon's royal battleship barely made it into the larger cavern from the smaller tunnel, creaking and groaning as parts of her rigging snapped and bent on the jagged rocks and stalactites. Several pieces of the main sail crashed down onto the weary crew.

Arrows flew from the jetty now, killing some of the scaled sailors, their screams mixing with those of the stranded Yeltans. The unexpected infra-red light signals in the cavern had interfered with the Hedra's night vision, just as it had Jal's, and Cimerato's heart lifted as many Hedra shots fell short or went wide of their mark. Most of the Yeltans were able to make it to the safety off the jetty before the Hedra eyes became accustomed to the conditions.

Unfortunately, there was no magic to help the Manimals and Yeltans this time and soon their supply of arms was spent. Black arrows splintered behind the crouching children and still more cracked noisily on the rocks in front of them. Blood trickled down from Michael's ear onto his dog collar and Ephie ripped a piece of cloth from her blue joggers, making a bandage of sorts, which she carefully pinned round his balding head.

Michael beamed at her. "Thanks again, Ephie. You're always coming to my rescue." Ephie simply smiled and let out a girlish titter.

Helen began to cry and Wee Joe gave her a big hug. "Never mind, Hewen, I stole some tabwet from her coat when we were in de cage."

As the arrows flew and the eerie screams filled the chamber, Wee Joe carefully unwrapped Galdinie's greaseproof paper and broke a piece of tablet from the bar for his big sister. He kissed her arm and patted her head. Jean pulled them both close. In the middle of the carnage, she smiled. Wee Joe offered a small piece of the tablet to Davado, who took it with a grateful nod. "You're a good boy, Joe," she whispered to him, "such a good boy."

"Back, we need to move back!" Cimerato cried. "They'll soon be at the jetty!"

They'd already lost too many of their number to the Hedra arrows, and with the tunnels to Nordengate now blocked, they would have to regroup in the city. Cimerato pushed his sword round the rock and saw the Hedra king in the reflection of the blade, a mere twenty feet from the shore. He saw Feldon smile as the torches revealed the devastation his archers had caused. The Hedra king's voice drifted over the black water as he pointed to a large decorative door and addressed one of his masters-at-arms. "Train all your arrows on that doorway. It's their only escape route. If any of those rats get through it, you will die. Is that clear?"

The Hedra master-at-arms turned and screamed the order. "All of you aim at the doorway! Shoot anything that moves!"

Cimerato pulled back his sword. "We're trapped! We'll have to wait until they come ashore, then fight hand to hand." Cimerato thumped his fist down on the nearest rock then grimaced as a fork of pain flashed up his arm. He gripped his wounded shoulder. "I keep forgetting about this stupid wound!" He scowled at Jal.

Lord Eldane crouched down beside his son. "We don't stand a chance. Those ships can each hold over two hundred Hedra and—"

His words were cut short by a sudden roar of water. Cimerato stuck his sword round the edge of the rock again and couldn't believe what he saw. The Hedra royal boat had been heaved to one side. It had cracked against the wall of the cavern.

The water around the boat began to boil and churn, falling away to reveal a huge Salt Troll, his neck lined with deep gouges. Two more Trolls burst from the waters of the lake and began to thump their heavy whale-tooth spears down onto the Hedra boats.

King Feldon yelled at his soldiers and ducked into his cabin. With a cold determination, the beasts continued to slam their weapons down on the first boat until it disintegrated, sinking beneath the cold waters along with its crew.

A few arrows glanced off the Salt Trolls' armour as they started plucking the screaming Hedra from the remaining ships and smacked them dead on the rocks.

Cimerato grabbed Jean's arm. "Quick, now is our only chance to get through the door."

Still unsure what was happening, they staggered to their feet and sprinted for the doorway. The Yeltans followed, their escape masked by the bedlam of the new battle on the Black Lake.

As he urged the others through the doorway, Cimerato kept his eye on the battle. One of the Hedra managed to catch a Salt

Troll's throat with a long boat hook. It was a skilful move, but the giant tumbled forward, smashing the boat and trapping the unlucky Hedra under him as he fell.

"Feldon!" the largest Troll bellowed as he began to tip the royal boat. His strength was immense and his black eyes burned with hatred. "Why did you not help us against the Osgrunf horde? Dendralon promised that you would help us!"

Like the slithering reptile he truly was, Feldon slipped free from the shelter of his cabin. "W...why did you attack the Osgrunfs in the first place?"

Cimerato recognised the Salt Troll as Sintor. And he could see that the Troll's focus was now on the blue crystal that swung from Feldon's neck.

"You were supposed to help us when we attacked!" Sintor reached down to grab the Hedra King, but Feldon sidestepped his clawed hand. "Dendralon promised us your help in crushing the Osgrunfs." Sintor swiped again and missed.

"I know nothing of this..." Feldon rolled over to his right to avoid another killing blow. "Please, believe me." Feldon's lies fell on deaf ears as he scrambled back into his cabin.

"Liar! You are in league with Dendralon! You still have your crystal!" Sintor smashed the cabin with his spear and found Feldon quivering under a fallen sail.

"I don't know what you mean," Feldon replied.

"Dendralon promised us victory and the city," bellowed Sintor. "He took my crystal. You only wanted our destruction!"

Feldon continued to hiss his protests.

"Well, I want my crystal back," roared Sintor, "but in the meantime I'll take yours!" Sintor snatched up the Hedra King and held him close to his leathery face.

As Cimerato and Jal slipped through the doorway, they checked to see that they were the last to escape. It was then that Feldon spotted Jal. The Hedra King looked confused and totally broken. "Jal! Hel—" he screamed.

But he never finished his plea. The Troll wrenched the chain from the Hedra King's neck so roughly that Feldon's serpentine head flew off and splashed into the water, followed, one second later, by his large, decapitated body. Sintor's heavily scarred hand closed round the blue stone, the largest of the three crystals. With a thunderous roar, he signalled to the remaining Troll to return to the depths and they sank beneath the surface of the Black Lake.

"Ssssss!" Jal sprinted up the stairs with Cimerato then stopped at the top to make sure no one was following.

"No Salt Troll will ever squeeze through that door," said Cimerato. He caught his breath beside the great barred doors of the jail where Dendralon had imprisoned him and then followed everyone else up the stairs that led to the city of Gwendral.

**

Two large Salt Trolls were wading out of the opening to the underground river. They splashed into the River Levan, then slipped under the surface.

Knowing something was not right, Dendralon muttered strange words and whispered magic prayers until he began to tremble all over. He gripped the Talisman and held it high above his head, unsure of the powers it would release.

Yellow pus oozed from between his scales and the Manimal skin began to lose its vigour. He felt a jolt and soon large portions of it sloughed off. Lifting the Talisman even higher, he thrust it forward and watched expectantly as a bolt of silver light spiralled downward towards the river. The light hit the surface with a sizzle, then disappeared.

**

Further down the river, a trail of bubbles signalled the Salt Trolls' progress beneath the waters. Sintor felt the stinging

166

sensation immediately. Gripping his throat in pain, his huge frame struggled out of the water, revealing himself all too clearly to the battling Hedra on the riverbank. The other Troll also emerged and stared anxiously at his master and King. "Sintor, we must get back beneath the surface," he pleaded, "They have seen us!"

But the Troll King's pain was all-consuming. Sintor twisted and turned in agony, oblivious to the Hedra nearby. "I'm burning!" he screamed. "Stop the burning!" Sintor dropped to his knees, still clutching the gold chain that held the Hedra crystal.

Seeing the Trolls' vulnerability, the Hedra quickly fired a volley of black arrows at the giants, and soon the river began to flow red. The Troll that had stood beside Sintor now staggered back under the onslaught and sank beneath the crimson waters. But Sintor was still gripped by the magic silver light that touched him. In the midst of his agony he pointed to a black figure, high up on the citadel. "Dendralon..."

Sintor had barely spoken the wizard's name when a feathered Raptor leapt from the riverbank and landed squarely on the Troll's massive chest. Digging in with its razor-sharp claws, it snapped and bit around flaying Sintor's neck until it found the golden chain.

***

Sintor's body was now full of arrows and he rolled, face down, onto the surface. At the same time, the last Osgrunf staggered backwards, falling dead into the water beside him. Both bodies bobbed on the bloody waters of the River Levan and would be carried off on the strengthening current toward the Gorton Sea. Not that it would matter where they were headed now, Dendralon recognised. Tealfirth was in its dying hours.

After watching Sintor's demise, Dendralon fixed his eyes on the Raptor, thrilled to see that it still held the crystal tightly in its mouth. He nodded with satisfaction and it cocked its head to one side as though in response.

As the Raptor bounded up the reed-tufted bank, it cried out to its master in the distance. The victorious Hedra on the riverbank cheered as the main bulk of their army, almost one hundred thousand strong, began to file onto the plain of Gwendral, unopposed.

Ignoring them, the Raptor forged ahead of the massing Hedra, picking its way through the corpses and flies of the muddy battlefield.

Watching the Raptor's progress, Dendralon thanked his own dark god for bringing him onto the balcony in time to see Sintor escaping with the last crystal, and for gifting him the Talisman and all its powers.

A simple beast to control, Dendralon knew the Raptor would bring his crystal to the city. He shouted down to his elite guards on the watchtowers, "Open the gates!"

The gates were some distance away, but his voice was loud and clear. Athelstone's Manimal elite guards began to wind the huge mechanism that would swing open the ivory gates to receive his special courier.

***

At the base of the citadel, James and the rest of Whindril's passengers heard Dendralon's command echo across the empty city.

"James, place your hand higher on the wall!" Mendel shouted, his voice full of urgency. James hoped the wizard knew what he was doing because so far there was no sign of any secret door into the citadel. Giving a little shrug, he reached higher.

Shhhooom! This time the wall shifted back at James's touch and a door appeared on the side of the citadel.

"About time too," sighed Craig.

"Quick, get inside now! Get…"

At that moment, an odd sound interrupted Mendel's command. Everyone in the group turned back and looked up at the huge blistering sun. Tealfirth itself seemed to be the source of the noise. Shielding their eyes, they shuddered as a low moan filled the air. It was a long, endless rumble that sent vibrations through every particle of Denthan.

James felt the deep bass tone in the pit of his stomach and it made him feel sick.

The sun was almost ready to explode.

***

Inside the city, the remaining Yeltans, Yukplugs and Manimals filtered up into the streets from the black lake below. Wee Joe was one of the last to climb the stairs to the surface.

Cimerato helped the young boy through the last door. But, as he left the shadows, a keening noise stopped him in his tracks.

Wee Joe tugged his mother's tattered skirt. "Mum, it's singing!" The little boy pointed up at Tealfirth. It looked like an angry boil, ready to burst at any moment. Its swan song was filling the beautiful city with the sound of death.

Michael shuddered and said, "It's like a requiem. The anthem of a dying world."

Jean bit down on her lip as a tear rolled down her cheek.

"There's Whindril!" somebody shouted. Cimerato saw the white dragon tethered in the courtyard below the main citadel. He hushed them all. "Quiet!" Another sound could be heard clearly over the steady drone of the dying sun.

"It sounds like chains," said Helen.

"They're opening the gates!" said Cimerato.

The huge fifty-foot ivory gates were beginning to move.

Michael found Ephie's hand. "I really pray we make it home, Ephie."

She held Michael's hand tightly and smiled up at him. "I'm not sure if we'll ever get home, but I need to tell you something—"

"Come on! Get a move on!" Cimerato cried. "We need to get into the citadel and up to the Council Chamber. Now!" Cimerato ushered Michael and Ephie across the courtyard. He took Helen under his good arm and signalled Jal to pick up Wee Joe.

Distracted by Cimerato's shouts, Michael glanced over at the beautiful, white dragon. "With any luck, Mendel and the boys will be in the tower already!" he shouted to the others.

Landris nodded to Cimerato. "I hope Michael's right. What do you want us to do now?"

"Close those gates," Cimerato ordered. "We need to stop the Hedra from getting inside the city walls. Take your best men. You go with them, Jal." The Hedra giant nodded his agreement. "The rest of us will climb up to the Council Chamber. We may be able to distract Dendralon while Mendel performs his magic."

With a salute, Landris began to lead the Yeltans toward the watchtowers. Before getting too far, however, he turned back and shouted, "Good luck to you all!"

Cimerato gave him a wave before jogging over to his father.

Lord Eldane stood motionless in the reddening light. Cimerato could see the pain on his face. "Time is against us, Father. Could you go back down to the tunnels and see if there's any sign of Elgry and the rest of our people?"

"Of course." Lord Eldane turned to go, but not before giving his son a long, doleful glance, as though he didn't expect to see him again.

Tealfirth's deafening drone intensified.

26 The Hairy One

James's group were still in the wall of the citadel, struggling up a steep, spiral staircase. The effort was beginning to take its toll on Bero's back legs.

Craig tried to encourage Bero as much as he could, but the old dog's hips had seized. He lay in an immovable heap, spread over three or four stone steps, blocking the way. "Hold on a minute!" pleaded Craig. He stared up at James. "He's never going to make it."

"Ee thinks ee can help." Eethan scampered back until he stood over the old dog. Cupping Bero's head in his small, blue hands, he blew straight into the dog's nostrils. "Whhooo!"

Bero sniffed and snorted, making a half-hearted attempt to snap at Eethan's mischievous face. Then the old dog's whole body shuddered.

"What are you doing?" said Craig in an anxious whisper.

Bero issued a small wheeze before his head thumped down onto the step. He looked quite dead.

Craig knelt down beside his dog, his heart beating hard. "Wake up, boy! Please…" Still Bero didn't move.

James felt his chest tighten. He tried too. "Bero," he whispered.

Then Craig stood up briskly, his eyes full of rage.

Eethan cowered.

"Wait!" James cried.

Bero's eyes had flicked open. His opaque pupils began to brighten. His feathered tail twitched and then began to wag. As they stared down at the old dog he began to change right before their eyes. His limbs seemed to stretch, grow more muscular, and the fur around his muzzle turned from grey to gold.

Craig's mouth fell open. "Bero?" He grabbed Eethan's skinny, blue arm. "He's alive! And he's not so fat now; his coat's all shiny! Is it still him? He looks…" Craig could hardly get the words out, "…so young!"

Bero yelped, then pawed at the ground, wiggling his back end in a fit of excitement.

"Ees about two years old now, ee thinks!" said Eethan. He sprinted up the spiral staircase, followed by Bero who bounded after him, panting and wagging his tail. Mendel's barrel bounced and swayed under the young dog's chin.

James heard Mendel's voice protesting at this rough treatment. "Eethan, what have you done? Slow down, Bero!"

"Slow down," yelled Craig.

"All this jolting is making me feel quite ill," moaned Mendel.

Cathy was puffing and panting now too. As Eethan and Bero passed close by, she flicked the little blue man on the arm. "I know we haven't always seen eye to eye, but…you couldn't knock ten or so years off me, could you?"

Eethan grinned and shrugged. "Ees possible, if you start to bee nice ladeee." He chuckled to himself and ran ahead.

"Very funny," grumbled Cathy.

"Stop!" Mendel's voice instantly filled their heads. "There is a room ahead." His voice became ominous. "There are bound to be a few traps and surprises along the way."

Hearing Mendel's words, Cathy fell back against the cold stone wall. She was breathing heavily. As her chest heaved she whispered to James, "You're going to need your puffer for this." She swung the small, green rucksack from her shoulder and rummaged for the blue inhaler.

"No, Mum. I told you before, I can breathe here just as well as any other boy…"

She eyed him suspiciously. "Were you just playing up with the whole asthma thing back home? Laying it on thick when there were chores to be done?"

"No, mum," gasped James. "It's just that—"

"Shush, James!" Mendel scolded. "Someone is near."

They all did their best to hold what breath they had left and listened. James could hear a shuffling, then a click, click, clicking. It sounded as though someone was hitting two hollow sticks together, louder and louder. Then suddenly the sound stopped. For a moment there was silence and then the whole thing started over again.

"Centides?" whispered James.

The sound instantly stopped.

Eethan put a blue finger to his thin lips and winked at them. He scuttled up the wall of the passage until he hung from the roof. The boys hadn't seen this particular trick before, and James marvelled as the blue man scampered, upside down, into the chamber beyond.

"I don't think it's a Centide," said Mendel, pressing a golden eye against the plastic window. "In fact, I can't say that I've actually ever heard that sound before." This didn't entirely surprise James – had he recognised it, Mendel would usually have given them the creature's Latin name and feeding habits by now.

James edged round the room's doorway to see if he could tell what was going on.

Eethan, still clinging to the ceiling, had just come face to face with a very strange-looking creature with a triangular head and a pair of crimson, bulbous eyes, like a dragonfly's. Eethan remained motionless, his smooth blue-tinged skin glimmering in the eerie light that filtered in from a small arrow slit in the wall.

Matching each other's movements, both creatures cocked their strange heads in unison.

Eethan's right hand slipped free of the ceiling and began to glow.

The creature pounced.

"Eeeeeeeee!"

"Firetongue!" yelled James, jumping into the room. Looking above him, he saw the thing chasing Eethan round above him. Bigger than a Centide, it looked like a cross between a Praying Mantis and a hairy Sun Spider. James's head thudded with pain as he shouted, "Wwwspiderwwwart!" But nothing happened. In fact, the spell only seemed to quicken the creature's pace. Eethan was rushing round a central chandelier, ducking and dodging a pair of snapping mandibles.

"Mendel, the spell hasn't worked!" shouted James.

Craig jumped into the room beside James, followed by Cathy and Bero. He lashed upwards with his spear and cheered when a long, hairy leg thumped to the ground at his feet.

Bero dived in and retrieved the limb, dropping it in front of Cathy.

"Yuck!" she gagged. "Go away, you stupid dog...and take that with you." She growled as she kicked the appendage across the cobbled floor. Her eyes widened, however, when the hairy leg jerked twice on the floor, then began sprouting its own limbs along with a mantis-like head. Within seconds, the newly formed creature was stalking Cathy, two bulbous, red eyes fixed on its prey.

James swiftly hacked the smaller creature's head off, but this too began to sprout its own legs and move towards him.

"Stop chopping bits off!"

"I was just going to say that!" shouted Craig.

Eethan tried his own magic, sending a flash of blue light into the monster's eyes. It stopped for a moment, then dropped off the ceiling right onto the boys.

"Arghhh!" James and Craig cried out in horror. They shoved the horrible thing off and leapt away, spitting long hairs from their mouths. Once clear, they turned and pierced its hard carapace with their weapons. Viscous, black blood that smelled of rotten entrails seeped from its sides. Eethan jumped down onto the creature's back and held on tightly as it tried to whip him off. He looked like some weird cowboy, riding the most disgusting bucking bronco ever.

The small, decapitated head and the severed leg were now two fully formed replicas of the original, and they had Cathy and Bero trapped in the corner of the room. The bigger of the two squirted a jet of yellow liquid from its mouth. The sticky stuff covered Cathy's leg and held her fast to the wall.

"Ah! You disgusting…!" Cathy yelped, fumbling inside the battered green rucksack for anything that might serve as a weapon. Eethan was still holding onto his attacker while Craig and James stabbed and prodded at the two others, trying to keep them back.

For his part, Bero barked and occasionally bit a hairy leg before yelping in retreat as he ducked from the various searching claws and mandibles. Cathy was still struggling with the rucksack, but then, with a cry of glee, she produced a small rusty, orange can.

Pssssssssssssssssssssssssssssss…

She held the tiny, white valve open, releasing the choking vapour into the room, spraying relentlessly until the can was completely empty.

They all began to cough and choke. James's eyes stung and he could barely see. He wondered if he'd been blinded. He cringed, waiting for the mandibles to find him…

Finally, their blurred eyes began to clear and they assumed defensive positions. They frantically peered about the room.

On the floor, they discovered all three giant insects, each as stiff as a board—all dead.

"Mum? That was fantastic! How did you do that?" asked James.

Craig stepped over the corpse of the biggest insect and took the empty orange can from Cathy. "It's Bero's flea spray!"

He punched the air triumphantly. "I knew it would come in handy somehow!"

James glowered at his friend. "Sure you did."

"Bero's fleas have just saved our lives..." Craig continued, ignoring James's put down.

"I was just about to turn them into stone," said Mendel. "There was no need to panic." The wizard sounded less than convincing.

"No need to what?" Cathy was still shaking as she knelt down beside the barrel and peered inside.

Mendel flicked his fins forward, pushing himself further back into the barrel, away from Cathy. "All the same, that was quite impressive, Mrs Peck. Quite impressive," he quickly relented.

Craig was just about to throw the empty tin into a corner when Mendel asked, "Um, what does it say on the can?"

"What do you mean? It says 'Flea Spray' of course," said Craig, adding a "Duh!" as he waved the empty can in front of the barrel's little plastic window.

"Yes, but what is the active ingredient?" Mendel splashed anxiously about in his plastic home. "I hope Garlon made this barrel airtight."

Cathy snatched the can back from Craig. "Give it here, dunderhead! It says..." James saw her trying to focus. "It says, 'triazinon'."

"Organophosphate! That's not too bad. Well, I mean, if it had been pyrethrum, the main ingredient in most flea sprays these days, I would be stone dead. It's quite deadly to fish, you see." Mendel made a splash inside the barrel.

"Quite deadly to big hairy spider things too," remarked Craig. "I reckon you're just jealous that Mrs Peck killed that thing without your help."

Mendel splashed. "Really, Craig, you have quite an imagination."

"Wees needs to geet going," rasped Eethan.

"Quite," Mendel agreed.

"Why didn't your first spell work, Mendel?" James asked as he ripped the yellow goo from his mother's clothes, releasing her from the wall.

"Oh, you probably didn't pronounce it correctly. Or..." Mendel paused. "...or perhaps Dendralon put some kind of magical shield round the creature. I suspect it was from the Acranidus family, just in case you're interested."

"We're not," Cathy muttered as she looked up the dark spiral staircase ahead.

"Here, here," agreed Craig. He winked at Cathy, but she was not in the mood to share the moment with him.

Eethan pushed past Cathy and the boys, clicking his fingers at the young Bero behind him. "Meee and Beero will go first!"

"When are you going to learn to talk properly, you useless freak?" Cathy demanded. "It should be, Bero and I!"

Eethan flicked something disgusting from his finger, which flew over his head and almost hit Cathy.

"Why you..!" She made after him.

"Ten yeeeers younger, indeeed," tittered Eethan.

Cathy skidded to a halt and swung the rucksack above her head. "You can take your ten years and..."

"Mum! Stop it!"

Well out of range, Craig whispered, "I think the Lugpus is wearing off."

Cathy eyed Craig suspiciously.

"I'm only saying," murmured Craig.

Eethan only chuckled and moved on. "Down to nine yeeeers now... No more. Eeee heee..."

27 The Gates

While the Yeltan crew and Jal raced towards the watchtowers to try and close the city gates, Cimerato herded the remaining Yeltans out of the sun's heat into the city hall nearest to the citadel. Elgry's wife and young son remained behind too. Both wanted to stay close to the tunnels to wait for his return.

Once inside, Cimerato squinted through an arrow slit and saw the Hedra army out on the ridge, attempting to pull themselves together and regroup as the much bigger force filed onto the plain. He thought that they might miss seeing the gates opening, but then one of them blew on a strange-looking trumpet and the rest swung round. Seeing what was happening, the newly reinforced Hedra began what could only be described as a mad race toward the opening gates.

Cimerato grimaced and cupped his mouth, shouting down at the Yeltans as they filed into the towers below. "Be quick, the Hedra have begun their charge!" Cimerato felt his heart sink as he stared hopelessly at the mass of creatures roaring down from the ridge like a great, grey river in flood. Hedra chariots carrying the Hedra elite rolled over the fallen on the Plain of Gwendral—they stopped for no one, not even their own.

***

The creaking of the giant cogs and chains that operated the gates was loud and grating. Jal hoped the sound would mask their movement and the guards would be unprepared for the Yeltan attack. They needed the element of surprise.

While Landris and Jal made their way to the top of the west watchtower, Garlon ran with the other half of the Yeltans up the spiral stairway of the east tower. When everyone was in position, Jal jumped into the guardroom and knocked several terrified guards to the floor. The Yeltans overpowered the rest of the guards and held them fast by their sheer numbers.

Hidden from the group in a shadowy alcove, a Manimal captain leapt out from his nook and slashed his curved sword down at the little Yeltan leader.

"Landris watch that one!" shouted Jal.

Landris rolled over twice, just managing to avoid the razor-sharp Gwendralin cutlass. He rolled again, then jumped up onto one of the cogs as it rotated round its giant spindle. The wheel turned slowly as the huge gate opened, taking Landris further away from his attacker. "Drop your sword!" Landris shouted. "We are here to help you. I am unarmed." He held up his empty hands, but the captain did not back down. "The real Athelstone is dead!" Landris shouted in desperation as the cog took him round towards the Manimal captain again.

Jal could see that the Manimal captain was unnerved by his presence.

"Do not try your trickery on me, Yeltan! You're in league with the Hedra," the Manimal shouted, pointing to Jal.

Landris had to keep stepping backwards as the giant wheel brought him closer and closer to the captain. Three Yeltans ran ahead of Jal and charged the Manimal captain, but the much bigger opponent easily knocked two of them down.

"Hold!" shouted Jal. He'd seen these Manimal guards throw their swords like spears before, and feared that the captain, in his highly threatened state, might use the same technique on Landris. The remaining Yeltan and Landris tried to reason with the distraught captain, but again he slashed down and they both had to jump to avoid his killing strokes.

Jal edged closer, but his foot hit a discarded sword, causing a clatter.

The Manimal captain whipped his head round.

Seeing the Manimal's distraction, Landris jumped, landing

on a small platform above the main mechanism. He teetered precariously on its edge.

Jal pounced forward to fell the captain, but the captain had already thrown his cutlass at the foundering Yeltan. It spun twice then stopped with a thud. Landris looked down in shock. The blade had pierced him through.

With a roar, Jal cut down the Manimal captain, though too late to save Landris. The Yeltan leader toppled forward, all the way down into the gate mechanism.

Garlon and his crew came running through the door just in time to see Landris fall.

"No!" Garlon cried as he fell to his knees in stunned disbelief.

The rest of the Yeltans rushed to Jal's side, but there was nothing that could be done to save their leader. He was gone.

Tears rolled down Garlon's face as the word, "Father..." slipped from his lips.

Sparing Garlon the horror, Jal peered down into the deep shaft. He could see Landris's twisted body caught in the chains, hanging, lifeless, like some gruesome puppet, far below in the gloom.

Shoulders slumped in grief, Garlon could only stare into nothingness as the low rumble that shook the whole of Denthan continued. Finally, he roused himself and numbly gave the order. "Make sure the gates are closed. I will not have my father die in vain."

Jal hacked at the thick ropes with his sword until they snapped. Slowly, the cogs and chains began to spin in reverse and the gates began to close. However, without the tower guards manning the levers and chains, the progress was laboured and the gap between the two gates was still about twenty yards.

Jal peered down at the Hedra army. Joined by thousands more from the south, they were at least ninety thousand strong. Their chariots to the fore, his kin were only five hundred yards from the tall, ivory gates.

Suddenly the gates gave a shriek that was momentarily even louder than the dying sun. They shuddered to a stop.

"What is going on, Jal?" Garlon cried "The Hedra are almost at the gates!" The Yeltan eyed Jal suspiciously. "Was Cimerato right to mistrust you?"

Jal grew angry. "Do not blame me for the gates, Yeltan! There is a second rope beside you. Cut it now!"

The Yeltans nearest to it began to hack at the main support rope that had slowed the progress of the gates. The screams and jeers of the Hedra grew louder as they worked. Dust from the plain billowed upward as the ninety thousand Hedra charged at full speed. They were trained to strike fear into the hearts of their enemies, smacking their shields loudly with their swords and spears as they ran. The first Hedra chariot was now only a hundred feet from the gate.

Jal dashed over and hacked into the thick rope with his own sword. "Cut harder!"

To the small Yeltans, the rope felt like steel but they hacked and hacked, again and again, until finally the cable snapped. There was a loud crack as the thick rope whipped out across the chamber and disappeared. The whiplash felled two more Yeltans, catching them unawares. But Jal could hear the heavy gates below slamming shut. He hurried back to the window and peered down. The first chariot had been cut in two, its lizard steeds crushed, its driver thrown against the ivory gates with such force that his body had bounced backwards and smashed into the chariot rider behind.

Seeing the gates closed, the screams of the Hedra army became absolutely deafening, the hellish din drowning out Tealfirth's death drone. But these were not screams of aggression, designed to scare an enemy; they were a clear sign that thousands of Hedra were being crushed as they were forced against the gates and walls of Gwendral by the ranks behind. To the rear, they began to fight amongst themselves, struggling to escape the deadly wave of bodies as the onslaught continued unchecked.

Jal lowered his head as those at the very back of the charge, mostly younglings and the old, simply dropped their weapons and sat down on the dusty plain. Resigning themselves to their fate, they stared up at the blisters of yellow and crimson that bubbled on the surface of their angry sun.

Only one creature had managed to get through the gates. Almost ten feet in height, it had hopped over the leading chariot into Gwendral. Jal watched it run towards the main citadel. Recognising what it was, he knew he would have to warn Cimerato immediately...

28 Stairs and Secrets

On the main stairway to the Council Chamber, Michael and Cimerato struggled with their charges. Wee Joe kicked against Michael's black, crumpled jacket, whining about days of travelling and no toys, while Helen complained about missing their hamster, Mufty.

"I want down to wook!" said Wee Joe, pointing at the rows of sculpted gargoyles that lined the stairs.

Jean tried to correct his pronunciation. "L... L... Look, Joe. Say it after me."

Cimerato saw the young boy struggling on Michael's shoulders and wondered how long the cleric would keep his patience.

"L... L... Wook!" Wee Joe repeated, stressing the 'W' as much as he could.

Unable to keep Wee Joe up on his shoulders any longer, Michael lowered the boy to the floor. Relieved of his burden, he walked on ahead, gasping in wonder every time he caught a glimpse of the city through one of the many stained glass windows. As a particularly spectacular view unfolded, he grabbed Ephie's arm. "You know, Ephie, I've been to every major cathedral in Europe, but I never dreamt that such buildings as these could exist. Just look at this stairwell we're in now," he said enthusiastically. "These arches are incredible!"

Ephie gave him a vague smile.

As they climbed, he continued to stare up at the five-point archways above them and marvelled at the tall columns that supported the vaulted roof above the massive spiral staircase.

Cimerato couldn't see how anyone could get so excited over bits of stone.

"I can't believe that all this will disappear," Michael went on. "I can't believe that all those strange animals and birds, which took millions of years to evolve, will just vanish. There must be some mistake, Ephie, there must be."

Hearing heavy footsteps behind him, Cimerato turned quickly, but was relieved to see that it was only Jal. "He will be more than happy to remind you that this great city was actually built by the Hedra."

Michael gasped. "The Hedra built this wonderful city?"

"According to legend," murmured Cimerato.

"Then surely you should find some kind of compromise. Work out a way of saving all the creatures on Denthan."

Cimerato gave Michael a look of complete disbelief. "Are you mad?"

"No... I mean..."

Jal was bounding up the stairs two at a time.

"You managed to close the gates then," remarked Cimerato.

"Yes," panted Jal, out of breath. "But we have an unwanted visitor."

A loud cracking noise up ahead distracted them. The stone around the gargoyles was beginning to crumble.

"Run!" Cimerato cried.

The group stumbled up the stairs as briskly as they could. In front of them was yet another large, five-point arch that led into an antechamber.

"This is the last arch before the Council Chamber," yelled Cimerato.

Jal tapped Cimerato on the shoulder. "The visitor... It's one of our Rapt—" But Jal's words were cut short yet again, this time by a movement ahead of them. Cimerato made sure that Wee Joe was behind him before drawing his sword.

Fifty yards on, the windows were almost shaking out of their frames. The strange gargoyle-like figures that lined the stairs were shuddering and dust was belching from the walls.

"The floor's collapsing!" screeched Ephie, trying her best

to stay upright.

"No," shouted Michael. "The citadel's not collapsing, it's the figures, they're moving!" He watched in horror as several squat forms jumped free from the cloud of dust. They walked steadily towards the trembling group.

Jean pulled Wee Joe and Helen close to her.

The freakish gargoyles crept down the last few stairs from the antechamber. Some resembled stunted men with the heads of animals. Others were more like snakes with the heads of men.

"This is dark Hedra magic," said Cimerato, testing his sword.

Jal roared and thrust forward, slashing down with his black-bladed sword, but the first of the gargoyles spun round with unexpected speed and knocked the sword out of Jal's hand. The Hedra was forced to jump high to avoid the gargoyle's stone mace, but still managed to duck down and retrieve his weapon. Again, he slashed downwards, but his blade stopped dead against solid stone and ricocheted from his hand a second time. He gripped his throbbing wrist and snarled.

Cimerato raced forward and slammed his heel into the face of a second snake-headed dwarf. The carved statue only slid back a few inches before regaining its forward momentum. The evil-looking creature had fixed its gaze on the children.

Jal turned to Cimerato. "They can't be destroyed with our swords. We will have to try and run round them!" As he sidestepped a third attacker, who had the head of a horse, it slashed at him with a stone flail. He dodged the blow, but ended up tripping over another of the creatures. Jal struggled to get to his feet as yet another gargoyle picked up a large stone and threw it down the stairs, narrowly missing Jean and the children.

The stone thudded against something soft and they all

glanced round to see what it was.

"Baacckkk!"

Just a few steps below them the large matted outline of the Mertol emerged out of the darkness. Its long hair was caked in dried blood and dirt, and his claws hung low at its side. They clicked against the masonry as the beast approached them.

Cimerato moved swiftly. He tried to shield Jean and the children from the Mertol below.

"Baacckkk!" the Mertol cried again, and they all braced as a black ball shot from one of the leathery pits in its left cheek. The Drumfintley group all ducked at the same time, but when the ball flew past Ephie's face and slammed into the stone attacker with the horse's head, they gasped with relief.

The gargoyle stopped, mid-swipe, as a thick sooty coating covered it. More balls flew from the Mertol, hitting the stone figures one by one. Everyone kept low to avoid the onslaught, pushing themselves flat against the stone stairs.

Beating its massive chest, the Mertol cried out excitedly, "Baacckkk!"

Not one of the gargoyles escaped its attack. Returned to lifelessness, the sooty coatings fell away to reveal damp, green moss. It shimmered in the strange amber light coming from outside.

Lying flat on the floor, Cimerato lifted his head from the stone and whispered to Jal, "It must have followed us here, all the way from the Eden Tree. I remember seeing it attack the Tree Troll, Ssslathat."

Ephie, fearful, said in a whimper, "It's come back to eat us."

Jal, his back against the wall, bent down to pick up his Hedra blade. "The Mertol is flesh and blood. It can still feel the sting of the sword!"

"Stop!" Michael caught Jal's arm. "If it had wanted to kill us, it would have done so by now. I think the Mertol wants to join us."

As though understanding the vicar's words, the Mertol retracted its razor-sharp claws and changed its call. It now issued a series of short grunts as the slits on his face opened and shut in intricate patterns. The flicking patterns had a mesmerising effect on Jal and Cimerato, so much so that they backed off.

Ephie steadied herself by holding onto Jean. "What's it doing?" she whispered.

"I think Michael's right," said Jean, "I think it wants to come with us."

To everyone's complete horror, Wee Joe pulled away from his mum, picked up a stone and threw it straight at the Mertol. His aim was perfect. It hit the beast square in the face.

They all cringed, waiting for a black ball to come flying at them.

The Mertol only grunted, blinked, shook its matted mane, and continued forward.

"Joe, for goodness sake…" whimpered Jean.

Helen caught her brother's arm before he could find another rock. "Don't do that again, okay!"

Wee Joe gave the beast a disrespectful "Hummff!" and stamped his feet. "I'll teach it to wock us up in a cage."

"No you won't!" said Helen, pulling on her mother's sleeve. "Mum, tell him."

Michael straightened and dusted himself down. "He's pointing to the archway behind us." He looked directly at the Mertol, then pointed up at the archway too.

The beast grunted twice then pushed past them all, pulling on Michael's black jacket as he went.

Cimerato covered his nose. The stench from the creature was unbearable. Reluctantly, he followed the Mertol through the last archway that led into the antechamber.

Once inside the room, Cimerato stared out the massive window to their left. The aperture was completely filled with the image of Tealfirth. "We don't have much time," he stated, as if anyone needed reminding.

"Mum, it's getting really hot," said Helen, as she walked into the antechamber of the Council Chamber. Ahead, a large, wooden door towered above them, cracked with time and worn from the touch of a million hands.

"I hope Mendel is behind that door," whispered Cimerato.

"Did you see that?" said Ephie. She'd jumped back from the window.

"See what?" demanded Jal, still watching the Mertol closely in case it made any threatening moves.

"I seed it too!" cried Wee Joe.

"What did you see, Joe?" Jean turned Wee Joe to face her.

"Mum," said Wee Joe, "it was a dwinosaur!"

Cimerato squinted out the window, the sun burning hot on his face. "There's only one creature that could scale the sheer wall of a citadel like this."

"That's what I've been trying to tell you," muttered Jal. "A Hedra Raptor made it through the gates."

"And it's just beaten us to the Council Chamber," sighed Cimerato.

***

Outside, on his balcony, Dendralon watched as the Raptor made its way up the citadel's smooth wall. The beast climbed the flawless alabaster surface, using its talons and sharp elbow hooks. The Raptor still held the crystal in its mouth, but Dendralon had watched the beast slip twice already during its climb, both times almost dropping the precious cargo.

Dendralon leaned over the parapet and reached down towards the Raptor's feathered jaws. "Come to me, my beauty. Only a few feet more. Bring it to me!" He urged the Raptor upwards, steadfastly ignoring the screams of the Hedra beyond the closed gates. He had to focus on the third crystal.

In the spiral staircase that wound its way up the great wall of the citadel, James wondered if they were getting any closer to the secret door that led to the Council Chamber. His mum was panting heavily, and had just opened her mouth to complain, when they all came to a halt. A smooth, black granite block marked the end of their climb.

"Now what?" moaned Cathy.

James sensed his mum was about to launch into one of her diatribes. "Mum, you're not feeling panicky in here, are you?" he asked, knowing this would distract her for a bit. It was strange that his mum had never once freaked out during her journey up the enclosed spiral staircase.

Cathy stopped mid-sentence and gripped the narrow walls. "Never even thought about that until now. My claustrophobia hasn't really bothered me since those little yellow imps gave me that stuff…"

"The Lugpus," Craig said. "Do you want a little more?" He fumbled in his pocket.

"No, I do not!" snapped Cathy.

Mendel splashed loudly. "We have more pressing issues to deal with!"

"I really don't like you, Mendel," said Cathy.

"Mum, I think he's trying to remember the spell that opens the hidden door into the Council Chamber," said James.

"And to do that, I need a little quiet," grumbled Mendel.

Eethan formed a puckish smile and placed a finger on his thin lips.

"Don't you shoosh me." Cathy gave Eethan a quick slap.

"EEeeeeeH!"

"Please," insisted Mendel, I need some peace to concentrate!" Mendel's googly eye appeared against the plastic window of the brandy barrel. It glared at them, crossly.

As they stood waiting, trapped in the stairwell, James

realised that the drone of the dying sun was growing louder and louder. And now that they were standing still, he could hear terrible screaming from outside. It sounded as if the Hedra were in trouble. "Have they taken the city?" he asked. But no one could give him an answer.

"I remember!" Mendel said suddenly. "James, put your hand on the obelisk."

Once more James felt faint as the knock, knock, knocking sensation began to build. He had to fight to keep from passing out...

29 The End of Athelstone

Out on the balcony of the citadel, Dendralon heard someone or something trying to force open the door of the Council Chamber. "Come closer, my pet. Be quick!" He almost had the chain in his hands...but the Raptor slid back down again, nearly falling off the citadel altogether. It hissed in frustration and sunk its hooks and claws back into the smooth alabaster, determined to heave itself up.

Mendel is close by, thought Dendralon. He could sense him. He leaned over the balcony to grab for the crystal but he still couldn't reach it. "Keep climbing! I must go back inside and defend the Council Chamber!" He spun round, cursing his dilemma.

***

The Mertol slammed its fifteen-foot bulk against the massive wooden door of the citadel's Council Chamber.

"Again!" cried Jal. "All of us this time."

As one, they ran at the door as hard as they could, slamming into the ancient timber. The door shook so roughly that several bolts sprang from the hinges and clattered onto the stone floor.

"That includes you two." Jal pointed to Michael and Ephie, who were busy chatting. "It's hardly the time for sweet talk."

Michael flushed crimson, then joined Jal, Cimerato and the Mertol in their effort to break down the massive door.

***

Back inside the Council Chamber, Dendralon headed toward the throne where the two blue crystals weighed down one side of a pair of giant, gleaming scales. Sitting snugly in their predestined slots, their cerulean glow threw long shadows across the seats.

In front of the throne, a patch of floor spread out in a semicircle from the edge of its ivory base towards the Council members' seats and the ancient, wooden door behind.

This strange stone semicircle of reptilian scales was, in fact, a Hedra vision pool. It shimmered now, alternating between dull, grey stone and the vivid, blistering surface of Tealfirth. Angry blood-reds and bile-yellows oozed between the fissures that lined the sun's blackened surface. Huge flares exploded then disappeared back beneath Tealfirth's tortured crust.

As Dendralon checked the crystals, a series of ear-splitting screams echoed from the vision pool, cutting through the air like the screeches of a million demons.

"The end is only moments away," declared Dendralon. He looked across to the main door of the Chamber. It buckled violently. He resisted using his magic on it, not wanting to waste a drop of energy when he was so close to creating the gateway. He had a feeling he was going to need all his power to operate the Magic Scales. Then he trailed his long fingers over the surface of the Talisman.

"No, I need that crystal!" he told himself, glancing at the door one more time before racing back through the curtain to the balcony.

He came face to face with the Raptor. It stood on the balcony's tiled floor, tilting its head to the side and snorting in his face. It snapped at him.

"It's me. Your master…" Dendralon's words didn't seem to register with the panting beast. It snapped at him, still holding the crystal in its jaws. The dark wizard tried to retrieve the crystal, but the Raptor barged past him, into the Chamber.

"Come back here!" Dendralon demanded, turning to follow.

***

"Wwwhedralanwwwa!" James placed his hand on the cold obelisk again and said the word one more time, with all the command he could muster. "Wwwhedralanwwwa!"

With a whoosh, the smooth, black granite slid upwards and the startled group fell straight into the Council Chamber.

A black-cloaked figure turned in surprise.

The stench of King Athelstone's decomposing skin instantly caught James's throat. He barely recognised Dendralon. He tried to imagine him wearing a pair of sunglasses back in the Drumfintley village shop, where they'd first met a few days earlier, but he just couldn't see any resemblance.

Hackles raised, Bero growled at the gruesome creature. Dendralon clawed a piece of Athelstone's rotting flesh from his scaled face and threw it at Bero's feet. "There's your great King, Mendel. It's too late for him. And now it's too late for you."

James spied the Talisman and gasped as Dendralon snatched it from his belt.

At the same moment, something ran out of the shadows behind Dendralon. It was a terrifying beast—half dinosaur, half bird. A few feet from the dark wizard, it hunkered down and screeched, revealing a thick golden chain hanging from its jaws. Distracted, Dendralon turned to face it. It hissed at him and cried out like a tortured seal. It seemed to be talking to the wizard.

"The last crystal is not yet in his grasp." Mendel's voice sounded louder and more forceful than James had ever heard it before. He felt the knocking sensation build in his head and knew he would have to stand and fight. Mendel needed him to be strong. But before he could push Mendel's spell from his lips, the wooden door at the far end of the Council Chamber exploded inward, showering the crouching Raptor with splinters. It yelped in pain.

Through the dust, James saw that a long shard of wood

had pierced the Raptor's thigh. Its jagged point dripped black blood onto the cobbled floor.

In less than a heartbeat, Dendralon jerked the shard from the Raptor's thigh and spun round towards the main door. He ducked behind the snarling beast.

In the confusion, Mendel failed to complete his spell. He pushed a googly eye against the plastic window of his barrel.

The Raptor stopped abruptly, its feathers flicking up on end. It had just seen something it didn't like – the Mertol stepping through the remnants of the shattered door.

James stared at the beast standing in front of Cimerato and Jal. Its matted orange hair was hanging down from its arms like a badly fitting angora jumper. It was outside this beast's cave that his father's fleecy jacket had been found. James's stomach heaved and his head swam with visions of the Herdigup and the doomed Hedra soldier, Garazar. Had it all been a cruel trick? The jacket, the compass...?

"Baacckkk!"

Jumping at least ten rows of the Chamber's seats, the Mertol slammed against the Raptor, slashing down with his claws. The Raptor screamed under the onslaught, but managed to push the heavy Mertol off with a series of violent kicks that cut into the bigger creature's ape-like belly. Falling back, the Mertol cried out and clutched its stomach. Blood seeped through its filthy, orange fingers as it swayed back to avoid the Raptor's snapping jaws. With another leap, the Mertol twisted in mid-air and kicked itself off the wall of the Chamber to land on the Raptor's back. Plunging his fangs deep into the Raptor's neck, the Mertol shook its ugly head.

The Raptor gave a strangled cry and the heavy golden chain that held the crystal slipped from its mouth, clattering onto the cobbled floor.

Seeing the crystal fall, Dendralon raced toward the battling duo. As he ran, the Manimal King's long, black hair slipped from the Hedra wizard's scalp. Sloughed and tattered, it caught on his collar and hung limply like a tattered shawl.

Seeing that Dendralon was distracted, James and Craig slipped under the wooden seats and crawled after him, weapons drawn.

As they neared the battling monsters, it was Craig who spied the blue crystal lying on the ground first. As the two beasts continued to knock each other about, he hunkered toward the glowing gem, the old timber seats disintegrating into clouds of flying splinters around him.

James followed a few feet behind his friend, drawing back when one of the Raptor's claws nearly caught his sword arm.

Craig reached out to grab the crystal, but the Mertol stepped backward to catch his balance and Craig had to roll out of the way of the giant foot.

A second later, James actually had the cool, smooth crystal in his hand, but he had to drop it when the Raptor pounced once again, missing him by inches.

"Get the third crystal, James!" Mendel kept shouting at him, not helping in the least.

"What do you think I'm *trying* to do?" James yelled back. Groping for the crystal, he sensed a dark presence moving his way. He glanced back to see Dendralon crawling towards him, now a hideous ghoul, half Hedra, half corpse. James shuddered. Had the dark wizard heard Mendel's voice too?

Bero dashed between the slatted seats, distracting Dendralon, who roared at the dog then lunged forward.

James could only watch as Dendralon snatched up the crystal.

He had to stop him! But the Mertol and the Raptor were still fighting. He and the others were trapped as the two beasts snarled and slashed at each other.

The end came suddenly. With a violent twist, the Mertol snapped the Raptor's feathered neck. With an ape-like roar of victory the tattered giant let the bird-like corpse fall dead to the floor.

Before Cimerato and Jal could charge, the Hedra wizard appeared behind the throne and laughed in triumph. Hearing the chilling sound, everyone stopped where they were.

James steadied himself against a cold stone pillar. The Mertol clutched at his bleeding stomach. Craig had found Bero's collar. Jal held back behind Cimerato, who looked ready to attack.

Thinking the worst was over, the rest of the Drumfintley group stepped carefully through the shattered doorway. Michael held Ephie close and stared blankly at the rows of stars and roses that adorned the ceiling. "It's like a harvest festival carved in stone," he said in a daze.

Cathy edged round and caught Michael's arm in a vice-like grip. "Shut up!"

Glancing between Dendralon and Cathy, Michael clamped his mouth shut.

Unsure what to do, James began to walk forward, through the debris. He raised his magic sword and looked Dendralon straight in the eye.

The wizard peeled the last remnants of Athelstone's skin from his face. It resisted, at first, then gave way with a loud slurp. It dropped to the floor with a thunk, revealing the wizard's true features.

30 The Fall

"Deceiver!" Cimerato cried, unable to hold back any longer. He rushed across the Chamber toward the Hedra wizard, but stopped in his tracks when he saw that the dark wizard was holding the third crystal up to the light.

"Marvellous, isn't it?" Dendralon sneered. "Here we are at the end of our world and I have the only thing that can get us out of here in time. So stop where you are!" He stared at Cimerato and then James. "Do not take another step!" Wielding the crystal like a weapon, he edged back toward the giant crystal Scales behind the throne.

James could now see the recess where the Hedra crystal would fit perfectly. He finally understood what the wizard meant to do with it. At the same moment, James spotted Eethan. The little, blue man had climbed along the roof timbers and now hung above the Dendralon's head.

The Hedra wizard must have sensed his presence, as he drew the Talisman from his belt and jabbed it upward.

A pulse of energy shot from the tip of the Yukplug horn and knocked Eethan down. With a thud Eethan fell at the wizard's feet.

Dendralon kicked the little blue man's limp body. "Thanks to you, my Hedra kin will never make it through the gates in time." He turned and pointed to the floor in front of the throne. "Look." The image of the dying sun appeared, pulsing like an over-inflated balloon about to pop. "We only have a few moments," he growled. "I suggest you let me continue with my spell if you want to live a little longer."

Dismissing them, he turned to go back behind the throne. With a roar, the Mertol leapt forward, but with a simple flick of the Talisman, Dendralon sent the beast flying backwards into what remained of the Chamber door.

James knew what he had to do. With a burst of power, he hurled his magical red sword at Dendralon. As it flew, it seemed to gather speed, then it sank deep into the wizard's left arm.

Dendralon spun round and everyone ducked. "Sticklebreath!" Dendralon's angry voice echoed across the Chamber. "The Peck boy has just threatened us all."

There was an uneasy silence, then a strange shuffling began. James gasped as all the wooden shards and splinters strewn over the floor of the Chamber came alive. Twitching at first, they moved together, forming three separate piles. Quick as a wink, the piles rose from the floor, each forming into a separate monster.

Dendralon pointed at James. "Kill him!"

Jerking forward, the twisted wooden skeletons stumbled at first, then turned to face James.

Jal and Cimerato dashed to block two, but the third went straight for James.

Cathy rushed over to protect her son.

The stick creatures came at them with their splintered fingers. James yanked his mum back behind him, unable to do anything else. His sword was still lodged in Dendralon's arm.

Before Jal could lift his sword, one of the creatures thrust three long, serrated fingers straight through Jal's chest plate.

Jal managed to push the thing back, but fell hard onto his knees, disbelief in his yellow eyes.

Cimerato dived to his left and cut through Jal's attacker's wooden shoulder. The creature tumbled lifeless at Jal's feet.

With lightning speed, one of the remaining shard-men slashed out at Cimerato's neck. He jumped back, then staggered, off balance and exposed. The wooden man hacked down with his knife-like fingers, but Cimerato regained his stance, side-stepped, and brought his cutlass down hard, cleaving its wooden head in two.

The third shard-man was still focused on James and Cathy. "Get down, Mum!" James cried, bracing himself for the blow. The wooden monster was bringing his jagged fist down to smash in James's head, but his hand froze in mid-air. Craig's magic spear was now poking through the wooden monster's body, shooting out bright green sparks that crackled up through its neck. Mouthing silent curses, it dropped to the floor and promptly fell apart.

With a frustrated frown, Dendralon lay the Talisman on the floor, waved both his hands, and chanted something in his Hedra tongue. A strange purple mist spread out from the Talisman to form a shimmering curtain.

"It's a force field!" shouted Mendel.

James's temples began to throb as Mendel attempted to destroy the shield forming round the wizard. "Wwwwaywwwormwfieldw!" As the strange word bubbled from James's lips, a flash shot out from Bero and hit the invisible wall like a firebomb.

Bang!

The wall shimmered and split for a second but soon reformed.

Dendralon narrowed his eyes and fixed his malevolent gaze on Bero. "I will skin you alive."

James whispered sharply to Craig, "He thinks that Bero is Mendel."

"He what?" Craig's eyes widened. Both boys ducked down and tried to coax Bero away from the dark wizard, hideous in his rage.

"Your powers are still no match for mine, Mendel," Dendralon boomed. "Do you think for one moment that I intend to let you live? We, the Hedra, built these walls, dug the wells, carved the foundations of this city from the bedrock beneath us. I will never relinquish this city to your kind. I have only to place this last crystal into the Magic Scales of Gwendral and we will escape this holocaust. After that, you will all die. As will any who do not bow to me as their god!"

The bitter words made James shudder, but what he saw next was worse. Near to the shattered door, Ephie and Cimerato were crouched beside Jal, trying to make him sit up. But it was no use. The Hedra's head slipped back onto the floor, a gasp spilling from his lips.

Enraged, Cimerato gave a shout and ran at the force field, his sword drawn, but he only slammed into the invisible curtain, falling backwards over the remaining chairs.

"Oh, please. No!" It was Jean. She pointed a quivering finger at something she'd just noticed on Dendralon's side of the force field.

James followed her gaze and saw that Wee Joe was standing beside Dendralon, trapped on the other side of the shimmering barrier.

"Joe!" Jean cried. She looked close to collapse. "Come over to Mum!"

Dendralon glanced down at the little three-year-old boy. "Ha!" he shouted triumphantly. "Thanks for the snack!" With a ruthless grin, he turned again to the Magic Scales and adjusted the mechanism.

Wee Joe, ignored for the moment, reached for the pretty golden chain that hung over the edge of the throne and pulled hard. The chain slid off and fell, along with the crystal, onto the hard marble floor.

The large blue crystal shattered and some of the pieces fell into the vision pool's blistering picture of the sun.

"Oopsie!" Wee Joe bleated.

James felt his mouth drop open.

Helpless, Dendralon turned and screamed. "NO!" He reached for Wee Joe's neck, his sharp claws extended.

"Leave him alone!" Cathy demanded, pounding on the force field.

Dendralon ignored her, swooping in on the boy. But before he could reach Wee Joe, a bright blue flash shone out from nearby, blinding him. He turned and slashed out with his sharpened nails.

James's head pounded as he blurted out Mendel's spells, "Wwwwaywwwormwfieldw!"

A bolt of green light shot from the barrel and slammed into the force field like a battering ram. Dendralon's protective shield shimmered, wavered, then fell. They all ran towards Dendralon, hoping to save Wee Joe.

Although partially blinded by the blue flash, Dendralon still managed to catch hold of Wee Joe's arm. He picked up the three-year-old and lifted him high above his head with his good arm. "We will all die now, thanks to this pathetic little runt!" Dendralon winced as James's sword seemed to bury itself deeper into his arm, but he did not falter. He held Wee Joe over the blazing vision pool.

The sun, Tealfirth, sang a single, high-pitched note as Dendralon screamed, "Mendel!" Having caught sight of Bero, he dropped Wee Joe at the edge of the vision pool and thrust his fist at the dog. Light shot from his reptilian fingers and blasted into Bero. The collar round his neck snapped and the barrel fell to the ground as Bero was drawn forward, yelping in pain.

Seeing their chance, James and Cathy rushed forward and snatched Wee Joe from the edge of the vision pool.

Jean grabbed her son's arm and pulled him close.

Dendralon picked up the Talisman and held it like a dagger, poised to strike Bero, who was sliding ever closer.

Taking his chance, Cimerato bolted in from the side and knocked the Talisman into the vision pool. He pounced on Dendralon, his sword flying. But the wizard again struck out with his fist, sending the Manimal sprawling onto the floor.

Bero scrambled to his feet. He pushed himself forward, helped by the impetus of Dendralon's spell, growling and barking at the wizard. But James could see that he was old again – his fur dull, his frail back legs dragging behind him.

Unseen by Dendralon, Eethan stirred. Cautiously, he crept over to the empty cup meant for the third crystal and climbed inside. The fulcrum of the ivory scales pitched downward.

The movement caught Dendralon's eye and he whipped round. As he did, Bero jumped and latched onto the wizard's wounded arm, clamping his teeth down hard. The force of the blow knocked Dendralon towards the vision pool. Cimerato stabbed upwards from the ground. But Dendralon managed to slash down with even more force, knocking the Manimal blade to the side. Dendralon teetered on the edge of the vision pool, Bero still clinging to his arm, James's sword glowing.

Cimerato screamed, and kicked the dark wizard as hard as he could.

Only then did Dendralon fall backwards into the vision pool, his black cloak already ablaze from the intense heat.

Bero let go and twisted round. He managed to grip the side of the vision pool with his front paws but his back legs dangled down into the furnace below. He whined at Craig and panted as the heat threatened to consume him.

"Bero!" screamed Craig. "Hang on, boy! Please...!"

As Craig shot forward, a scaled claw came out of nowhere and grabbed hold of Bero's tail.

With a grip like a vice, Dendralon jerked the old dog towards him.

"Bero!" Craig wailed.

Bero howled, only once, before Dendralon's tortured voice echoed up from the inferno. "Die with me, Mendel..."

Cimerato caught hold of Craig.

James stared at the spot where Bero had been, then

watched in stunned disbelief as the vision pool turned as black as night.

Behind them, sitting in the little hollow meant for the third crystal, Eethan was actually glowing. A bright iridescent blue radiated from his sparkling skin. Strangely, his weight exactly matched the two crystals on the Magic Scales. For an instant, his whole body shone as bright as any sun.

A thundering noise forced everyone to their knees. The floor fell away beneath them and they all screamed.

As Tealfirth imploded, the room began to spin ever faster.

James's strong link with Mendel allowed him to see everything that was happening, as if looking down from a great height. What he saw was both terrible and awesome...

Outside the city walls, the Hedra looked up at the sun one last time before instant obliteration. All conscious life on the planet had been aware of its imminent demise for a few seconds at most, then, with no time for regret or pain, everything simply stopped. In a heartbeat, Denthan was covered in an all-consuming fire; seas instantly steamed and boiled, mountains were swept clear of trees and earth. The whole planet shuddered and cracked all the way to its core. For a moment, its mantle expanded like a balloon, then Denthan exploded. Along with its five sister planets, it simply turned to dust and disappeared, sucked into the black hole that had once been Tealfirth.

James shuddered as he watched a trillion zillion tons of stardust pour through the abyss. Tears rolled down his face as an infinity of souls appeared before him then flew away to an infinity of destinations.

He hadn't wanted to, but he'd seen and felt everything.

31 Almost Home

As James slowly opened his eyes, blue flashes danced across his field of vision. Everything was still blurred, but the most noticeable thing was the complete and utter silence. It was simply amazing after the raging chaos and James didn't want it to stop. He didn't feel scared or frightened or upset; he felt comforted, peaceful and calm. The sensation held him, cradled him, and he wondered if this was what being dead was like. Then he felt a cold tear roll down his cheek.

A small voice interrupted the stillness. "Are we in heaven, Mum?" asked Helen. She yawned and rubbed her eyes.

Jean sat up and touched her daughter's arm. "I don't think so, darling."

"We're not dead," said James, quickly wiping his face, "but I'm not sure why," he added. He looked round for the small plastic barrel.

Hearing voices, Michael sat up and slid over toward Ephie and Jean. "God preserve us and keep us." Michael mumbled another small prayer as he gazed round the half-demolished Council Chamber. He looked like a startled hare and James felt himself smile.

Cimerato was still lying on his back, close to the vision pool, just a few yards from Wee Joe.

Craig hadn't moved from the spot where he'd seen Bero disappear. His head was bowed and his body was still shaking with long, deep sobs. "Why did he do that? Why?" Tears covered Craig's freckled face.

The realization of what had just happened hit James with a jolt. "I'm sorry, Craig." He looked into his friend's bleary eyes and tried to hold back his own emotions. "Bero saved us all. He was very brave." But there was no consoling Craig. James felt awkward, unsure whether to hug his best friend or leave him be.

Craig saved him the bother. Edging back from the vision pool, he moved as far as he could from the group.

Michael crawled over to where the little plastic barrel sat, about five feet from the vision pool. "Mendel, are you in there?" he asked. "Where are we?"

Close by, Cimerato grimaced as he stretched his arm. He nodded toward James. "You can hear Mendel when others cannot. Is he still here?"

James stepped over to the barrel and picked it up. He peered inside the tiny window. "Mendel...? Everyone wants to know where we are."

"We are where we should be, of course," replied Mendel, matter-of-factly, as if he'd planned every single moment of their adventure and known the outcome all along. "Thanks to Eethan and Dendralon, the whole city has been transported back to Earth – back to Drumfintley, to be specific."

"We're back home?" said James, the words trailing slowly from his lips.

"Drumfintley?" echoed Cathy.

Jean Harrison bristled. "What! We can't possibly bring these, these..." Jean looked away from Cimerato. "Well, this whole..." – she waved her hand round her head – "...*thing* back to Drumfintley. I mean..."

Cathy's eyes blazed. "You mean, what will the neighbours think? That's what you mean, isn't that right?"

James flushed with embarrassment. The last few days had not changed his mum's demeanour. Nothing ever would. She couldn't help it. She was fine for a few hours, even a whole day sometimes, but eventually the anger would erupt. It was always there, smouldering. Nobody ever dared to tell her that her behaviour was unacceptable. Not Mendel, certainly not his dad.

With a resigned sigh, James decided that his mum's anger was a necessary part of her; the power inside that made her unique and strong. People found her hard work, but that was mostly because they envied her, he decided. His mum said all the things they felt but never dared to say themselves.

As Jean gathered her kids about her, James saw something flash in his mum's eyes. He could tell she was thinking about his dad.

Cathy's eyes glazed as she looked straight at him. "Where is he when we need him? Where, James?"

James's mouth fell open, but nothing came out. He prayed that his dad hadn't been left behind on Denthan.

Father Michael issued a loud, relieved sigh. "We're finally home! Thank God." He turned to Cathy and beamed. She scowled back at the vicar, and James knew that the moment between his mum and himself had passed.

Michael's smile faded as he looked over at James. "Can I ask him something?"

"You mean Mendel?" said James.

Michael nodded. "Yes, yes, if that's alright. It's kind of personal."

A few bubbles trickled over Mendel's little window. "Yes, Father. Only James and you can hear me for the moment."

"He can do that," explained James, in a whisper. "I forget how, but—"

Mendel sighed. "It's called 'inter-atomic selectivity'. I have explained it all before."

James looked at Michael and shrugged.

Michael flinched. "Um, yes. Um, where did all those creatures go? I mean after the end of Denthan—I'm assuming the planet is gone."

Mendel sighed and pushed a golden eye against his little window. "They went wherever they believed they would go."

"What do you mean?" asked Michael, lifting the barrel up

to his face.

"If you believe something strongly enough," Mendel continued, "it often becomes your own, personal truth."

"The truth! What *is* the truth?" whispered Michael, his voice wavering.

"The truth is what you believe it is," Mendel replied calmly. "But remember, just because I believe something doesn't make it your truth, or anyone else's for that matter. It's just my truth. For example, you might see true beauty where no one else sees it. If so, that is your truth."

"Ah...I see," said Michael, glancing over at Ephie.

James thought it all sounded very complicated.

Michael stood up and took Ephie's hand. "Well, at least we're all safe now."

"We're not all safe..." Craig interjected, looking forlorn.

The Mertol's matted, red back emerged from the debris as though Craig's words had conjured him up. As it turned to face them, its cold, black eyes blinked and its pitted face rippled in strange patterns. The wounded beast faltered, then dropped down onto one knee, clutching its stomach.

"Stay back, and don't threaten it!" Cimerato's hand went to his sword hilt.

James watched in trepidation as the beast issued a muffled "Baacckkk!" before slumping against the wall nearest to the shattered door. The Mertol closed its eyes and Cimerato sheathed his sword.

"I want to go howme!" Wee Joe's voice echoed round the Chamber, cutting through the tension.

"And so you shall, Joe. So you shall," said Mendel.

Judging by the looks on everyone's faces, James could tell that Mendel could be heard by all of them. They all began asking questions at once.

"Shhhh!" the wizard scolded. "What I'm about to say is very important." He splashed in his barrel. "First I want you to gather round and look into the vision pool. You see, it's not just a picture, it's a portal."

As the others shuffled toward the lip of the pool, James felt Mendel home in on his mind alone. "Stay here a moment. I need to tell you something, just you."

James stopped where he was. "Go on," he whispered.

"The pool is how Dendralon managed to steal your father's things. He probably sent a Herdigup to do it."

"You mean the compass and his jacket? But why?" James spoke quietly, a bit of hope beginning to burgeon inside him.

"Dendralon knew where Sleven met his death and put two and two together. He probably watched through the vision pool as you confronted Sleven on your roof. He retrieved some of your father's things in order to lead us on a merry dance. He must have read your thoughts and sensed your pain when you held the crystal up to the light in your bedroom."

"You mean the time you shouted at me," James whispered.

"Yes," admitted Mendel, "but I suspect that Craig probably toyed with the crystal even before that. Dendralon would have been able to read your thoughts, or Craig's, whenever either of you held the crystal up to the light."

"Really?" said James, a bit louder than he meant to. He actually saw the goldfish give a little nod behind the plastic window of the barrel. "So if that was all a trick, where's my dad? He wasn't in Denthan, was he? Don't tell me he's dead!"

There was an uncomfortable silence in James's head as Mendel hesitated. James could see that the others were growing restless at the edge of the vision pool.

"He's not dead, James," Mendel finally replied.

James tensed. "How can you be sure?"

"You must join the others now," Mendel directed, refusing to answer.

When James got there, the vision pool was mostly dark, though there were a few points of light flashing across its surface. When he peered closer, he realised that he was seeing moorland below them. "Are we flying?"

"Hovering," Mendel corrected.

"A whole city?" whispered Helen.

"There's something down there," said Cimerato.

Ephie shuffled in beside the Manimal captain and said, "Torches! I think they're torches!"

"Yes, and look!" James cried, pointing down at the dim landscape below. "It's the Jesus Rocks!"

Cimerato's cat-like pupils dilated suspiciously. "I have never seen torches like those!"

Craig joined James. "Look, Craig! Do you see that person down there?"

"I do!" Michael answered before Craig had a chance. "It's... it's..." He peered down at the scene. "It's Archie!"

"Archie MacNulty," whispered Craig.

James was amazed when the small figure below looked straight up at them, though he didn't seem to see them.

"Why is he standing between those two policemen?" James's eye-brows lifted.

Michael gasped and tried to push forward. "He's handcuffed to them!"

"Don't go too close to the edge," said Mendel. "If you fall without my help..."

Everyone took one step back from the vision pool.

"Don't forget, we've been missing from the village for the best part of a week," Ephie reminded everybody. "They probably think we've all been murdered."

Cathy spoke up. "Let me get this straight. You mean to say that Gwendral, which must cover at least two square miles, is floating above the Jesus Rocks and nobody can see us?" Cathy's voice sounded derisive.

"Three and a half square miles would be more accurate," corrected Mendel. "Don't forget that we have one and a half thousand Yeltans and, I hope and pray, another fifteen thousand Manimals in the city with us as well."

"Not to mention a forty-foot white dragon," added James, remembering Whindril.

Craig had been very quiet through all this. James saw Jean move over beside him. "I'm sorry, Son, but Bero probably saved us all from that...that thing."

James felt his own tears well up as Craig pushed his wet face into his mum's shabby mohair cardigan and sobbed.

With his friend crying beside him, and seeing Bruce Moor again— the last place his dad had been seen alive—James, too, started to weep. He couldn't stop himself. "I'm sorry we took Bero with us, Craig!" His shoulders shook and his chest heaved. "It's all my fault. I'm sorry!"

Without answering, Craig pulled away from his mum and moved over to the ivory throne.

James watched him for a moment but was distracted by a scuffling behind him. He thought—hoped—it might be his own mum come to comfort him.

But when he turned, he saw a Yeltan standing in the doorway of the Chamber. "Garlon!" James quickly wiped his face on his sleeve and cleared his throat. "Is everybody alright?"

"Most of us are fine, but..." The Yeltan's voice trailed off into a deep sigh.

"Where's Landris?" James asked, but as he did, he saw the answer in Garlon's deep blue eyes. "Oh no, Garlon. How...?"

"My father died a hero's death." Garlon bowed his head and moved over to the vision pool.

James looked down at Garlon and whispered, "Bero did too. He saved us all."

Many more footsteps filled the antechamber and James saw Lord Eldane pick his way through the broken seats. "Son!" he cried, clapping Cimerato on the back. The old Manimal was flushed and out of breath, but obviously happy to see his son.

"Elgry and the soldiers from the lake met our people walking back to the city. They didn't feel safe in the tunnels with all that shaking and rumbling going on."

"How many made it?" breathed Cimerato.

"More than ten thousand."

"What about Mother?" he asked reluctantly, as though afraid of the answer.

"She is safe," his father reassured him.

Mendel cleared his throat, his yellow fins beating against the little window in the barrel. "James, only you can hear me. Listen carefully. I am going to return us all to Drumfintley. All, that is, except the people and creatures of Denthan. There is another world that will suit them better than yours. Eethan will know what to do. More importantly, I think it would be best for everyone concerned if I relieved them of their memories."

James couldn't believe it. "What?"

"Of Denthan, of this whole adventure," Mendel continued.

"No!" James felt everyone's eyes upon him after his sudden exclamation.

"Shhh!" Mendel's voice was like a whisper floating round inside James's head. "It's for the best. Not you and Craig, of course not. You've both proved yourselves and...well, there may be a chance of me returning to my own form on your world, just a small chance. I may yet need your help. The rest of the group, however, will be better off if they return without these memories."

"I need to tell Craig," said James.

"Of course. But be quick about it," said Mendel.

Craig was slumped against Athelstone's throne, wiping his nose with his sleeve.

"Craig, I need to talk to you."

Craig looked up.

"Mendel is going to erase everyone's memory, apart from ours," said James.

"What do you mean? Erase everyone's memory?"

"Basically, they'll forget everything that happened in Denthan, the whole lot. But, you and me, we won't forget a thing," explained James.

"What's the point of that? What about Bero? How do I explain that to my mum?" James looked down at the brandy barrel in his hands. "Mendel?"

"It's for the best, Craig," said Mendel.

James stepped back as Craig let go of Athelstone's throne and pulled himself to his feet. "Mendel, you can't just wipe their memories of Denthan. I don't want them to forget the whole thing. I don't want them to forget what Bero did."

James noticed that Craig's sharply whispered words had reached Father Michael. The Reverend hurried over to the boys.

"Please, Mendel," Michael pleaded, kneeling down in front of the barrel. "I don't want to forget. I'm in love, and so is Ephie, and we might never get a chance like this again. Besides, there are things I believe in now that I never could have before."

Mendel made a little splash. "Sorry, Michael, but..."

"Remember you told me about truth?" pressed Michael. "This, and everything that has happened to me in the last five days, has become my own personal truth."

"We'll see," sighed Mendel. "Just get the rest of the villagers ready. You'll all have to jump into the vision pool when I say so, understood?"

James wondered what Mendel would do.

"I mean it, Mendel," said Michael. "I need to know what happened."

Father Michael looked almost angry as he motioned to the others. "Gather round, now. Mendel wants us to stand right here." James stuffed the brown plastic barrel into his battered, green rucksack and closed his eyes. "When Mendel says jump, we all have to jump into the vision pool," he said.

Beside him, Helen held her mother's arm and pulled Wee Joe in close. "But it's a long way down. We'll get hurt," she sniffed.

"You can either trust Mendel or stay here in Gwendral," said James, "It's your choice."

With a mixture of shrugs and scared expressions, they all nodded back at him. They seemed to have resigned themselves to the absurdity of the situation.

Mendel splashed about inside the rucksack. "Please hurry! We have to be quick."

Hearing the urgency in Mendel's voice, James glanced over at the balanced Scales where Eethan had transformed himself. He noticed the blue glow falter for a second. "Mendel, just tell us when to jump." James looked round the room. "Goodbye, Cimerato!" he called. "Bye, Garlon." He smiled at Lord Eldane, then his eyes landed on the wounded Mertol. He offered the creature a small nod. "Goodbye, and thanks for taking care of that dinosaur."

"Baacckkk..." the Mertol replied weakly, its cheek holes opening and closing in unison.

"Ssss," a voice hissed from behind him, "Goodbye, boys!"

Every one of the Drumfintley group turned round to look. Jal, the giant Hedra warrior, was trying to sit up. James twisted away from the vision pool, but Cathy caught hold of his shirt and heaved him back into position. "We've no time, James."

James squinted round anxiously. He saw something that resembled a smile forming on Jal's lips.

"I've had worse, boy," said the Hedra.

James grinned. "Get yourself well, Jal." He felt better seeing Cimerato move over to Jal and help steady him. He was, after all, the last of his kind now.

Feeling Mendel's magic, James called out, "Get ready!" The Drumfintley crowd edged closer to the vision pool and looked down. Instinctively, they joined hands.

Predictably, Cathy fidgeted. "For goodness sake, let's get this over with!"

Mendel's voice was loud in everyone's head. "Jump!"

What they'd all experienced and seen in the last few days was completely beyond imagination, so being told to leap into a pool within a huge alien city, hovering about one hundred feet above Bruce Moor, actually sounded pretty normal.

Without hesitation, they all jumped into the abyss.

32 Wee Joe's Secret

James shivered in the cold morning mist that tumbled across Bruce moor. But the chill wasn't the worst of it. In front of them, a search party, consisting of sniffer-dogs, policemen and a very wet-looking Archie MacNulty, were stretched out in a straight line across the moor.

While the others were coming round, James reached into his rucksack and felt for his blue inhaler. His back against the cold stone, he inhaled the fine, white mist and held it in his lungs for as long as he could.

One of the searchers called out, "I've got something!"

James coughed out the rest of the mist, then tentatively peered round the Jesus Rock as he crouched. Not far off, Constable Watt held up a plastic bag that contained something resembling a hardened lump of dog poo. "We might be able to match this with the ones we found in the Harrison's back garden."

"Wather you than me, Sonny," said Archie MacNulty, pulling on his handcuffs, which were attached to Sergeant Carr. The action made the sergeant glare at MacNulty. The hatred between the two men could never have been more obvious.

"Archie?" Michael called out. The line stopped. Michael put his hand on James's shoulder before moving forward. "Archie, it's me!"

Archie pulled on his chain, almost yanking the sergeant off his feet. "Weverend?"

"Keep still!" said Carr, but when he saw Father Michael appearing out of the mist like a ghost, he juddered to a halt.

Dazed and unsteady on their feet, the rest of the tattered group followed the vicar. With each person's appearance, the sergeant's eyes widened even further.

Wee Joe and Helen were shivering, so Jean pulled them close into her matted cardigan.

Cathy gave the policemen a withering stare. "Well don't just stand there gawping, get these kids some coats!"

Five or six policemen jumped to attention, pulling little silver foil bags from their day-glow rucksacks as they ran toward the dishevelled group.

"Are you alright, Madam?" one of them asked Ephie. She looked a bit worse for wear.

"Absolutely fine, thank you," answered Ephie.

Archie MacNulty stared at her, and then looked over at the vicar. "You war holding hands wif Miss Blake, favar."

Father Michael only smiled.

The officer in charge looked James straight in the eye. "Can you tell me where you've been, boy?"

James pointed at Ephie. He was just a kid. There was no reason why he should be the one to come up with a quick answer. Ephie looked, in turn, at Father Michael.

"Um, we were walking, officer," answered Father Michael. "We've been walking and um..."

"Yes, that's right," Ephie took over. "We've been walking, just got a bit lost."

"Lost? You've been missing for *five days*," blurted Sergeant Carr. Oddly enough, he looked disappointed.

"Looks like MacNulty's off the hook, Sarge," said the young constable, sniffing smugly.

Sergeant Carr's eyes blazed as he turned on the constable. "Shut up, Watt. Just shut up!"

"Yes, well..." said Father Michael. "It's certainly not Archie's fault that we got lost, is it?"

"Are you all okay, Mrs Harrison?" the officer in charge asked, as he approached Craig's mum and her kids.

"Yes, um, we're fine," answered Jean.

James thought she sounded confused.

216

Wee Joe was shivering. "Mum, I'm cold."

A smirking Constable Watt unwrapped another foil blanket and put it round Wee Joe's shoulders.

"Mum!" James called out, but she looked surprised to see him.

She whispered her reply. "James?"

He knew now that she had no idea where she was and, more importantly, she had no idea where she'd been.

"This is Bruce Moor, Mum. Don't you remember?"

"I know it's Bruce Moor," she snapped. "I just don't know how I got here. Is your father here?" James's heart grew heavy. In the chaos of the last few minutes, he'd actually forgotten all about his dad. How could he? A dark wave of realisation washed over him as he relived the destruction of Denthan. "I hope so, Mum," he answered.

"Have we been looking for him?" His mum didn't seem to notice his distress.

"Kind of..." James felt his chest tighten. "But I don't think we're any the wiser." The cold air was beginning to make him wheeze. Coughing, he stepped back into a strange indentation that reminded him of Sleven's three-toed footprint. He was sure it was the same spot where he'd seen the squashed stoat.

Craig joined his own mum, Helen and Wee Joe. "Come on, guys. Let's go home," he directed, though his voice sounded hollow.

"Why is this man still in handcuffs, Sergeant Carr?" demanded Father Michael.

Archie gave a little tug, and James saw Constable Watt stifle another snigger.

"Well sir, I mean, Father. We thought he might have had something to do with your disappearance, being the last person to see you all, as it were, and..."

"And, nothing! Release him!" snapped Father Michael.

"But sir, there are procedures to go through before we

can..."

"What procedures?" pressed Michael, "We're all here, aren't we?"

"That is still to be ascertained sir, and there is the matter of Mr Peck, who also disappeared, and was last seen here on Bruce Moor."

"Don't be ridiculous, man. Father Michael turned to Archie, "Where's Patch?"

James had forgotten all about Father Michael's little Jack Russell Terrier.

"She's been wif me," answered Archie. "She's safe and sound, but she'll need fed."

The plainclothes officer shrugged his broad shoulders and gave the order. "Release him for the time being, Sergeant Carr." He addressed Arche: "But don't go disappearing anywhere, MacNulty. Okay?"

"But..." Sergeant Carr protested.

"Scoutff honour, your officership." Archie held three fingers up to his right ear.

***

Back in the village of Drumfintley, just before they went their separate ways, a dejected James turned to Craig. "Have you heard anything from Mendel?"

"Not a peep," said Craig, "We'd better check he's alright." Before doing so, though, Craig pulled back his ripped sleeve and turned his palm upward. "Look," he whispered, "no tattoos."

James glanced at his right hand. His palm was clean and unmarked as well. *What does it mean?* He fumbled for a second, eventually producing the plastic barrel with *Wundadoz Chemicals* etched on the little glass window. James held it up to the light and peered inside. "Mendel?"

At first there was no movement and James feared Mendel

hadn't survived the fall. Then, out of the blue, came the words James had been longing to hear since their whole adventure had begun. "I think I know where your father is."

James's heart began to pound; he was sure Mendel was going to tell him that his dad had been killed on Denthan when it had exploded.

Mendel's voice was laced with excitement. "Sergeant Carr said that your father was last seen on the moor. When, exactly, was he seen there?"

James, gobsmacked, stuttered his reply. "Th...th...the first of June."

"Twenty-six days ago. Just as I thought," said Mendel, his deep voice smug.

"What does that mean?" said James, his hands starting to shake.

"Hurry up, James," his mum moaned. She was already at the front gate of number 45 Willow Terrace.

"Not just yet, Mum!" pleaded James, peering inside the barrel.

Cathy's eyes narrowed. "What did you say?"

"Nothing, nothing. I'm coming, Mum!" said James.

She turned and headed up the path.

Mendel continued his reasoning. "At the end, Dendralon thought I was Bero. But he sent me from Denthan as I am now: a goldfish, Carassius auratus."

"Hurry up, Mendel!" With a thumbs-up, James tried to placate his mum a second time as she glanced back at him, scowling.

"Well, he must have thought that I'd been affected by a phenomenon called thought transference," continued Mendel.

"What the heck is that?" James asked bluntly.

"When you use a gateway – or for that matter, if you are close to a gateway when it is being used – it is a very bad idea to think about any other animal or living thing," Mendel explained, "because there is a slight chance you will take on that form. Dendralon obviously thought I had turned myself into a dog, either by mistake or on purpose. Though I can't think for the life of me why I would choose an old Golden Retriever."

Craig's eyes widened indignantly.

"Right, we get the point," James said hurriedly. "Why didn't you just think of your own form when he sent you through the gateway in the first place?"

"That doesn't work and—"

"Okay," snapped James, "so how does this affect my dad?"

"Your father was on the moor on the same day, possibly at the very same instant that I came through the gateway. There is a slight chance that he was affected by thought transference."

Cathy gesticulated to James from the front door.

James waved back at her and smiled, trying his best to calm her. He lifted the barrel up to his face. Mendel's golden fins flashed past the plastic window. "You mean he might have been thinking about some animal just when you appeared, and he's been that animal ever since?"

"Exactly!" Mendel cried. "Now you must tell me what animal he may have been thinking about."

Cathy began marching back down the garden path towards James. She looked particularly angry.

James was losing patience with Mendel, and running out of time. "How am I supposed to know what kind of animal my dad was thinking about? He was up on the moor. Alone."

Wee Joe, sent by his mum to fetch Craig, started tugging on his big brother's sleeve. "Hamster!" the little boy suddenly shouted.

James and Craig both looked down at Wee Joe and were about to tell him to shut up when he explained, "James's daddy got me di hamster for mees birfday. I heerd mummy say it. Mr Peck got it. And now wees got two!"

James looked down at Wee Joe in utter amazement. At the same time James's mum grabbed his arm and yanked him back from the gate. "In! Now!"

As James half tripped, half staggered his way up his garden path, he heard Craig quiz his little brother. "What do you mean we've got two hamsters? We've only got the one… Mufty."

Wee Joe looked up at his big brother as they walked and gave him a little wink. "Mufty's got a pal, and Mum doesn't even knows it! I found it in the garden and catched it!"

As James was packed up to his room, Mendel spoke to him again. "Well, that solves that mystery. I think we must assume that your father was changed into a hamster up on Bruce Moor. After that, he simply waited there, probably in a state of confusion, until that stoat turned up."

"And…" James prompted as he sat down on his yellow duvet.

"And it's a good job Sleven came when he did," said Mendel.

James shook his head as he lowered Mendel into the tin bath.

"You mean Sleven appeared just as the stoat pounced at dad, and squished it flat?"

"Oh, dear," said Mendel. "That means you killed the very creature that saved your father's life."

James couldn't speak.

Mendel sighed, sending up a trail of bubbles. "Sometimes fate has a very cruel way of unravelling, James. But in this instance…" he paused, "I think your dad has been very fortunate. Very fortunate, indeed."

"But you're guessing. You don't know anything for sure. Wee Joe only heard me mumbling about my dad." James took a sharp intake of breath as a terrifying thought tumbled from his tired brain. "What if my dad was thinking of a stoat? What if Sleven stamped on…"

Cathy popped her head into his bedroom. "What are you wittering on about?"

"Nothing, mum." James began to wheeze. He reached into the rucksack for his inhaler.

His mum looked unconvinced but withdrew nonetheless.

"Let's stick to the hamster theory for now," said Mendel as the door closed. "After escaping the stoat, he must have scrambled back down the hill to the village."

"But why didn't he come home? Why go to the Harrison's house?" whispered James.

"Let's leave it there for now," said Mendel.

"But..."

"Rest... We need to rest..." Mendel's voice petered out into a bubbly sigh.

33 One Marriage, Two Hellos

His mum had been up several times during the night, pottering about, mumbling to herself. Even so, James was convinced she'd forgotten everything. It was just as Mendel had said it would be. She hadn't once mentioned their adventure in Denthan.

James, himself, had been totally hyper the entire night. He hadn't slept a wink for thinking about the possibility of his dad having been squished by a Swamp Troll – by Sleven. He really hoped that Mendel was right. But even then, to be stuck as a hamster, in Wee Joe's cage, behind bars...and with Mufty...

Finally, the sky outside reddened enough to be seen through his thin curtains. He raised himself up onto his elbows and threw off his duvet. "Mendel? We need to go round to Craig's house and see if my dad's there. I can't stand it any longer."

There was a splash from the tin bath. "Of course, but..."

"But what? There are no buts," said James.

"Well," said Mendel, "I've thought about it long and hard and there is, perhaps, a chance for one of us." Mendel sounded very serious.

"What do you mean by, 'one of us'? Stop talking in riddles all the time."

Mendel darted behind the plastic castle and looked up at James through a window covered in green slime. "First things first. Check your rucksack. Empty everything out."

James picked the well-worn green bag off his bed and turned it upside down. Out fell the empty orange can of flea spray, his inhaler and, to his surprise, a piece of blue crystal.

"But how?"

"Wee Joe popped that in there at the last moment. I asked him to. It split off when the Hedra crystal broke on the floor of the Chamber. Of course, the chain and the main portion of the crystal fell into the vision pool, but this fragment..." Mendel poked his golden head above the water. "This one shard may be enough to do the job."

"Do what job, Mendel?" asked James.

"Well," said Mendel, "it might be enough to return one of us back to our original form".

"That's if Dad's really at Craig's house, and hasn't already been eaten or squashed flat," James reminded him. "Tell me more."

Mendel circled the castle. "There's not enough of the crystal here to help us both, but one of us – your father or myself – might be able to change back into their original form."

"Mendel," said James, "my dad wouldn't be a bloomin' hamster, or whatever he is, if it wasn't for you coming here in the first place!"

The water in the tin bath rippled.

"Yes, yes, I know that. And that's why, if your father is indeed in Wee Joe's hamster cage, I will give up my chance and turn him back instead."

"You will?" James instantly regretted his outburst.

"James! What have I told you about shouting!" His mum's voice blasted out from her bedroom. "It's barely dawn!"

"Sorry, Mum. Can I go to Craig's for a bit?"

"At this time?" James heard his mum issue a long-drawn-out sigh before she said, "I want a lie in. Be back by twelve."

"Okay! Thanks, Mum." James picked up the plastic barrel and placed it in the tin bath for Mendel to swim into. "Quick, while she's still in a good mood. They don't last long..."

***

Outside the Harrison house, James could hear Mrs Harrison through the kitchen window. She was frying up some breakfast. "Look, I'm going to phone an advert into the paper – *'Golden Retriever missing, distinctive brown ear. We will be pleased to pay a £25 reward for information leading to a reunion. Please phone Jean on 01389…da, da, da.'* How does that sound?"

James heard Craig's reply and felt another pang of sadness.

"Look, Mum, he's gone for good. Trust me, he's not coming back."

"I don't like the da, da, da bit," Helen piped up.

Ignoring her daughter, Jean continued, "Don't be so negative, Craig. He'll turn up. You'll see. Bero is a boy-dog. They go off wandering sometimes. They can't help it."

James thought about his dad briefly and then decided to put Craig out of his misery. He rang the doorbell.

Craig answered the door and shook his head. "She just keeps going on and on about Bero. It's doing my nut in."

James cut to the chase. "Have you checked the hamster cage?"

Craig sighed. "You know, my great theory about your dad escaping to a better life in France could be a load of tosh after all."

"He never went 'off wandering', so just tell me!" pressed James.

Craig nodded. "Wee Joe's right. Mufty's got company."

James pushed his way inside.

Craig followed him up the stairs, talking all the way. "Every time I open the cage, he scampers away from me. But get this, when he does eventually poke his nose out of the shredded paper, he holds his right paw up to his ear just like a Scout salute. I can almost hear the Scout pack shouting, 'Dib, dib, dib.'"

James skidded to a halt outside Craig's room. "Hardee-har. Look, you better not be kidding me."

Craig forced a smile. "He's probably just cleaning his ears."

"How come your Mum didn't notice an extra hamster?" asked James.

"Mum only lets that lot have pets on the condition that she doesn't have to clean out their cages," said Craig, jerking his thumb towards Helen and Joe's room.

"So, the cage is still in there?" pressed James.

Craig shrugged. "In their room? Of course."

James eased the door open and stared across at the yellow hamster cage, a sense of trepidation building in his chest.

Craig edged past him and knelt down. "Phew! They stink," he muttered, flicking the water dispenser until the bubbles disappeared.

"No, they don't. It's you who stinks!" Helen and Wee Joe called out, practically in unison, then laughed.

"How did it get here?" asked James.

Wee Joe gave James a particularly derisive stare and tapped his nose with his forefinger.

"That means he knows but is never going to tell," explained Craig.

"Mendel, what now?" asked James. He began to wheeze as he pulled the barrel out of his green rucksack.

His chest tightened as he moved even closer to the yellow, plastic cage. It contained a blue wheel and a small white house with a red roof. The hamster house was stuffed with pink shredded paper. James coughed nervously as he pinged open the cage door.

"Mendel, please. Help me." James was frightened at the prospect of finding his dad and also anxious that he might be too late. Mendel's voice filled his head. "Put the crystal down beside the cage and make sure you take the hamster out."

"Wee Joe says that it doesn't like to be picked up," said Craig, tuning into Mendel's voice.

Mendel sighed in exasperation. "James, could you please

explain to Craig that it might prove a little painful if your father were to try to stand up in a one-foot-high metal cage."

"Ahh…" James scratched a spot on his neck and tried not to imagine his father being sliced and grated.

Craig winced, then took Wee Joe's hand and sat him down beside the hamster cage. "James wants to see the new hamster." He patted Wee Joe on the head, only to receive a brisk kick. "Wee Joe's the only one who can prise the new hamster from the cage, aren't you, you little…" Craig stopped himself in time.

A little piece of white, fluffy hamster bottom appeared at the door of the plastic house.

"There he is!" said Craig.

"It's mees secret and it's only me that can holds it! Hmuhh!" Wee Joe sassed smugly, then opened the little door a few inches before plunging his hand into the doorway of the plastic house.

"It's not a lucky dip, Joe. Be gentle," cautioned James, grimacing as he watched Wee Joe pluck the big hamster out from the shredded paper. The creature's little black eyes were nearly popping out of his head.

Helen intervened. "Give him here! You always try to love him too much."

"But I do wove him," said Wee Joe, reluctantly passing the struggling ball of fur to his big sister.

The sunlight filtered in through the net curtain and James immediately recognised something familiar about the hamster's face. He took a deep breath and asked, "Dad, is that you?"

James's words seemed to fall on deaf, fluffy ears.

Seemingly annoyed at the attention shown to the other hamster, Mufty took to her wheel and soon built up to maximum speed. The racket was like a machine gun.

Wee Joe put a finger to his lips. "Wufty, shhh!"

"M... M... Mufty! Not Wufty," said Helen.

"M... M... Shut up!" replied Wee Joe, sinking his teeth into his sister's outstretched hand.

The hamster dropped onto the floor.

"You animal!" Helen screeched, stamping her foot in anger and narrowly missing the hamster.

"Watch what you're doing!" yelled James.

Mendel stayed calm. "Put the crystal on the carpet beside your father, James."

"Right, okay." James was shaking. He placed the broken piece of crystal beside the hamster and stood back.

"Look out the window. Can you see Ben Larvach?" asked Mendel.

"He won't be able to. Wrong window. But you can see it from Mum's window at the front of the house," explained Craig, rubbing his sister's mauled hand.

Helen seemed confused by the disjointed conversation.

"Fine," said Mendel. "Point the sharp end of the crystal towards the spot on your wall where you think it is. Imagine you can see Ben Larvach out of your mother's window from here."

James repeated Mendel's instructions as if they were his own.

"That's easy!" said Helen, twisting the crystal round in the direction of their built-in cupboard.

The hamster twitched his little pink nose and looked up at the children. He cleaned his whiskers with a tiny pair of white paws and sniffed across at the cage.

"It's wooking for Mufty." Wee Joe knelt down and tried to pry Mufty from her wheel.

"Not just now, Joe!" snapped James.

Craig caught Wee Joe's arm. "Mufty might get hurt. It's safer for her in the cage, just for the moment."

James felt the knock, knock, knocking sensation build

inside his head and his lips quivered in unison with Mendel's. The bubbly, fishy-sounding words filled the whole room- "Wwwwretwwurnwwwwwtoselfwwww!"

Like most little kids, Helen tried to copy the strange words by pinging her lips and speaking at the same time.

The crystal began to glow blue before turning a brilliant white, as bright as any sun. Then it hummed powerfully.

They all covered their eyes and turned away from the light. Only James still dared to look down at the hamster.

The animal stopped cleaning itself and began to shake uncontrollably.

"Stop it! You're hurting him!" shouted James, but it was too late. There was another dazzling flash of light.

"Arghhh!" A loud scream filled the room, but James couldn't see a thing. Blinded, he rubbed his eyes in vain. Everything was just a mass of blue and white flashes.

"James?"

He couldn't see, but James knew the voice at once.

"Dad!" Blindly, James stretched out his arms and gripped onto the soft, familiar texture of his dad's fleecy jacket. "Dad, is it really you?"

Slowly his vision cleared and his dad came into view. James's heart was pounding. He was shaking. His dad looked exactly as he remembered him. He had the same mousy brown hair as James. The same ears – one rounded and one pointed. James reckoned his hamster diet must have been good for him because he'd certainly lost a few pounds. His grey eyes looked bleary but he seemed unharmed, just bewildered. "I can't believe it's you." James caught hold of his dad's hand and squeezed it tightly. Normally he would have been embarrassed to show such affection, but right now he didn't care.

"Of course it's me. Why am I covered in sawdust and...?" David Peck eased his hand free of James's grip and put his index finger between his teeth. Confused, his dad poked a finger round in his mouth before producing several sunflower seeds and a half-eaten peanut from the inside of his cheek.

"What the heck...?"

Now there was another noise in the room.

Scratch! Scratch!

"Ooww!"

The children jumped onto the bed while a bemused David Peck stared across at the bedroom cupboard. "What have you got in that cupboard, James?"

"Nothing!" James blurted. He was still reeling from the bright lights and the shock of seeing his dad, but his eyes were adjusting now. His dad didn't look particularly happy.

"Well, there's something in there!" his dad shouted. "I hope you're not being cruel to some poor animal."

Mendel's voice found its way into the boys' heads. "Could one of you open the cupboard door?"

Craig jumped off the bed and pulled on the brass handle of the cupboard.

"Oohh! It's hot!" he cried, blowing on his fingers. He grabbed one of Helen's dolls. Holding it by the legs, he pushed the handle down with the doll's head.

"Tsssssss!" The face of the plastic doll began to melt and a black, acrid smoke spiralled toward the ceiling. The handle gave and the door sprang open...

"Woof!"

James couldn't believe it. There, sitting on the chipboard floor of the kids' toy cupboard, was a little Golden Retriever puppy, wagging his tail and panting just the way Bero had.

James slid off the bed. "He's got the same brown ear!"

His dad's nose twitched as he waved the smoke away from his eyes. "Craig, it's not like you to be cruel to animals. Why did you lock the pup in the cupboard?"

Not listening, Craig crouched. "Come on, boy. Come on!"

James pulled on his dad's sleeve and gave him a 'don't

say another word' stare. Somehow, he knew that the dog in the cupboard was Bero. He was also sure he'd heard Eethan's wispy laugh while the crystal fragment was doing its magic. The little, blue man seemed to possess supernatural abilities that even Mendel couldn't match.

"Bero!" As soon as Craig said the name, the pup bounded out of the cupboard and leapt up into his arms.

Mendel's voice cut into James's thoughts. "Eethan never fails to surprise me."

Helen began to pat the puppy too. "It's a baby Bero!"

Wee Joe beamed up at James's dad. "When dee big Bewo comes back wees will have two doggies!"

"That was a good trick, Mr Peck!" Helen ran out her bedroom door and shouted down for her mother. "Mum! Mr. Peck's doing a magic show!"

James snapped out of his state of shock and wrapped his arms round his dad. "I love you, Dad."

His dad drew back in surprise. "I love you too, Son, but..."

Jean Harrison opened the bedroom door. "Craig, Cathy Peck's on the..." She stood stalk still, fixed to the spot. "... phone," she eventually finished. "David?"

"It's my dad!" James hugged his dad once more.

Looking shocked, Craig's mum handed David Peck the mobile phone. "It's your wife," she whispered.

"Hello. Cathy?" he said.

There was no reply.

James knew this was going to be tricky for his dad to explain. He snatched the receiver from his dad and listened. "Mum?"

"Eh, I think I can see her running down the street," said Craig. "Look."

This was *definitely* going to be tricky, thought James.

"I'm a bit confused, I have to admit," said David.

"Things are a bit like that just now," said Jean, timidly.

"Still, it's nice to see you again, David."

There was a loud knock on the front door.

"I think…" Jean paused. "I think I'd better answer the door."

James heard the Harrison's doorbell dinging uncontrollably, a continuous racket that signalled trouble.

James was too frightened to move. As soon as his mum appeared at the top of the stairs his worst fears were confirmed. Her face was ashen grey.

Jean gave David Peck a small pat on the back, and produced a particularly false smile. "Cathy's missed you…"

James heard Jean's words trail off as his mum's expression hardened.

James watched as his mum approached his dad. Uncharacteristically, a tear was tracing its way down her cheek and, for a moment, James thought she was going to hug him. But the moment was short-lived. She sighed and then drew her hand back to slap him.

"No, Mum!"

David winced.

Cathy grunted as her hand stopped an inch from David's face.

Jean Harrison had intercepted the blow and now had a tight grip on Cathy's wrist.

No one moved or made a sound. In that one moment, the tension seemed to stifle everything. It was all too much. The mixture of emotions James was feeling bore down on him like a trillion tons of rock. He just wanted to run away.

"You will not hit him. Not in my house, in front of my children."

"It's abuse to hit people," added Helen, her cheeks pink.

Cathy's eyes blazed with fury as she jerked her wrist free. Then she focused in on David and pointed towards the bedroom door. "We should go."

"Um, James," said Craig, cutting through the tension.

"Don't forget your rucksack."

Glad of the excuse to step back from his parents, James grabbed the bag and popped the barrel inside. To his relief, without saying a word, his mum and dad made their way to the bedroom door.

Wee Joe tried to stifle a giggle.

This was the way James remembered his parents – at odds, diminished by each other, but a couple again, nonetheless.

Cathy Peck led the way. She seemed to stare blankly at some spot in the distance as she walked toward the stairs.

James had hoped that she might have changed after her time in Denthan, but how could she have? Her memory had been wiped. For an instant he flushed with rage. Why had Mendel made her forget their struggle, their whole, incredible journey? They'd faced monsters, armies of lizards, wizards and more just to find his dad... He stared hard at his mum, willing her to remember everything. He'd dreamed of some big celebration upon finding his dad...not this.

David, bewildered, followed Cathy down the stairs.

James smiled and shook his head before waving the Harrisons goodbye. "I think we're off home," he said. "Good luck with the new pup, Craig."

"What new pup?" asked Jean, more confused than ever.

Craig lifted the little retriever pup up to his mum.

James heard him shout down after them. "Thanks, Mendel!" James twisted round and smiled up at his best friend.

"Thanks to you too, ye numpty," added Craig.

"It looks like Bero, doesn't it?" said Jean, voice wavering.

As he stepped onto the bottom landing, James saw the young Bero lookalike licking and nipping Mrs Harrison's nose in a frenzy of excitement.

Following his parents back to his house, James heard Mendel's voice in his head. "Well, all's well that ends well."

"Mendel?" said James.

"Yes, James."

James tightened the straps of his rucksack. "Shut up."

***

Two months later, James sat down to write in his diary:

Michael and Ephie were married today in St. Donan's Church. The whole of Drumfintley was there to see the new, slimmer Ephie Blake, walk down the aisle with Father Michael. Ephie's weird brother, Kwedgin, gave her away and Archie MacNulty and Patch were Best Man and Best Dog respectively. I was there with Mum, who's just allowed Dad to move back into our house again, which is a big relief. Dad says that he must have fallen and bumped his head, or something, as he can't remember a thing about his missing time. Mum says 'Yeah, right!' and other stuff that makes me think she doesn't really believe him. Craig was there too, along with his mum, his sister, Wee Joe and their dad, who, according to Craig, has finally returned from a stint in a submarine under the North Pole. Craig seems to be much happier now that he's got his dad back too.

When he stands on his back legs, the 'new' Bero is nearly up to my belly button and he continues to get madder by the minute.

As I write this, Mendel is splashing about in his tin bath, but I can tell that he is getting more and more restless every day. He's promised to rid me of my asthma when he regains his full powers again but, in the meantime, he helps me to relax and breathe much better than I ever did before. He still drives me and Craig crazy with all his Latin names and stuff when we take him on walks. Only yesterday, he told us that Eethan had managed to get the city of Gwendral to another world but, apparently, not the one he'd planned.

Craig and I often wonder how the Mertol is settling in, and if Jal has recovered from his wounds. Back here in Drumfintley, the local paper reports that the police have now closed the case on our 'missing time', but the villagers never stop chattering about it. Gauser says it was a mass hoax, but he's the village drunk, so no one really listens to him that much. Mrs Galdinie tells her customers at the ice-cream shop that we were most likely abducted by aliens. She's closer to the mark than she realises.

There's not a day goes by that I don't think or dream about our adventure in Denthan, but the main thing for me is that I have my family back again, warts and all.

Ps – they don't really have warts, but you know what I mean.

James put his pen down and closed the diary. The moon was shining brighter than usual above Drumfintley and everything was still and quiet. Alone in his little room, he looked out his window at the stars that filled the summer-night sky and wondered if one of the far-off specks of light might now be Gwendral's new sun. Perhaps Cimerato and Garlon were looking up at their stars too.

James stretched and let his diary slip off his bed, too tired to care as it bumped onto the wooden floor.

The water rippled in the old tin bath as his mum's dulcet tones filled the night. "Who's Mufty?" she demanded.

James wondered how his mum could possibly be jealous of a female Chinese Orange hamster; but then, as long as his dad continued to mumble Mufty's name in his sleep, and as long as he failed to come up with a plausible explanation for doing so, his mum would no doubt continue to throw a wobbly now and then.

She did at least seem sort of glad to have him back. And 'sort of' felt like some sort of improvement on before.

Poor Dad, James thought, smiling to himself as he snuggled into his duvet.

Poor Dad...

The story continues in…

Tyrant

Book 3 of *The Peck Chronicles*

Publication: Summer 2016

Go to **www.stridentpublishing.co.uk** for details.